SONS OF EMPIRE

Book IV of the
Imperial Chronicles

THE COMING YEARS WOULD TEST THE COURAGE
OF CITIZENS AND SUBJECT PEOPLES, OF
LEGIONARIES AND SLAVES, OF THE MEN AND
WOMEN OF THE EMPIRE; AND DETERMINE
WHETHER THE NATION CHOSEN BY IMPERIUM
WOULD FULFILL ITS CALLING: TO RULE OVER ALL
THE WORLD.

—Primo Alleus, national historian, writer of *The Imperial Chronicles*

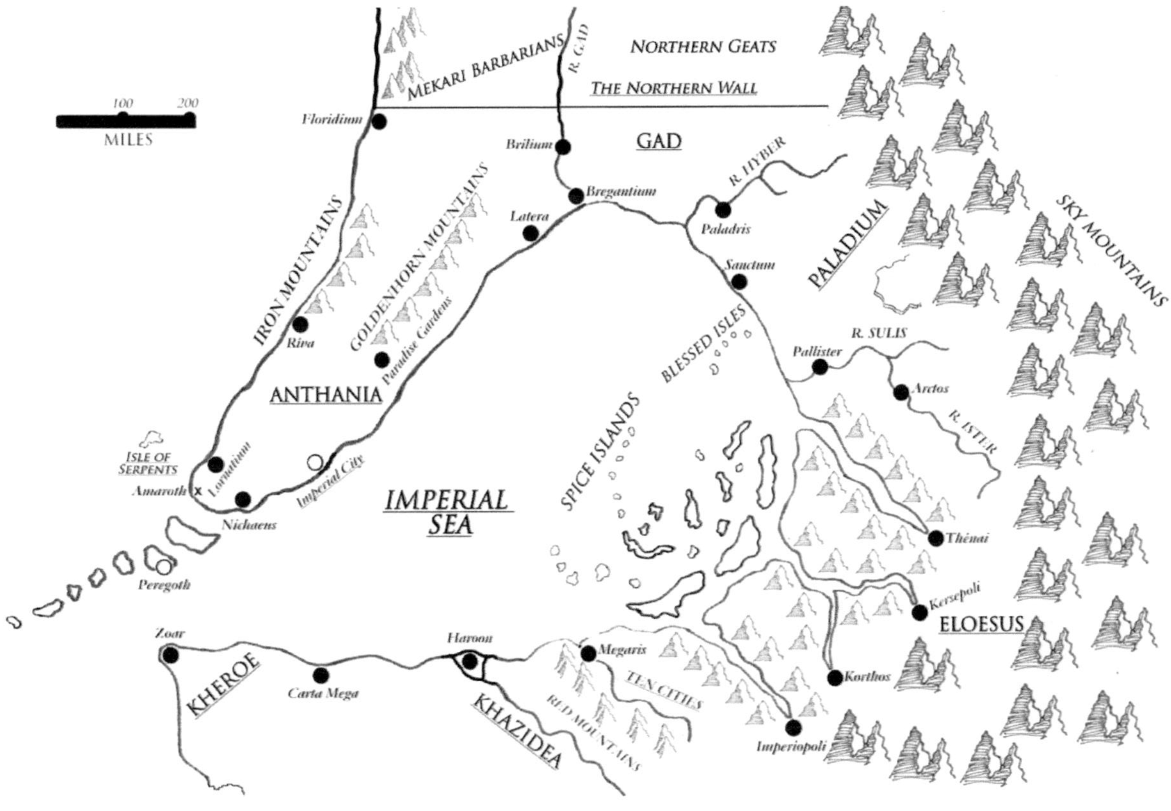

MILES
100
200
MEKARI BARBARIANS
NORTHERN GEATS
The Northern Wall
R. GAD
Floridium
Brilium
GAD
Latera
Bregantium
R. HYBER
Paladris
PALADIUM
SKY MOUNTAINS
Sanctum
Pallister
R. SULIS
Archos
R. ISTER
IRON MOUNTAINS
Riva
GOLDENHORN MOUNTAINS
Paradise Gardens
ANTHANIA
Theimi
BLESSED ISLES
SPICE ISLANDS
Kersephili
ELOESUS
Korthos
ISLE OF SERPENTS
Amaruth
Lornathun
Nichaeus
Imperial City
IMPERIAL SEA
Peregoth
Zoor
Harrau
Megaris
TEN CITIES
SHADOW MOUNTAINS
KHEROE
Carta Mega
KHAZIDEA
Imperiopoli

Imperial City

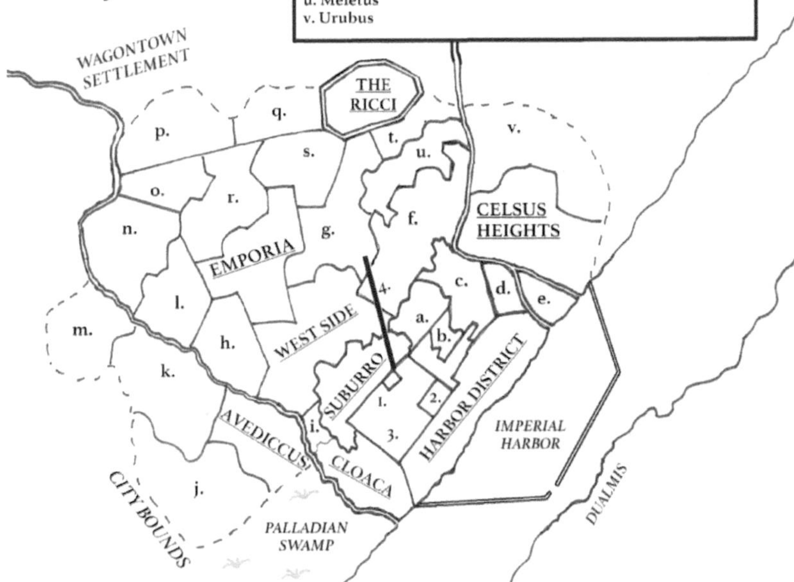

PROLOGUE:
THE SOURCE OF ALL ILLS

Julian Tyrenas

Summer, 1085

The night that changed Julian's life began as most every night had before. In their spacious stone home just north of Bregantium, his grandmother entertained him with stories by the fire—a tale perhaps too scary for a seven-year-old boy, "The Wolf Man of Norbrook," followed by his personal favorite, "The Worm of Reha." Outside, through the iron-grilled windows, twilight was setting in, painting the forest of hardy oaks in shades of gold. All seemed well that fateful summer night, and the thought that everything might change never crossed Julian's mind, until it did.

In the late evening hours, chaos erupted downstairs. "Be calm," his grandmother said, stood up on her feeble legs, and hurried out of the room.

Julian waited a few moments, too worried to do anything, but soon his solitude became too much to bear, and the shadows cast by the fire seemed more threatening than the shouts downstairs. He bolted out of the room.

On the ground floor, Father had drawn his sword. The iron-hinged door had burst open, with shards of wood lying all over the room like it had exploded. A man stood in its wake, his head bald and white like an egg, holding a long wooden stick in one hand. He wore a scarlet robe. Two men stood at his side, men with roughshorn hair and unshaven faces.

Bandits. But who was the man in the scarlet robe? There was something terrible about him, far more terrible than the bandits.

"Signor Tyrenas," the red-garbed man rasped. "The folk of this town call you Helm."

"Helm is my name," Father thundered back. "What is the meaning of this, intruder?"

"Do not search for meaning where there is none. My name is Malleon, and I have heard you own great stores of gold and silver."

"I am a veteran. I am a master of the sword. I served the god Claudian in his wars. I would not test my skill—"

"And I serve the god Meltoth, Prince of Slaughter, who aids my magic."

"I will not have a magic weaver in my household," Father boomed. Mother came running in from her bedchamber. *"Get out!"* Father screamed.

"What is going on?" Mother screamed. "Get away from my family! Who are—"

A twisted fork of purple lightning blasted from Malleon's hand. Mother screamed, then fell silent as she hit the floor. Father roared and charged forward with his sword.

"Run," Grandmother snapped at Julian.

"No," Julian snapped back.

One of Malleon's lackeys charged Father. Their swords kissed twice in the span of a second.

"Run," Grandmother growled, frantic, "or as the gods as my witness, I will skin you alive! Run, Julian, for your father's sake. Gods in heaven, *run!"*

For Father's sake, Julian thought. The lackey's head hit the floor, sliced off by Father's sword. *He could kill the bandits. If it weren't for magic, Mother would still be alive.*

"For your father and mother's sake, by the gods in Heaven, as Heaven as my witness, *run!"*

Grandmother kicked him forward, and this time Julian obeyed. He sprinted out as the sorcerer's lightning struck Father head-on. He whimpered as he bolted out the door into the cool of the summer night.

~

Julian ran, and he didn't know how long he ran or where, only that he had gone at full-sprint until finally his little body gave out, and he had collapsed onto the pavestones, sucking in air like a dying fish, throat burning and heart pounding out of control. Footsteps passed him by. Sometime in the dark of night, a foot prodded him awake. When he looked up, a man towered above him, wearing a hood that hid everything except his mouth.

"Is something wrong, little one?"

"Everything," he rasped. "Everything is wrong."

"May Hieronus guard you, and may Amara soothe your wounded heart."

The initial fear of strangers melted away with the realization that this was a priest, a man of the gods. Weakly Julian stood up, still trembling all over. He could scarcely breathe. "My mother and father… they… they can't be dead."

The priest touched his shoulder. "Be calm. I am going to the Magisterium. I believe Hieronus has put you in my path for a purpose. Little one, how would you like to become a brother?"

"A priest," Julian breathed, still unable to make sense of it all. His thoughts returned to Mother and Father, by all accounts now dead. "A sorcerer broke into our house. He killed my mother and father with lightning from his hand."

"Magic," the priest said, "is the source of all ills. Now come with me."

1099

Primo Alleus, National Historian, Writer of the Imperial Chronicles

The summer heat lay heavy over the streets of Imperial City, forming a visible haze. Primo Alleus was not completely a pauper—if he wanted to, he could quite easily leave the confines of the cramped metropolis and retreat to cooler climes. Gods knew, his son Matteo had done as much. But Primo Alleus had just begun making headway on his history books—the ones he called the Imperial Chronicles—and in the choking heat of the upper-story apartment he had set out several jars of black ink and reams of paper.

Yet he had only reached halfway through the second book, covering the life of Empress Irena—the only woman to hold the title of emperor in her own right—in the dark days of the third century Y.E.

"In the wake of the murdered Imperial Council, many thought the Empire would falter," Primo wrote. *"The emperor was dead by the hands of an assassin; we were locked in a losing war with the greatest power of the day. Yet the greatest strengths of the Empire—our inability to give up, the rallying of our spirits in times of trouble, and our unwavering love for our nation—would allow us to prevail despite impossible odds, and with the aid of Imperium, enter the fourth century stronger than ever before."*

Primo Alleus paused. Even now the Empire seemed at its zenith—nay, an uneasy plateau. In the wake of its battle with the lawgivers, the Fharese Empire had only slightly resurged, still remaining a pale shadow of what it had been in the days of Claudio-Valens Adamantus.

Claudio-Valens Adamantus, Primo thought, and sighed. The Empire had not seen a man of his mettle since his death. Who knew if—in this new peace—no great souls would be forged in the fire of strife?

But Primo Alleus had an unshakeable feeling the peace would

not last, and he questioned, when it finally broke, whether the Empire would truly emerge victorious, stronger than ever before.

6

CHAPTER ONE:
THE RETURN

Theon Arkadios

The past few years had been an opium dream.

He still recalled when he had first set out. A rich blueblood from Eloesus, he had craved more than the mansion and the life of leisure his father had ensured him. On a whim he had left south, pledging to follow the Silk Route to its furthermost extent. Against horrible odds, he had persevered; crossing deserts hot and cold, climbing snowy peaks, and traversing dangerous plains rife with bandits. He had spent uneasy nights with bad company, holing up in the caravanserais of eastern Fharas and the furthermost desert lands. At last, he reached the western shore of the Sea of Stars. He had gone to the Jade City, and enjoyed the favored eye of the Celestial Emperor; to the folk of that land he was as foreign to them as they were to him. And it was there that he had tasted true freedom. The supposed liberty of the Empire could not compare with what he found in the land of the Furthermost East.

Among the misty lands of the Forgotten Isle he had studied with its sages, learned the ancient war-craft of its knights, and achieved a new state of mind free from the worries and cares of the so-called real world. The world that Theon Arkadios had once called real was not half as real as he had believed.

By the time the months-long journey had ended, he had forgotten much of the past few years, and most of the specifics; it had become an opium haze to him, but he knew he had changed forever. He wore the orange silk robe of a sage, painted with intricate draconic symbols, and strung along his belt were the square coins of the Eastern Empire. Strapped to his back was the single-edged slashing sword of the Forgotten Isle warriors, layered with a film of lacquer. In a pouch clipped to his side, three-dozen throwing stars were within reach of his hand. But these tools were his last resort; before he employed the weapons of the inferior material world, he would use the wisdom he had gained as a sage, pondering mysteries in the tea-gardens of the Forgotten Isle.

By the time he had reached the terminus of the Khazan River, where it split into a hundred lesser streams, Theon Arkadios wished he had never left the East.

~

The South Gate of Haroon lay open and he passed through easily, gaining several curious looks from passersby. In the shade of the red sandstone temples with their onion domes and thin towers, Theon Arkadios walked these streets which he had visited so many times before. *But I am not the same.* He would never be the same. In some ways, Theon Arkadios would never walk these streets again, for he had become someone totally different.

The speech of the citizens reached his ears: Khazidean—in the southern and northern dialects—and Kheroan, both languages he did not understand. Even the guttural tongue of the Far North barbarians was represented among the mass of voices. The two languages he did understand—Eloesian and Imperial—he had not heard in what seemed like a lifetime. But as he walked, traces of their conversations came back to him, and little by little he began to understand what had gone on in his absence.

A new emperor, they said—Severus had died, gods rest his soul—yet it was not Claudian or even an Adamantus that sat on the throne. Emperor Janus, they said. And a pretender to the throne. Some, in hushed tones, said the name "Adamantion." And the name "Astarthe" was the most common word spoken. The brother-kings and sister-queens had not been seen in hundreds of years.

What are they talking about?

"Did you hear, Phadros?" an Eloesian asked. "The northman-king is coming to the Empire, with his wizards…"

"Wizards?"

By northman, they surely did not mean the northern barbarians. The barbarians did not have a king, only a war chief.

Imperial soldiers had a thick presence throughout the city. The Imperial war-eagle flew on all the turrets, so why all this talk of Astarthe? It seemed obvious the sister-queen did not reign again; the Empire's control, here, was palpable.

Theon found himself in the market-square, overlooking the stone embankments and the blue waters of the Imperial Sea.

A waft of perfume enveloped him. "Stranger, where did you get those clothes?"

Theon turned around and found a Khazidean woman—short, though tall for a Khazidean—standing before him. Her luscious lips were smeared purple, complementing her oiled copper skin. She wore a hood of red satin that made her seem matronly, but no lace veil of marriage. "Does it matter, s-signora?" After all this time away, it was difficult to even speak the language of his birth.

"It matters to me." Her Khazidean accent, her dewy eyes and smooth skin caused Theon's body to respond, despite his best wishes otherwise. "Tell me where you got that lovely silk robe, those gold and silver trinkets—"

"Coins," he snapped.

"—and that strange sword, and I ensure you, you shall be richly rewarded."

"There is nothing you can offer me, signora. Leave me be."

Her lips formed into an irresistible smile. "Not even the queen's favor would sway you?"

"The queen? What are you talking about? There has been no—"

"You have been gone long," the woman said, stealing his words. "Much has changed in the past ten years. And that has told me much by itself. You have gone on a long journey, a journey of months and years. Yes, the queen might like to hear of your travels. She loves nothing more than tales from far-away lands. She is the consummate gossip."

"The queen—"

Again she stole his words. "Queen Astarthe sits once more on the Red Throne. She does not have soldiers, nor does she in truth rule. She has wisely submitted to the Empire and the emperor, and now she may live as she will."

In dalliance and luxury and sensuality, Theon would guess, if the tales of the sister-queen held true. Among the sages of the Forgotten Isle, things of this world—physical sensations, dark pleasures and rich foods—were corrupt snares and traps that prevented one from achieving the true reality and the perfect self.

"She would delight at hearing from you, signore."

Theon felt his eyes narrow. "I am not one who wastes his time."

"Then come."

Theon turned to walk away.

The words of the woman followed him as he tried to escape her: "If you change your mind, signore, then go to the gate of the palace, and say the queen's handmaid Nama sent you."

Though he walked away, her words followed quick after him. Her words were snares, traps tempting him to forsake the Way. But as he left her, he realized he did not truly know where he was going. *Home*, he had told himself, but was his home even there anymore? Did the mansion in Thénai still sit on the high hilltop, and would his parents take him in, after he had scorned them and brought shame upon their household?

Why did I leave? The past years had all been an opium dream, and he in truth could not remember. Of all the chance memories and recollections of the far east, not all brought pleasant emotions to his mind. The Celestial Emperor had given him much attention there— Theon's foreignness and strange appearance made him an object of great interest—and some members of the court despised Theon for it. Among the sages of the Forgotten Isle, he recalled firm instruction at the end of a stick—shaping him into a wiser being, they called it, bringing him closer to the true world unseen by the simple folk—but also their grave concern of a storm growing beyond the Sea of Stars.

Choh, one of the sages, told Theon that he'd gone to the port-city of Xia to research in its library. There, traders told him they'd sailed to the lands of the people they'd called the *dai ma*, and the great mountains on the edge of the sea—once empty and silent—raged with a great fire-storm. The world had lost its adherence to the Way, Choh had said, and things were beginning to come undone.

"Signore!" the male voice startled him from his idle reflection.

He turned for the second time that day, and found a soldier in full Imperial dress standing before him. The sunlight illuminated a fair-skinned face. "You look Imperial, but your garb is most certainly something else."

Not again. Theon blew out a sigh. "My business is my own. Please leave me be."

"What is your name, signore?"

"Theon Arkadios, it once was," he answered. "Now it is Wayfarer."

"Wayfarer, is it," the soldier said in a dark tone Theon wasn't sure he liked. "I would like you to come with me to the garrison."

"The garrison? But wha—? Why?"

"You are wanted in the city of Thénai."

"Wanted? Impossible. I've done nothing wrong."

"As every criminal before you has said."

"*Criminal?*"

"Your father Tharon is a man of impeccable honor. Seven years ago you fled his household. You were his only son."

"And who are you?"

"I am a soldier, nothing more. But Tharon is a good friend of the First Harak Legion."

"I'd bet he is." Father was the richest man in Thénai, perhaps even the whole of the Imperial east. "I'm sure my father would not wish me harm."

"On the contrary. He has adopted another son and married *her* to the Marcovi girl… the one you scorned."

"Marcovi…" He remembered Elsa Marcovi, a spoiled and intolerable young woman. Being the daughter of a great legate was her only virtue. Father was ever the schemer. "I am sure he will understand."

"He will not, signore. He asked that I bring you, bound in chains for a formal disownment and perhaps the magistrate's justice."

The blueblood inside Theon stepped out of the timid shell. "And what authority do you have, Signor—"

"Signor Lucus Marcovi, you may call me, First Harak Legate." A wide smile formed over his face.

Theon took a step back and fingered the pouch of throwing stars.

"By the will of Imperium, and the authority invested in me by Emperor Janus himself, I place you under arrest. Come with me, Theon Arkadios."

Lucus Marcovi had not finished saying Theon's name before he disappeared into the crowd.

~

At the portcullis of the Red Palace, a guard from inside narrowed her eyes. "Who is this, babbling? What is your name?" Theon eyed her over, seeing a thin chain shirt over her chest and a sword buckled to her side. He had seen few women warriors in his life, but she looked fierce.

"Theon," he began.

"Only women and Godlings are permitted in the Red Palace, save the queen's consorts and children."

"The handmaid Nama sent me."

"Nama." The woman's eyes narrowed. She turned and stalked off.

Theon glanced back every few seconds in the time that passed, checking for Imperial soldiers, but before Marcovi's men found him the gates had opened, and he was walking hand-in-hand with Nama toward the queen.

CHAPTER TWO:
THE NORTHMAN KING

Maximian, Marshal of the Guard

Today promised to make history. Emissaries often came from the far north, bringing tidings from a land far from the Empire's power, which few citizens visited or desired to visit. In the reckoning of most, the lands of the "north-beyond-north" were only slightly more civilized than the barbarians who massed outside the wall.

But seeing King Bretonnius—a tall man, strongly-built, his brown beard having none of the unshorn dirtiness of the wild barbarians—Maximian could not help but wonder if they'd been wrong all along. His brocade robe—gold on one side, green on the other—was studded along its entire length with fiery rubies, celestial sapphires, and intense emeralds. Bretonnius' crown had none of the intended humility of the Imperial Circlet; it was a thing completely forged of gold, glittering with rubies and diamonds, with purple velvet in the center. The man's fingers gleamed with jeweled rings.

If we killed him, Maximian mused darkly, *we could pay the court's expenses for a year, just with the gold he's wearing.*

The northman king's ostentatious outfit and his smelly gaggle of servants were not the thing that most concerned Maximian, however. Bretonnius had brought with him an old man, taller than himself, with a white beard that touched the floor. In his wrinkled hand he clutched a staff, carved of gray birch, with a jewel at its tip that radiated light. In his eyes, Maximian saw cunning and a calculating mind. They called him Lemuel, and Bretonnius had said he was an advisor, nothing more.

Emperor Janus stood up from the White Throne. "Bretonnius."

How diametrically opposed they are, Maximian thought. Janus was young, his face clean-shaven and his dark brown hair cut short. The northman king sported a full-beard and a thick head of hair, and could not be any younger than fifty. "Please," Bretonnius said through a thick, syrupy accent. "You must not be so formal. Call me Gylles."

"Gylles…"

"Gylles vis Bretagne." When Lemuel spoke, it seemed the very earth shook. The man was an inch taller than King Bretonnius, yet his powerful presence made him seem twice the height of everyone in the room. His robe went down to his heels, made of flannel and dyed a slate blue. "His Majesty has just inherited the Lion Throne. A formal visit by the King of Zarubain has not been made to the Empire in over a century; you should count yourself lucky."

Maximian laughed at the presumption; Janus remained tactful. "And to what do I owe this visit?"

"His Majesty—"

"Let me speak," King Bretonnius cut Lemuel off. "My father Cyrien had sold much wool to your nation in the past, and bought much silk, and he had always intended to visit your nation. But he put it off, and soon he was old, and suffering from hag's eye and the gout, and unable to leave the Royal Palace. I intended to visit your nation while I am still well."

There is something else he wants, Maximian thought. And if he had to guess, it involved this so-called 'advisor' of his, Lemuel.

"And what do you think of our fair nation?"

"Word of your wealth and strength has reached Vale Royeau and my own household. Your city is so incredibly large and congested." King Bretonnius obviously struggled to contain his derision. "And forgive me, sir… is it true that, in your nation, the lowborn *choose* their leader?"

"I suppose it is," Janus said, looking more amused than offended.

King Bretonnius admirably managed not to gasp. "That is so very… interesting. And is it true that men here have more than one wife?"

"No it is not," Janus laughed. "You are thinking of the southrons. I've had only one wife, Signor Bretonnius. Eloesa was a lovely woman, rest her soul. I hope I shall get the pleasure of meeting yours."

"There is no woman lovelier than Lanabelle."

"And where is she?" Janus intoned.

"She took a liking to the pretty statues on—what do you call it?—the Walk of Glory. My knights shall protect her in my absence."

The pleasantries faded from Maximian's conscious thought, and he found himself examining the face of Lemuel. The man's dark eyes darted this way and that, as if he were searching for something. Maximian had no idea what the man wanted, but he was determined not to let him get it.

After Janus and Bretonnius departed the throne room for a tour of the White Palace, Maximian took his place at the right of the throne, hand on the hilt of his sword. Out of the shadows a wind rustled his hair, and an augur appeared, a high-ranking member of the Collegium. Silvana, he recalled, the augur whose traces golden hair flowed from her winged cap. "Maximian," she said, "keep a watchful eye on the emperor. I do not trust these folk."

"Guarding the emperor's life is my duty, signora." Maximian smiled. *How I'd like to run my hands through that hair of gold.* "I assure you I will not let the king nor his advisor touch him."

"Advisor," Silvana sneered. "His aura is overpowering. He is a weaver of power, much stronger than myself. The Maestro could feel him from miles away."

Maximian's smile vanished. "A magic weaver, you say."

"A *wizard.*"

"Wizard." The room seemed colder, now.

"In all I do not know what a wizard wants with Emperor Janus, but you can never leave his side. *Go.*"

An encouraging wind blew as Maximian hurried down the corridors.

The tunnel to the council chamber—newly rebuilt after the accident years ago—proved a barely-sufficient space to contain Lemuel. Maximian caught up to them in the council chambers themselves. For the councilors it was the favorite time of year, the hot days of midsummer when they retreated to the cool of the foothills or the relaxation of the island resorts. Their presence was not badly missed. Janus would probably be gone as well, if it weren't for this grand interruption.

"What lovely woodwork," Lemuel said, but his scanning eyes were not truly fixed on the wooden chairs.

"And stonework." Bretonnius was gazing at the high domed ceiling.

"Sir Emperor," Lemuel intoned, too ignorant or perhaps unwilling to address him as His Undying Glory. "I would love to see the artwork in your private bedchamber, if you would let me."

"Enough!" All three of them snapped their heads to look at Maximian, as if they hadn't realized he'd been there all along. "You have been rude enough to the lord emperor, but this crosses the line. The emperor's private quarters do not—" Their silence stopped him, and his face flushed. Janus looked baffled; King Bretonnius stared at him like a rude, unwelcome country peasant. Lemuel's ancient face held a trace of a smile, as if he knew Maximian's concerns and also that Maximian could not act upon them.

"Maximian, we are merely talking," Janus said. "Perhaps you should excuse yourself. There is still daylight left."

Maximian would not leave Janus alone with Lemuel. But eventually the combined stares drove him away, back toward the White Chamber. His face burned with embarrassment. Laughter followed him as he left the council chambers.

~

When he returned to the White Chamber, a nymph stood

there, admiring the titanic throne. The scent of flower-oils and fragrant perfume billowed out from the blonde-haired woman. A gown of gold cloth fell to her knees, revealing tight linen hose and slippers. Her forest-green eyes met Maximian's, and she glanced away bashfully. Her cheeks turned red.

Others had entered the chamber: soldiers, clearly not Imperial. Iron plated armor covered the whole of their huge bodies, and steel greatswords were strapped to their backs. There were about a dozen in the White Chamber, each of them larger than Maximian. Compared to them, he felt unprepared, a lamb to the slaughter.

He fixed his gaze again on the radiant nymph before him. "Signora…"

Her timid green eyes met Maximian for a second longer, this time, but quickly darted away. "I… I do not speak…"

This had to be Lanabelle, the northman king's wife. For once Maximian wished he spoke their strange tongue. Of all the women he had ever seen, none compared to this dainty figure before him.

A wind blew across the room; the augur Silvana had stormed off through a corridor. Jealousy, perhaps, but in this moment she no longer seemed half so important.

"Lanabelle, is it?"

She nodded and Maximian stepped toward her. "I am Maximian, Marshal of the Guard." He fell to one knee.

A storm of voices and footsteps filled the hall.

"Lowborn, step away from my wife!"

The shock of fear quickly morphed to anger. *Lowborn.* He had been called worse in the taverns of Imperial City, but the word nonetheless stung. He found himself backing away, watching as Bretonnius gathered his wife by the hand as he would a troublesome child. "In my country," the northman-king said, "a lowborn would not so much as breathe in the same room as Lanabelle. She is, after all, of the House Bretagne."

"What makes you think I am lowborn?" Maximian risked saying. Beyond him, Lemuel had an amused smirk.

"Who is your father? Who is your grandfather?"

"There is no nobility in the Empire," Maximian said. "I earned my position. I suppose, Signor Bretonnius, that is the difference between you and me."

"Stop," Janus said. "Pardon him, Signor Bretonnius. We do not know your customs. Do you and sweet Lanabelle know where your guest rooms are?"

"I can show them the way," Lemuel boomed.

Together, he, the knights, the king and the queen left the White Chamber, at which Maximian breathed a sigh of relief. But Janus did not have a relieved or even welcoming look, only irritation bordering on wrath. "You certainly acted strangely, Maximian."

"These men have ulterior motives, I know it. Nevertheless, forgive me, Your Undying Glory." He fell to his knees, and when he looked up, most of the anger had left the emperor's eyes.

"All of us have motives, Maximian," Janus said. "I do not trust these northmen any more than I trust any other foreigners. But I must say, his wife is very pretty."

"She is," Maximian said. "They seem happily married." *Words that need to be spoken, regardless of truth.*

"Do they? I am not so certain." There was scheming in Janus' eyes, and his lust was legendary.

"I would concern myself with Lemuel…"

"Then do so. I will concern myself with Lanabelle."

Maximian bit his lips. Secondo Janus was used to getting what he wanted.

CHAPTER THREE:
SCATTERED

Caro, Legionary

As a poor boy, the son of a shepherd, Caro never thought he would leave the isle of Kerundis, much less travel the world. His father had barely scraped by. He had named his son Caro, which could not have been any less fitting. Caro, the grand legate who had conquered the East, had died in golden halls, and now—by anyone's account—Caro would die here in the far south, away from home. The cataphracts had broken the legion, and Caro had fled under the orders of his centurion. They had intended to strike Seshán and reduce it to rubble before the fortifications were complete, but the partially-finished wall had been irrelevant. The padisha emperor, who called himself Pharzanes the Empire-Hater, sent all his forces to fight the legion. They'd broken like chaff in the wind.

"The Empire does not retreat!" Caro's legate had screamed as his men broke rank and fled, and seconds before an arrow took him in the throat.

Caro's century had been one of the last to fall back. But the night had grown late, and they were still alive. Warhorns still blew, echoing through the darkness, and the thunder of horses' hooves—though growing fainter—still rolled over the mountainous hills. Caro himself had never been the bravest of the legionaries, but still his trembling legs embarrassed him. Some of the men had gotten what they called murky-boots, caught from the long marches through wetlands and the rain. The southrons didn't have roads like the Imperials did; theirs were primitive, made of dirt, muddy and miserable, not ideal for a soldier's march.

A screech lit up the night, and a shadow passed over the moon. The Sand Drakes lived nearby, and of late they'd gone after human prey. There was a rumor that Pharzanes the Empire-Hater had trained some of his warriors to ride on the drakes' backs. But that was too terrifying a thought for Caro to contemplate. If he ever did manage to train the Sand Drakes and harness the power of their corroding breath, the Empire was done for, as far as Caro saw it.

Another shriek lit up the night. Caro jolted and forced himself not to whimper. His friend Taurus had gotten a bad case of murky-boots; he could barely run more than five minutes at a time, and the trembling was nearly constant. Taurus was half Eastern, half Anthanian. The century called him Halfblood, but he didn't seem to mind. After all, they called Caro Sheepbrain.

The thunder of horses rolled up and down the dale, all throughout the hills. The aftermath of the slaughter at Seshán would only worsen. But if Imperium willed it, they'd regroup and survive to fight again. One thing was certain; they could not go north, 'til they had their victory crown. A coward or deserter that showed his face was likely to have his throat slit, if he was lucky, and more likely crucified. Their centurion was well aware of this, and he had seethed with rage when the ranks broke. The cowards, if they returned to the Empire, would get what they had coming to them, as far as Caro saw it. After all they had doomed the legion to failure, and a slow painful death was much as they deserved.

The sounds of the slaughter began to fade into the night darkness. The hills of north Fharas became silent, and the century found shelter in a stone ruin.

In the light of dawn, Caro awoke to Taurus' groans of pain. He had removed his boots and was massaging his flaking feet. It seemed he had washed off the mud, but even then there was some dirt you could never remove, not to mention the grayish growth where the murky-boots had started to spread.

"Taurus." Caro reached for his canteen, but picking it up, it felt empty. His tongue was dry. *The soldier's life isn't for the weak.*

Taurus' only response was another groan of pain.

"Taurus…"

"Go do something useful, Sheepbrain," Taurus growled. "Get Septimo."

"Aye."

The century—all ninety of them—lay among the stone arches and broken foundations of the ruin, sleeping lightly, ready to startle awake at the slightest disturbance. Above, the golden light illuminated a clear cloudless sky, with the moon and stars still clearly visible. In his youth, he considered dawn the happiest time of day, full of possibility and promise—not now.

Septimo, the medic, was from the Isles just like Caro, but he came from Seldanis, a much more prosperous and civilized island, and Caro never heard the end of how the Kerundi were all goat-humping shepherds. Septimo was a master of herbs and poultices, and he had the stomach for what he did—even amputations—when Caro most certainly would not. He had a little salve for murky-boots that took the pain and itchiness away, but it didn't last.

He lay there, snoring on his bedroll, still wearing his robe, a thing of linen fabric so caked with dirt and dried blood it was difficult to discern the medic's star symbol.

A light kick was all that took to awake him. "Ah, Sheepbrains."

Though pledged to Sollust, god of healing, he used the same vulgar nicknames as everyone else. "Murky-boots," Caro said, chuckling despite the terrors of the past night, the abject failure of their mission and the doom that awaited them on either side of the border, Imperial or southron.

"Murky-boots," Septimo breathed, and opened the case of medical supplies at his side. "Old Halfblood will be the end of me."

The salve Septimo used for murky-boots was poisonous if ingested, but smeared on the scaly gray feet, all the pain on Halfblood's face melted away.

"Thank Sollust," Halfblood sighed.

"Don't thank Sollust. Thank milk-of-the-nightblossom."

Until Septimo, Caro had never met a priest so disrespectful to his patron god. It was hard to witness sometimes.

"But don't really thank milk-of-the-nightblossom, either. You won't really get healed for this until I find some kernsroot." Septimo drew his white hood above his head, a symptom that the day had begun in earnest.

Caro wondered what would become of their century. The legion had scattered to the four winds. Panic breeds panic, and they'd likely never regroup. There was only death ahead of them, as far as he could see.

"Where are we?" Halfblood breathed in between the sighs of relief.

"In a ruin," Septimo answered as he continued smearing the salve. "What's more, I think this is a ruin of the Svarthal…"

"The wha—?" Halfblood gasped, caught unawares by the sudden burst of relief.

"A people that lived here long ago… the southron dwarves."

The norgs, the legendary Little People of the Forest, were said to have descended from dwarves. Stories said they lived in an enchanted wood near the Wall. They sometimes eked out a living among humans, though Caro had never met one. He turned and surveyed the land around him as they continued to talk.

Dry, pebbly grass and low rolling hills stretched as far as he could see. They were hidden from obvious view, but Caro knew they were not alone. There were herders here, of cattle and sheep, and not long before they had come upon the ruin they had passed through wheat-fields.

"The Svarthal were great workers of metal," Septimo went on. "They were friends of the efreeti."

"The efreeti?" Halfblood gasped as the salve continued to

work its wonders. "Surely you don't believe that nonsense."

"I don't believe it or disbelieve it," Septimo stood up, finished with his work. "I only repeat what I've been told. They say the efreeti passed on from this world, into another. The magi still revere them."

Halfblood grabbed his muddy boots.

"I'd walk barefoot, if I wanted my feet to heal. You need dry air if you want to cure murky-boots without kernsroot powder."

Halfblood snarled and shoved his feet into the muddy boots anyway. "Only a madman marches barefoot."

Caro smiled. If you wanted Halfblood to do something, you told him the opposite. By now, Septimo should know that.

As his fellow soldiers quaffed down their rations of road-biscuits and dried fruit, Caro looked around the ruin. Most of it was a bare foundation, but some freestanding structures remained: pointed arches that might have once been gates, square slabs of marble, and broken pillars as low as tree stumps. He wondered what had happened to the Svarthal, but in truth there was no point in worrying about it, as he saw it. History is history, as they said.

Masimo, their centurion, had already donned his armor and horsehair-crested helmet, and was ordering everyone to prepare to march. It was anyone's guess where he wanted them to go. The Empire would kill them as deserters, if the southrons didn't get to them first. Caro didn't know who would give them the least painful death, but Caro wasn't set on dying. He had joined the legion for the promises of loot and treasure, and maybe one day a house in the north, where no one could bother him with their company unless he asked them to. But here, in the Southern World, that dream he'd had as a fresh recruit seemed so impossibly far away now, so far removed from his mind in the intense heat of the sun.

CHAPTER FOUR:
THE STAR OF THE ARENA

Raulus No-Name

From the day his domina rescued him from certain death—lying exposed as an unwanted infant—Raulus had been groomed as a gladiator. Everything done had been toward that end. He barely had the ability to walk when he held his first wooden sword. His domina, Leto, had not spared a moment since then. From age one through nineteen, everything he had done he had done with the Arena in mind. Leto had remained his domina, and he her slave; but Leto never struck him unless he truly deserved it. And her strict training had produced the desired results; now, Raulus No-Name had become the Imperial Eagles' most valuable gladiator.

In the team battles, when they used the alchemical gaming swords, Raulus rarely fell to his opponents. In the games of blood, he never took a single wound against the ceremonially-executed criminals, even when the gamemaster ordered them armed. Whether he fought near-blind as the heavily armored Myrmidon, quick on his feet as the spear-wielding Harak, or armorless with the net and trident of the Thartan, his weapon always found its quarry, and none but the most skilled could last long when Raulus focused on them.

Only recently was Raulus—a man of nineteen, forbidden to go anywhere without the express consent of his ever-wise domina—allowed to pray in the Temple of Imperium without her supervision. After all, he was preparing for the game of his life.

The emperor himself—Janus—had ruled the nation, for the most part, with competence, or so Raulus' loving domina had said. But something—Domina Leto said—was also seriously wrong with him.

Before the giant hall of Imperium, in sight of the towering War-Eagle statue, Raulus knelt and asked for absolvement of the sin to come. The emperor, Secondo Janus, in his best moments, had ample wisdom and a shrewd command of the nation. In his worst moments, he was hopelessly insane. It was in this fit of insanity that he proclaimed himself the son of Lorenus the Sea God, and challenged Raulus to a gladiatorial duel to the death. Raulus knew how it would end: a spear, or trident, or sword through the emperor's chest.

And what graver sin against Imperium could there be, than slaying the very one the Spirit of Empire chose to rule?

He had hoped Janus would regain his judgment and retract the offer. But when Domina Leto asked, he remained firm. He said he would fight Raulus as a gladiator. Even in his sanity, it seemed the pronouncements he made in his fits of madness prevailed.

"What troubles you, Signor Raulus?" The voice of the priest echoed throughout the chamber.

"How do you know my name?"

"Who doesn't? You are a famed gladiator. Everyone knows who you are, my signore. You are the best gladiator in Imperial City, perhaps in the whole Imperial World. Which begs the question, why are you here in the Temple of Imperium? You look like one who is asking forgiveness."

Raulus stood up and turned to face the priest.

The man's hair was gray, but his eyes seemed young, perhaps even wild. His priestly blue robe touched the floor, cinched with a rope-belt of bright gold. In his wrinkled right hand he clutched a staff of wood, its tip carved in the likeness of an eagle. This was a man devoted to the Spirit of Empire, a man who dedicated his life to Imperium, the national cult, and the very idea of Empire. Would he understand?

"I am, in a way," Raulus said. "I fear what I must do. I love our nation. I love the country where I was born. I love the Spirit of Empire and I wish more than anything to act according to the Will of Imperium."

"Speak, Signor Raulus. Tell me what troubles you. I know you are a patriot. I know Imperium smiles on you. You do not need to convince me of that. Tell me what troubles you."

"The Hand of Imperium has challenged me to a duel to the death… in the Arena. I know I will have to fight him, else I would disobey him. But how can I fight the Hand of Imperium, knowing I will succeed? It would be the gravest sin of all…"

"It would not be against the Will of Imperium," the priest answered. "If you fought his Hand, and slew him, it would fall under his Will."

"But then, I could not live with myself. I deal in death. I have slain murderers and criminals and foreigners, but I can't bear to slay a good citizen, let alone the bloody emperor."

"The Will of Imperium is hard to see… it weaves intricately through the lives of the citizens, always bringing the Empire to greater glory. The Spirit of Empire forgives you, Signor Raulus. Imperium will still smile on you, should you slay its Hand."

"Bless you, Signor Priest. But still, even if the Spirit of Empire should forgive me, I will never forgive myself. I have never met the emperor Janus, but I have viewed him as the father I never had… the ruler of the Empire is the father to all—that is what they say."

"And the father of the Empire is subject to the consequences of his decisions… even death by the sword of his unwilling, but still-beloved son."

Even the forgiveness of the priest, the assurance of Imperium, would not prevail against his looming guilt. After he slew the emperor whom he loved, he would never be the same; he would die as a guilty man, bitter and deeply sad because of what he had been forced to do— even if it was, in truth, the Will of Imperium. "Thank you, Signor Priest. I appreciate your words." But still, they did not heal him, and they would not heal him. The guilt would run deep throughout all his days.

Forgive me, Imperium, and forgive me, all the gods of Heaven. He turned and left for the temple's double-doors.

~

When he returned to his home—a multi-room dwelling on the ground floor of one of Imperial City's many apartment blocks—Leto was waiting for him.

At times, Raulus despised his domina, but those bouts became increasingly rare. Leto, a blonde woman with the coldest blue eyes he'd ever seen, nonetheless had a very warm and tender side to her when she deemed it appropriate.

She reclined on the couch, a silver goblet of wine in her hand—probably the expensive Korthian red she bought with Raulus' winnings. "Have you atoned, sweet Raulus?"

The sarcasm was not lost on him, but she meant well. She understood her slave's devotion, even if she could not understand why he devoted himself so fervently to the cause of Imperium. She was a devoted woman in her own way: devoted to maximizing profits, storing away gold and purchasing apartment blocks to rent out—building a life for herself, she said, but not willing to live in the moment and enjoy the life she already had.

"I have," Raulus answered. "The priest said I am absolved… I am guilt free… Janus may be the Hand of Imperium but he must live with the choices he made…"

"So do we all, sweet Raulus. Though you did not choose the life you had. Your mother was one rotten lupa, to leave you to die. But she did not destroy you. She sent you into the loving arms of your sweet domina, and you made the best of what you have. Your name is famous across the whole Empire."

"And perhaps, soon, it will be infamous."

The bright midday sun shone through the bright silk curtains of green and yellow. The smell of cooking food and the mixture of human smells from the street still had a hold over Leto's home, though she had tried her best to disguise it with incense and thick perfumes.

"Infamous is still famous," Leto said. "I do not know what you are so worried about. The emperor challenged the best gladiator in the whole of the Empire. You are not responsible for another person's madness."

"Another person. The emperor is something else… the Hand of Imperium."

Leto puckered like she'd tasted a sour grape. "Oh, Issa's loins, Signor Raulus, please spare me. Not even the Magisterium believes Imperium is a true god."

The statement was more wounding than if she had said nothing at all. "What does the Magisterium know?"

Leto's grimace relaxed into a smile. "Ah, my sweet Raulus, the Magisterium is a joke, and a bad joke at that. I do not care what you believe. I know it is difficult for you… I know slaying your god's mortal agent is more than you can bear. But you must remember, the Imperial Arena will be packed. Every seat will be taken. And that means more libra than ever… we will be drowning in gold, when you receive the victor's sum."

"Is it worth it, though?"

"Yes," Leto answered. "Yes, it most certainly is. And I will not hear your refusals. The gods have showered us with a great bounty… dropped it into our lap like a silver idol from Heaven. If you refuse it, then surely your Imperium will condemn you to hellfire."

Raulus turned so that he did not have to look at her. "You do not understand."

"I will not hear of it anymore."

"Then I will leave."

"Farewell, sweet Raulus. Come back before dark."

For a moment, he despised her again. For a moment, he wanted to wring her neck. But she was not entirely a villainess. She was only uncaring, unwilling to understand her slave—the one she said she loved as a son—unwilling to consider Raulus' feelings, concerned only for gold.

He left his home thinking that he hated her, but he knew, in time, that would change.

The streets of Imperial City exhibited the Empire's ascension. Now, the unchallenged Master of the World, it drew aspirants from every corner of Varda. Stepping outside the apartment block that Leto owned, two Fharese men in turbans walked by; an Eloesian, quite clearly a social climber—his finespun woolen tunic studded with gems—probably a lowblood in his own nation but eager to make something of himself; and then there were some other people, the likes of which Raulus had never seen before.

They were bloodless and white as any Getan—three, in number—one with red hair, another with black and another dark brown, clearly from nowhere nearby. They had trimmed, clean beards and thick mustaches, and their armor was something unlike Raulus had ever seen.

It covered them head-to-toe, forged of thick steel plates and decorated with gold filigree in the shape of lions. Their swords were giant head-cleavers of weapons—like the northern barbarians, but of better quality steel, hilts of fine leather and gold pommels—and they spoke in a guttural tongue amongst themselves. Raulus wondered if these were the Elders—the folk from the Far-Beyond North—but then he remembered the Elders were creatures of magic and great wisdom. It seemed these folk had only their swords as weapons, not the Elders' legendary powers of blinding light. They walked with a confident, almost arrogant gait as they passed Raulus by.

He wondered what would happen if he faced these foreigners in the Arena—larger than Raulus, with huge swords that could chop him in two but might very well prove bulky and unwieldy—but then he reminded himself that he would not have to deal with these folk at all. Like the other foreigners, these "far-northerners" would be gone soon, and the Empire would continue on as it had, the unchallenged Master of the World.

Still, he had never seen such folk in the streets of Imperial City before. He wondered if their presence was a portent, an omen of Imperium—the god that Leto mocked. At the thought of his cruel domina, Raulus ground his teeth.

CHAPTER FIVE:
PALADIN

Julian

"Before us is a true warrior of heaven, a hammer in the Just God's hand." The priest who officiated the ceremony wore a hooded robe of bright-white linen. The smell of incense hung thickly over the room. "In his duties to the Pontifex he has proven himself strong and brave and faithful to the tenets of the Just God. He has never feared evil, only bashed it with his mace. Now, let him be called Malleus, Julian the Hammer, servant of Hieronus, paladin of god. Let him be beholden to no man or priest or Pontifex. He is now a free agent, accountable only to himself and to Hieronus. May the Just God guide his hammer to always strike home; may the skulls of the evildoers be smashed like jars of clay."

Julian fell to one knee. The white-robed priest sprinkled oil on his bare head. He had worked all twenty-one years of his life for this; now, he was perhaps the youngest paladin in the order. Except on direct missions of the Pontifex, he had never left the walls of Sanctum. Now, he would be unsupervised, liable only to the Just God and the petty laws of the Empire. He would be a free agent, a hammer in the hand of god.

"Rise, Julian Malleus Ultor," the priest said.

Julian did just that. A templar, Dorimer, handed him the warhammer. He accepted the heavy weapon without any struggle. The head of the warhammer, made of iron, came to a sharp point on one end, useful for breaking through the hardest of iron. All along its edge, fine ironwork detailed a scene from a nearly-forgotten holy war: the struggle against the river people, worshipers of a death goddess they called the Midnight Crone. Julian had learned about them in history lessons, but the subject lent itself to forgetfulness.

"May the Just God guide you," the priest said.

Julian nodded.

"Go. Crack the skulls of the evildoers in the name of god."

Julian left the Magisterium's doors as a paladin.

His horse, a giant white charger, awaited him. The priests had provided him the beast as a farewell gift. As he heaved himself on its back, dressed in the eagle-emblazoned chainmail, he gave one look back to the Magisterium with its great white domes, pillars and spires; then, he rode off.

The words of the priest echoed in his mind: Go. Crack the skulls of the evildoers in the name of god.

Years ago, he had learned who the true evildoers were. Magic caused all ills, and those who wielded it were, by nature, evil. He did not know who he would wreak havoc on first: the Augur Collegium, the hierophants or theurges. First, of course, he had to crack the skull of the one who had killed his parents. Finding him would be difficult. Torture of all kinds was prohibited to the paladins; because of that, the magician should count himself incredibly lucky.

He rode north out of the gate, galloping out of the White City, with the sun setting to his left.

The causeways across the moors of South Paladium wove through the province like a web. At certain points, flyspeck villages appeared—small settlements of a dozen families at most, built on upraised layers of wooden piles—some of which Julian recognized from his outings. But in his theological studies and physical conditioning, he had little time to himself, and those outings had been exceedingly rare. He still remembered a summer night at seventeen, when the humidity was nigh unbearable. He had traveled to the largest town in the moorland, a city called Solace. There, all the rigid laws of the Magisterium had no effect. There were spice houses, gambling halls and taverns, brothels, but worst of all to Julian, an outpost of the

Augur Collegium where magic weavers practiced their dark art unmolested. That night in Solace, his friend Kyros, the most gifted warrior Julian had ever met, tried Haroon spice for the first time. He never left Solace; from what he heard, the addiction had ruined him. The other fellow student he traveled with—Barkha, a god-fearing Khazidee—had visited one of the brothels, the cheapest one and the only he could afford. The pox he contracted would stay with him the rest of his life, but Barkha nonetheless was on his way to becoming a full monk militant, celibate but forever living with the consequences of that one mistake.

As the last bits of light faded, Julian Malleus kept an eye out for an inn. Gods knew there were few of those in the moorlands. The town of Paladris still lay impossibly far away.

Darkness fell and he rode alone across the causeway. A moor-dog howled. There were, of course, no villages nearby and thus no dogs; the dog was a phantom, a product of the dark times. That was what the Order of Hunters said. The thought of demon-worshipers attacking him did not strike him with fear, only stir the desire to crack their skulls.

Still, the night grew increasingly lonely and quiet. The darkness hung heavy, and the hours blended into each other. He thought of sleeping on the roadside, amid all the swarming midges and worse creatures rumored to lurk underwater. A dozen times he began drifting off only to suddenly waken. Then, at some point during the long night, lights appeared: candles in a window, a small village, an inn.

For a town in the moorlands it was quite impressive in size; in all a dozen buildings clustered together, and in the center, on the roadside, lay an inn marked "The Red Dragon." Before Julian had the chance to knock, a servant opened the door—a young lass of no less than fifteen—and sprang out. "Signor Traveler, we have ale and hot food—well, not hot, seeing as I made it a few hours ago, but still warm.

You'd do us honor if you stayed at the Red Dragon, signore."

"Indeed, I would," Julian said, and found himself hopping off the saddle.

~

The hearth burned warm, turning the humid air nigh unbearable, but once settled in on the divan, and after the serving wench brought him a glass of chilled sweetwine, all the discomforts of the inn and his prior journeys melted away. She sat down across from him on the other divan. She was plump, with a full bosom and lush red lips. Her blue eyes had a fire to them, and her expression had a simpering look he'd seen so many times before. "Ah, signore, you are so handsome," they would say, and he had learned to turn them down. He had pledged himself to the Order of St. Dorimer, not a celibate order by any means, but bedding a girl without wedding her first was grounds for termination; and once wed, there could be no divorce.

"That hammer is too big for you, signore."

Julian kept silent.

"Where do you come from?"

"The Magisterium," he answered.

"Ah, you are one of those folk." Her expression became dour, disappointed. "So rarely does a handsome young man come in, and he is one of those priestly folk… touched in the head by the gods, yes, but *touched*."

Mocking words had long failed to upset him. "Where is the innkeeper?"

"Do not worry about Signor Pieter."

"I am not worried."

"Well, some might be… some claim he is a demon-worshiper, a black theurge, a disciple of the dark arts."

"If he is," Julian said, "then I will kill him."

"Ah, I pray to Issa for a brave, handsome man… and she grants it, yet she makes him a priest. Why does she torture me so?"

"A good Paladian woman worships Issa?" The goddess of fertility was the domain of the Khazidees and southrons, not folk so far north.

"I am her most fervent devotee in all Paladium."

"I do not doubt it."

"I have made a pilgrimage to her temple in Imperiopoli… even tried to join her priesthood."

The thought turned Julian's stomach.

"A sacred concubine must be chosen by the goddess at a young age… I thought nineteen was young, but the Mother Priestess disagreed." The simpering smile returned to the serving wench's lips. "Between Signor Pieter the so-called black theurge, and me, the worshiper of Issa, perhaps you understand why the Red Dragon has such a poor reputation."

"Let us hope only one of those rumors is true, signora. The goddess Issa is a being of Heaven, but a magic weaver… that, I will not abide."

"I do not think it is true, my signore," the wench said. "Though the noises at night are quite odd… you'd think there is a menagerie of animals in his room, though all he has is his dog." She was warming to him, that much was clear; a spur for Julian to leave. "My name is Mathise… I have not asked yours, braveheart."

"Paladin," Julian answered. "My name is Paladin."

Next, Mathise brought in the meal, a bowl of crawfish that had grown cool and pungent. Julian ate it quickly, and Mathise watched him as he did, making him ever more and more uncomfortable. To any man of lesser conviction, Mathise would be impossible to resist. But according to the Order of St. Dorimer, he could only have one woman his entire life, and he would not join himself to a worshiper of Issa.

"I shall get the signore some more wine…"

"I am fine, Signora Mathise," Julian answered. "I had so much

I don't think I will ever thirst again."

Mathise smirked.

The night deepened, and the divan—cleaned and kept free of grime—was a more promising place to relax than the beds, which Julian had no doubt were flea-ridden, miserable things. Thus he stayed, and eventually his adamant will frayed; he shared a glass of chilled sweetwine with Mathise, then another, and the saucy lass revealed ever more and more about herself. Perhaps she trusted priests implicitly, thinking they'd never harm her; perhaps she was right.

"The innkeeper has strange company… in all honesty I do not know if the rumors are true. Even *you* would be afraid of the folk that come in here."

Julian knew he wouldn't.

"I think they truly might be magic weavers. There is a fellow… he came in, from the north."

"Bregantium?" Julian still hungered to find the blackguard that murdered his family.

"No… further. Brill. Had the look of a madman in his eyes… was babbling nonsense, but you knew enough to be afraid of him. Folk said the man could enchant people, make them like him. That is probably the only way he could…"

Julian remembered the magic weaver… he had come from the north, and might possibly be mad—as any murderer is loath to be— but his powers of magic were lightning. He exhaled at the dead end. Then he took another deep sip of his chilled sweetwine, finishing the last of it. *I will avenge my father.* That is what he thought in the darkest of times in his training.

But he would never give up. Julian never gave up on anything if he committed himself to it. And he would not rest until his hammer had avenged his family's blood.

"They say when the Signor Innkeeper walks by the moor-dogs howl."

Julian stood up. "I must go." He would not abide a magic weaver, even less a man who aroused the moor-dogs' howl.

~

As he rode out of the village, the flickering torchlight painted the face of a man walking in from the moors. In his hand was a staff, and he was dressed in black. It could only be the innkeeper, and he had the look of magic to him. Julian had an urge to put things right in this village, to deal death to him as all magic weavers so rightly deserved.

CHAPTER SIX:
THE LOTUS COURT

Theon Arkadios

Not long after Theon Arkadios entered the Red Palace, passing through the red pointed arches and taking in the sweet, intoxicating scents of the garden, he met the queen herself. Her eyes were large, set against a thin, small nose. She had the copper skin of a Khazidee and an elegant swanlike neck. She could not be any older than seventeen.

At her feet, beside the Red Throne, was a child of no more than six. Astarthe was kneading his scalp with her thin fingers; Theon wondered if he ever left her sight.

"Out of the crowd comes a man tall, dark, handsome," Astarthe breathed. "Fharese, he might be, but no—the goddess toys with me, sends me a man of Eloesus. Yet it seems he is not; he is dressed like a barbarian, or at least like a people very far away."

"Your Grace—"

"You will speak when I ask you to speak!" Astarthe snapped, and Theon felt himself shrinking away from the spoiled girl's air of majesty. "In olden days, before the glorious Empire took me in his lovingcare, the country smallfolk of Khazidea would not even dare to look at Astarthe, daughter of the goddess, for fear they'd be blinded. The Empire in his infinite wisdom allowed the books of history to remain in the royal library; I have read them religiously."

"You speak of the Empire like he is a man."

To his surprise, she did not lay into him. "The Empire I consider as a loving husband, to whom I give all my excess grain. He rules over my people, and I delight at his affection when he so lovingly gives it. The Empire is my lord, the one I serve only after my mother goddess Issa…"

"The Empire gave you a child?" Perhaps the legendary

madness of the Queens of Haroon had affected her.

"Look at the one before you, and tremble! Adamantion has a god's blood in him. His father is Claudian, whom I bore a child by my fertility and his wondrous, unforgettable love."

Only then did Theon focus on the child before him. The tone of his skin was a comely mixture of the red Khazidean of Astarthe and the olive Anthanian of Claudian: a light yet virile bronze. His nose was aquiline like the Anthanian's, but less pronounced. Most of all, his eyes had a stern look, the legendary intensity and judging fire of a conqueror, like the Adamanti were said to have.

Theon guessed this combination of features would make him a handsome man, indeed.

"He so rarely sees other men," Astarthe said. "I do take lovers, my sweet signore, but it is not good for a boy his age to know too much of love."

Despite her obvious spoiled and pampered lifestyle, it seemed Astarthe had an intelligence and a command of words beyond her age. Indeed she was a queen by blood.

"My handmaid Nama only brings truly interesting people into the Lotus Court—for that is what we call our court this year. Even rarer does she think a *man* is worth bringing here… she knows my standards for them are near impossible to meet."

"I am Theon Arkadios," he answered, though in truth he was called Wayfarer.

"Arkadios," Astarthe said, and stood to her feet. "That is a name so rich, the saying of it likely produces gold. Achaeus Arkadios was a merchant of Eloesus… back when the common people of Eloesus ruled themselves, when they called themselves *citizens* instead of subjects."

"I think you know more of my history than I do," Theon ventured, but the comment did not receive a laugh, only a hint of a smile.

"It is said Achaeus Arkadios grew so wealthy he became a

king. But a king is only by blood. Do you agree?"

"I… I do not know…"

"The Adamanti by rights should rule the world. The man who rules now is not by blood a ruler… he is a mere man. The councilors say the Adamanti line is extinguished… Ha! They are wrong and I have my proof right here. Secondo Janus may be a Knight, but the Jani do not rule, the Adamanti do. Do you agree, my sweet signore?"

"I… I guess… Yes."

"Oh, you are so delightful to watch, trying to please me. I do not know why I have such power over men."

Astarthe was beautiful, but she was ambitious, and that child she bore—far from being an asset—may well prove the end of her. The Empire abounded with schemers like maggots on spoiled meat, and an Adamanti-born would be the first to the knife.

"Tell me, my sweet signore, where you come from… or I shall go over there and pinch your cheeks and force it out of your mouth." She turned to one of her orange-robed handmaids. "Jesmiya, some tea, at once!"

"I come," he began as the handmaid scurried off, "from a land I do not remember… from a life I do not recall, or that I only recall glimpses of. From far east, so far east I followed the Silk Route to where it ends. It took so long that when I got there I was so relieved… but I could not speak a word of their tongue. I came to a city larger than any in the Empire, larger than even Imperial City. There were parrots and winding streets and a stench like you wouldn't believe. Everyone was looking at me curiously. The rest… the rest is an opium dream."

"You are already boring me, signore," Astarthe said. "You are lucky you are so devilishly handsome. A handsome face can cover a multitude of flaws, as I see it."

Theon looked down. He did not want this. He did not want to be in this "Lotus Court." But what better hiding place could there be? Here, the legate wouldn't find him, nor his father's false son. Here, he was safe.

"I have never heard a firsthand account of the Far East," Astarthe purred. "The ones I have sent I have never heard from again. Perhaps they too were lost in an opium dream… and they are not strong like you. They have never recovered."

"Or perhaps a sabre-tooth cat laid into them, or a Dreshen Monster, or a great lizard… the Silk Route goes across the Plain of Megiddo, and if you aren't careful, the wildlife there will—"

"Hush. Do not speak so much, signore. You are much more pleasing to the eye than the ear." She giggled. "Oh, I jest, signore. But believe me, I know all there is to know about the Southern World. The Plains of Megiddo are as wild as the horse-folk who ride across them. There is no better place for a hunter, but he had best come prepared. An arrow to the neck isn't enough to overcome most of the vicious beasts there."

"So you have left the Red Palace."

"I have spent more time outside the Red Palace than in it, signore. As a child I spent time in the tiger-city of Saidoon… and before that at Qarn-El, on the easternmost edge of the Wild Plain. Do not presume to lecture me, my sweet, handsome fool."

"Do not call me a fool, signora," Theon half-spoke, half-snarled.

"Do not tell a queen what to say and what not to say, my sweet, handsome fool."

Theon groaned at her words. She was shapely and beautiful, a copper-skinned goddess in living form, and his physical side may soon overcome his spiritual self, but one who lived fully in the physical world would never achieve freedom from the cycle of death and rebirth—that is what the sage Choh had told him all those ages ago. He marveled at how little he remembered of all those years, but it is said a westerner who ventures to the ancient lands of the Far East did not return the same person. He wondered if one of the Celestial Emperor's elementalists had cast a spell of forgetfulness over him, or if it—in truth—had really been the opium.

"What are those square tablets on your belt?"

"Coins," he answered her. "The Easterners use square money. It is much more practical than ours."

"More practical than mine?"

"I will not play games with you, Your Grace."

"You had best do whatever you can to please me, my sweet fool. My handmaids are my eyes and ears around the city. My soldiers—the Anakhil—are not armed by Imperial decree, but they listen and tell me all. The First Harak Legate is looking for a man named Theon Arkadios. And I have him right here."

Theon felt the blood drain from his face. "Ah, signora—Your Grace," he corrected himself. *An Illumined One knows no fear,* Choh had said. "Forgive me. I shall do nothing more."

"Ah, but you will do something, my sweet fool."

The thought of spending the night with her—forsaking the spiritual world for the false physical realm—terrified him more than his father's false son.

"I am making an appearance in Imperial City. The ships set sail in two days. A proper Queen of Haroon cannot be without a consort; else the common farmers of the river will think her infertile, and fear dreadful things to come." Her hands began to knead little Adamantion's hair again. "My child—the son of Khazidea and the Empire—comes with me. You shall not call him Adamantion there, but Anakh. At least, until I tell you to. I expect in Imperial City we will eat sumptuous foods and enjoy all its entertainments. There is a game coming up, after all. My eyes and ears in the city say that Emperor Janus is performing in the Arena, against the best gladiator in the whole of the Imperial World."

The ambition behind her words were palpable. "An emperor, competing in the Arena… he may as well perform naked in a pantomime, or prostitute himself…" He had begun to remember how the Empire worked.

"Things are changing. Things have always been changing, and they will continue to change. Besides, he would not be the first emperor to go wildly against tradition. It is admirable, do you think, to shirk responsibility, to do as you wish without regard for custom?"

"No. I do not think that, at all…" Though Theon was a son of the Empire, the Far East had become deeply part of him.

CHAPTER SEVEN: ALL-SEEING ORB

Maximian, Marshal of the Guard

In the solitude of his bedchamber, Maximian ran his hand along the length of his blade. The hard, unbreakable bluish metal—adamant—made it worth more than a king's ransom. And the more King Bretonnius stayed in the Imperial Palace, the more he ingratiated himself toward Janus while his "advisor" Lemuel snooped around, the more Maximian wanted to hold these northmen for ransom.

Janus was a young man, inexperienced in the world. He did not see these folk like Maximian saw them, as potential enemies and dangers to the realm. Silvana, after all, had confirmed his suspicions. The "advisor" Lemuel was a wizard, and he wanted something the Empire had.

Maximian grasped the adamant sword by the hilt and slid it into its sheath. Janus himself had granted it to him, as he'd outfit every member of the Imperial Guard. Some received cheaper swords of adamant alloy, but Maximian—as marshal, the chief member of the Guard—had received the best-made of them all. The smith had named it *Imperium's Rebuke*. When struck with enough force, it shattered the highest quality of steel. If they outfitted the whole of the Imperial army with such weaponry, no one could stand against them, especially these northmen. But the making of adamant weapons was prohibitively expensive, and might stop soon altogether—from what Maximian heard, the Alchemist Collegium had nearly used up all the required material. To smelt adamant ore and shape the metal required a flame so hot that rare and increasingly depleted ingredients were necessary.

In many ways, Maximian thought, *I am lucky.*

"I think I know what he is after." For the first time Maximian remembered, the voice of Silvana came before her wind. "There is a tool of magic power… the All-Seeing Eye…"

Maximian pivoted to face her. She was a welcome sight. Traces of blonde hair fell from her winged leather cap. Her blue eyes held strength and intensity, but also warmth. "And what shall we do, sweetling?"

"Do not call me sweetling." Her eyes narrowed, losing all warmth, and her lips twisted in anger. "Janus is blind to their machinations. The wizard Lemuel is asking all sorts of questions. It is only a matter of time before he uncovers the location. Then, he will steal it."

"We should tell Janus."

"No." Silvana shook her head. "I already have, and he won't listen. He is too enamored with Bretonnius' stories."

And his wife. "Does he know about the All-Seeing Eye?"

"He does not. Nor does he know how to use it. But he has allowed Maestro Fausto to use it, and he seems unwilling to accept that it's an invaluable asset… unwilling, or complacent. Fausto's warnings have won us many battles… even those we have not fought."

"Perhaps we should exact justice ourselves. Rebuke is thirsty for blood."

"Lemuel would fry you to a pulp. He is a great wizard. His aura is stronger than mine… twice the aura of even Fausto."

"A knife in the dark would silence him before he cast a spell."

"Those oafish knights guard Lemuel day and night. And I have no doubts he is protected with wards."

"Wards?"

"Booby-traps that would burn you to ash in half a second. The only thing we can do, I fear, is take the orb from its tower. But it is terribly heavy, Signor Maximian."

"Do not call me 'signor.'" Vengeance for 'sweetling.' It is remarkable how much that stung. "Are you asking me to carry it?"

"It would be too heavy for even you."

Maximian laughed darkly. "I think you underestimate me, sweetling."

Her lips twisted into a half-snarl. "In an hour, we require you to stand guard over the north wing, and let no one by on threat of death. If Lemuel comes, you must not let him pass."

"And if he continues anyway?"

"You must fight him."

"And have him roast me?"

Silvana said nothing.

"Very well, sweetling. I will do as you say."

The rest of the Imperial Guard sat around a table in the mess room, cups of cheap sweetwine strewn around as they rolled dice. Of late the Imperial Guard hadn't much chance to fight and improve upon their swordsmanship. Except in moments of public address or lavish banquets, dice and sweetwine was the order of the day.

"Signores… we finally have something to do. I'd suggest you get on your feet and ready yourselves."

Niko, an Eloesian, snickered. "Ah, yes. I wonder how long we'll have to stand and do nothing this time."

"Let us all hope, not for long."

They formed a wall on the north wing, which thankfully was rarely entered or crossed with foot-traffic. The line of guards would certainly attract suspicion, the last thing Silvana would want. Still, all fourteen members of the Guard stood there, with Maximian at the head, waiting for the first sign of trouble.

The minutes ticked by. The Guard fell into idle chatter, and no one came. Three times Maximian snapped at them to keep silent and watchful; three times they slowly but surely began to talk again. At last Maximian thought it not worth the time to correct them. There was no one coming; there was no danger. Lemuel had no idea what Silvana was doing; the strained sounds of the All-Seeing Orb removing from its place.

Then Lemuel appeared in a twirl of his slate-blue robes. "Imperial Guards. Just what is it that you are guarding?"

"That is not your concern, Signor Lemuel."

An amused grin crept over the wizard's face. "Please, my good sirs. I mean no harm. I have some business to attend to.

"Do you?" Maximian said flatly. "I wonder what you have to do in the north wing, where there is nothing. Please go on your way, signore."

"Nothing, you say. So I presume you are guarding nothing. Are you touched in the head, my good Signor Maximian?" His 'signor' was laced with derision.

"You are not permitted to go wherever you please. In the Empire you must follow the Empire's rules."

Lemuel's bushy eyebrows narrowed. "Ah, quaint. A man of no nobility—by magical talent or blood—presumes to tell me what I can and cannot do." Out of the folds of his slate-blue robe he procured a white crystalline rod.

In an instant, the air in the room chilled, and Maximian's skin ran wild with gooseflesh. He drew *Imperium's Rebuke* and in the same motion leapt for Lemuel, slashing hard.

Throes of magic burst from the rod—orbs of emerald green, deep ruby red, nimbuses of white and daisy yellow, and twisting spirals of ocean blue. The colors danced in the air, a light-show before their very eyes. Maximian imagined this was like the Otherworld, where the satyrs and nymphs played in a garden of brilliant radiance and sensual bliss. He tried to grasp at the strands of emerald but they passed through his hand like vapor. The yellow orbs floated by his ear, but those too had no material consistency.

Lemuel was gone.

"Issa's loins, I'll kill him!" Maximian shouted. Some of his fellow guards had not woken up from the spell. But he bolted down the corridor, swearing he'd bury *Imperium's Rebuke* in Lemuel's heart.

A sprint up the stairs carried him to where Lemuel and an augur had engaged in a heated argument. Both had their staffs at the ready, and the cold, sugar-sweet smell of magic chilled the air. Behind the augur a dozen of his underlings had removed a giant blackish-green orb from its place and had rolled it a quarter-way down the stairs.

"You southlanders must think so very highly of yourselves, if you presume to use an All-Seeing Orb so recklessly. Do you know, my dear sir, that the tool of magic you use is tainted? That using it poses a threat to your mind and soul? With it, you can see the world. But the Dark One can see you."

Maestro Fausto laughed. "Let him see me. The Empire is not at war with the Dark One. The Empire is at war with Fharas, and perhaps… if you keep up your meddling, we will be at war with you."

"You are not at war with the Dark One, you say," Lemuel scoffed. "Few men have such an impressive lack of shame."

"Go back to the northlands, Signor Lemuel. You are not wanted here."

"Oh, I do intend to go back… with the dark tool you so wantonly use."

At the words Maximian charged him, preparing to thrust the adamant blade straight through his chest. But at the last moment, Lemuel turned around, eyes blazing fierily. The adamant sword flashed green and was gone; a loud whirr echoed through the stairwell. Fausto blasted a gust of wind, but Lemuel himself flashed green and appeared at the top of the stairs. Out of his robe—now looming above them from his high position—he pulled another white crystalline rod.

Below him, the augurs trying to roll the orb away looked up at him, frightened.

What chance do we have, against someone who can make our very swords disappear?

"I would not test me, dear sir," Lemuel intoned. "The Council of the Twelve is the most powerful body of magic weavers outside the elven nations."

"Elven?" Maximian breathed out, though Fausto seemed less

bewildered.

"Elven," Lemuel darkened; he seemed to grow taller, and the room shrunk before them. "The Elder Council could destroy you in a moment's span. They have access to the Wonders of the ancients… just as you so foolishly use a tool of darkness. All I have done, I have done by the authority of the Archwizard. If you resist, I must warn you, my wand holds the power to blind you irrevocably. The one who infused it is none other than Estarion Lunitar, Chief Lightbearer, who also brought your grave misconduct to the Council's attention."

To Maximian, he spoke nonsense, but Fausto's response seemed not confusion, but anger. "You are awfully presumptuous, Signor Lemuel. You treat us like you—"

"I treat you as children, Signor Fausto, because that is what you are. You are unlearned. You wield magic as the wild-men wage war; pure instinct, without skill or refinement, unpracticed and unlearned in theorems and techniques. I would not test me, sir, if you value your vision."

"What a great negotiator you are," Maximian said darkly, but he could feel himself inching down the steps, falling back toward the door. The magic in the air had grown so heavy that he could almost hear it. It hummed, a primal and immaterial sound.

"Children. Children!" Fausto sounded barely coherent, and it seemed all reason and thought was giving way to anger. "The Imperial people have subdued every nation on earth; even Fharas trembles at our might! If you act wrongly, Signor Lemuel, the north and south will meet, and not in peace."

Lemuel chuckled. "You silly man. Yes, the north and south shall meet; I am sure of it. And the Empire will fall; it is already crumbling. Your peasants choose your leaders, I hear… you are crumbling under the weight of your own liberty. If the Empire wishes to hasten its demise, then go… come face the knights and wizards and fey priestesses of the sovereign king, and I assure you it will fall."

Fausto sent a blast of focused wind at him, one that could

topple an ox; but the wind seemed to hit an invisible wall, a shield of force.

Maximian shielded his eyes, and light blasted all around him. When he looked up, his vision was blurred but nonetheless he could see. The augurs were at their knees on the stairs, feeling around the walls like blind men. The only one who had the sense to shield her eyes was Silvana.

As his vision returned the All-Seeing Orb glowed green and was gone. Then Signor Lemuel himself disappeared, leaving to who knows where, with all this destruction in his wake.

CHAPTER EIGHT:
AN ANCIENT LAND

Caro

Together, the sixty-strong ragtag band—still called, despite their casualties, a century—set out across the dry sunbaked hills of Fharas. The salve that Septimo, the medic and halfhearted priest of Sollust, had rubbed on Halfblood's feet took away his pain and constant itching, it seemed. Caro didn't hear Halfblood complain a bit, and he seemed happy as he had ever been. He began calling Caro "Sheepbrains" again, and when he was his mocking self that meant he had become back to normal. But Septimo hadn't cured, him, he'd made it clear, and within a day the murky-boots would set in hard again, and he'd be back to the discomfort and constant itching. Septimo said murky-boots got worse in the rain or in wet areas, which for a moment made Caro thankful they were in the hot baking sun of Fharas.

Their centurion was not a fool; he knew that regrouping was impossible, since they had most certainly spread out in all directions. Returning to the Empire in defeat was not an option; therefore, he said, they would have to return in victory. And since victory was out of the question, too, he said they had to return with something akin to victory—wealth, stolen from an ancient, nearly-forgotten Fire Temple a three-day march away. As Caro saw it, he had come up with the best plan he could possibly think of. It was still a long shot; a store of ancient gold was a small price to pay for retreat.

The Empire never retreats, they said. If the Imperial Army did retreat, it was an unnatural thing, repayable only by death. But gold has a way of convincing the most strident of emperors—that's what their centurion Masimo had said, and Masimo also said that Emperor Janus was no honor-bound, duty-obsessed emperor like the Adamanti that came before him. Janus, he said, loved gold more than honor.

The journey began through the dry grassland sun, and they had only the water in their canteens to replenish them. Soon they ran out, but the centurion Masimo ordered them to keep marching, and who was he to disagree?

In midday a large rock-hill appeared. In its shadow lay the ruins of an abandoned town, like the ones he had seen before. Out of its mouth, a doorway had been chiseled.

"There are no guards," Caro observed. It was an obvious statement, but as soon as it left his lips he realized he had made a more profound point than he thought.

"Yes," the centurion Masimo said. "There are no guards. I once spent months in Fharas, Signor Caro, during the Uneasy Peace. The northern Fharese dread this place like none other. But there is gold here, in the deep vaults, they don't wish to touch. Their superstition will make me a rich man… *all of us*, rich men."

The words of Masimo only worsened Caro's uneasy feeling. What could these Fharese fear, he wondered. He supposed, in this strange and ancient land, there were things to fear more than the lances of the cataphracts and the arrows of the horsemen-nomads. He thought of the Svarthal—the so-called southron dwarves—and the efreeti, evil beings of fire and destruction. He would follow his brothers-in-arms into the gates of Hell if need be; but that did not mean he wasn't afraid.

CHAPTER NINE:
RUMORS

Julian Ultor, Malleus

The road from the Magisterium to Paladris was a road that few took. Between the unbearable summer humidity, the biting midges and insects, and the long stretches of nothing but flyspeck villages and the marsh's wide expanse, most everybody preferred to take a ship wherever they wanted to go. For Julian Ultor Malleus, the road was the only way he traveled. A paladin was nothing without his horse and hammer. A warrior of god did not fear long roads or bandits. A warrior of god did not fear, and a warrior of god did not tire. Hieronus the Lord of Justice and Just War would guide his hammer. When he again returned to the town of his birth, he would find the dark sorcerer who killed his family, then put an end to his vile life. From then on he would fight as a warrior of god, putting an end to the source of all ills—magic, and those who wielded it.

Many days later he reached Paladris and its mighty white bridge, spanning the whole extent of the River Hyber. A dome rose above the city buildings, topped with a towering thin needle of gold— the Temple of Hieronus the War-Caller—that served as a resting-place for Traber and Bolimer and a half-dozen other warrior-saints. The streets were thick with monks in ash-gray habits and vestals in white hooded robes. Templars in full armor wandered also, but soon all the noise of Paladris passed him by, and he was again on the road. When he crossed the bridge, and the hooves of his charger were in the province of Gad, he felt something change within him.

He had not been in this province since all those years ago, in that evil night of his childhood, when he had run from the scene of his family's massacre. The words of the traveling monk had stuck with him. The Magisterium had been his salvation. Magic had been the source of all his ills, as it was the source of everything evil in the world. If the Pontifex judged with a right mind, he would declare a Holy War on magic weavers of all stripes. But instead, the Pontifex did nothing; he had not gone as far as allowing magic weavers into the holy orders, but he had proven his weakness through inaction.

But the Magisterium was far behind him. He had left the marshes of Paladium and the white temples of the holy orders. He had returned through distance and through time. He was back where all his troubles began, where all his dreams of a life had been shattered by magic; where all the innocence and happiness within him had been broken, turned to mourning and despair.

He was back in Gad.

~

The marshes disappeared, and with them the aggravating bites of the midges and insects. The air remained warm, but at least it was not so horridly humid. His teachers in the holy order had taught him to be thankful for everything you had; else, the gods would shame you by taking it away, and you would learn to be grateful. Julian had taken his lesson to its uttermost extreme, and thanked the gods for everything that was not a curse. It had served him well; he was still alive, still strong, still able to wield his hammer and crack the skulls of evildoers.

As he continued, trees began to line the road, growing larger and more numerous. The forests relieved him from the elements, yes, but they also instilled in him a growing sense of dread—dread he had not felt since the infant years of his training. A paladin has nothing to fear, his teachers had told him. But if he traveled to the House of Tyrenas, he questioned whether he could handle the ghosts of his past, the ghosts of that evil night when everything changed for him. The Dark One would tempt him to despair.

He was halfway to the River Gad when an inn appeared by

the side of the road. *The Greenbeard Inn,* under the shadow of two great maple trees, had a nearly tangible pall of rumor hanging over it as soon as he entered. Beside a marble statue of Kernunnos, the Green Man, two men spoke of a "foreigner" and "dark magic." The innkeeper, a large heavy-set man whose thick hair and beard made him look like an avatar of the Green Man himself, stood behind the desk. "Ah, a paladin, have we? I hope you do not mind a worshipper of the Wild God."

"All gods are good," Julian repeated one of the Magisterium's most common phrases. "And besides, a true worshipper of the Wild God would not live in a house of stone and wood. He would live in the forest near a Sacred Well, clothed in nothing but deerskins or woven leaves…"

"Aye," the innkeeper boomed. "I suppose the religious studies aren't only about stodgy old Hieronus."

"Do not speak of my god like that, Signor Innkeeper. A paladin is deadlier than a Vestal or Monk of Peace."

The innkeeper's grin widened. "You speak much truth, Signor Paladin. The cost for one night's stay is a mere denar. For wildberry pie, I shall add a mere four aesa… the rooms are quite—"

"A rumor, Signor Innkeeper… is there talk of a magician?"

"A wizard, yes," the innkeeper said. "A man of dark powers came from the north… stole something valuable, they say. Left Imperial City, and now is headed back to his home-country."

"A wizard." The wizards were an exotic thing to the Empire, a rich fodder for tales. Like all magic weavers they deserved death. "Someone must kill him, then."

"Well, Signor Paladin, if you wish to do the honors I'd be careful. Do not go after a wizard unless you are wet and difficult to light."

"Do not jest, Signor Innkeeper. The wicked man may have many powers in his arsenal, but not even a wizard can stand against the hammer of god."

He would not go to the House of Tyrenas north of Bregantium; at the next road-fork he took the northward route to Brill. He swore to Hieronus, then and there, he would either crush the wizard's skull, or perish in the act of trying.

CHAPTER TEN:
THE QUEEN'S ARRIVAL

Theon Arkadios

Theon arrived in the harbor of Imperial City, a queen in his right arm and a robe of flame-orange silk falling to his feet. He was, to the folk of this squalid metropolis, a foreign king. In truth he was a mere consort, a puppet of Astarthe. But nonetheless he rode on the Queen's royal ship, flanked on either side by the Anakhil warriors—bare chested and wrapped with links of fine gold chain, carrying bronze chopping-swords in both hands. Above his robe of flame-orange silk he wore a turban inset with a giant sapphire. His dusky Eloesian skin, combined with the southron attire, might cause people to mistake him for a Khazidee from a distance.

At the harbor, the people of Imperial City had gathered to observe the legendary Sister-Queen of Khazidea; a descendant of the Astarthe whom Claudio the God had beheaded, whom his own son Claudian had reinstated and—unbeknownst to most—given her a child.

The toddling Adamantus wore a miniature turban and a robe of silk painted with lotuses, making it exceptionally difficult to see the Imperial blood in him.

"Call him Anakh, when we are in public," Astarthe had told him, intending to disguise his father. For all her lax and luxurious lifestyle, Astarthe seemed to have more wits than Theon had estimated at first. An Adamantus would be a challenge to the very rule of Secondo Janus, who had achieved the White Throne after all the Line of Adamanti had died off.

Amid the crowd, it seemed the Imperial government had formed a welcoming party. There were old men, no doubt Augusts, wearing the purple sashes of high governmental offices.

The Imperials hate kings, but it seems they are fascinated by them.

Theon eyed his arm, hooked into Astarthe's like a woven pattern. *And they think I am one.*

The sailors scrambled to tie the boat to the docks. The giant ship still tossed in the waves, despite the calmer seas behind Imperial City's breakwater.

Together they departed from the ship, and the line of thirty Anakhil with their topknots followed a step behind. Trumpets blared from the deck. The Imperial citizens began to chatter, and all were staring wide-eyed at the foreign monarchs, the strange soldiers with their outdated bronze swords and bizarre attire. Some knew a little of Khazidean history; others only heard that the "queer people from beyond the sea" had arrived. The people of Imperial City loved a show, whether a bloodbath in the Arena or a victorious triumph. Now, it was Theon of all people who would provide it.

Hand hooked in Astarthe's arm, he led the queen to the men in purple sashes. They bowed their heads slightly—a small show of respect, compared to the groveling the queen's people gave her, but she did not seem to mind. Astarthe, after all, said she had fallen in love with the Empire; and considered the nation that ruled over her as her husband.

"Queen Astarthe," one said. "I am Crispus Servillius, Speaker of the Council."

Astarthe bowed a bit more deeply than he did, but not by much. "It is a pleasure. I have never visited King Anthans' city before. It is quite lovely."

The stone edifices stretched high above—apartment blocks, temple spires, and towers—even more than Theon remembered during his long-ago visit in his youth. The peasants live on the ground; the civilized live in the air—so said the sage Choh during one of Theon's visits to Xia, but what would he think when the buildings were so high? The Way seemed so distant now, as distant as the road that led to the Eastern Sea. *I have left it behind.* But he touched the pouch still fastened to his belt, and remembered the tokens he had brought would make it nearly impossible to forget his past journey: throwing stars, a common weapon for the warrior sages, but a thing of wonder in the West.

"Quite lovely, you say," Crispus continued. "I assure you, we have provided you with the best of accommodations, my good Signora Queen. The House of Lenora was built many decades ago… but the lady Lenora was a great lover of all thing southron. I expect you should feel at home there. There are wall-paintings… lily-blossoms of the Khazan, crocodiles, river-horses, and Sand Drakes too."

"I am sure I shall feel welcome no matter where I stay," Astarthe answered. "The Empire has shown me great hospitality and grace throughout my entire life. Without the Empire, I would have surely passed on."

Crispus was silent a while; his smile grew stale. "Well, then, Signora Queen. I am sure you will be of great interest to the Augusts. I will escort you to Kings Terrace, and a grand reception will follow."

"Thank you, Signor Crispus," Astarthe answered, and—arm locked in Theon's—followed the councilor down the road. "I have brought a white bull from Khazidea as well. I would like to offer it to Imperium in his temple, and pray that the Empire reigns a thousand thousand years, over all Varda."

"You delightful thing," Crispus said, his tone patronizingly sweet, as if he spoke to a naïve child.

But if Astarthe sensed the derision, she made no sign. Instead, she walked ahead at the same confident gait.

~

Crispus had not lied; the House of Lenora astounded Theon, even when compared to his father's mansion on the highest hill of Thénai. Paintings of the Khazan River—lit, as they were, with steady-burning lanterns—had an almost exact representation of what he had

seen before. The paintings in his father's house could not compare—
-they, after all, were painted in an era of lesser artistic sophistication—
but Queen Astarthe's reaction was muted. Adamantion shouted and
clapped with glee at the paintings—especially one of the Red
Mountains and the scenes of Sand Drakes breathing blasts of fire.

"They have done their best to please me," Astarthe said. "But
if I wanted Khazidea I would have stayed there."

"And where would you have liked to stay?"

"Imperial City… with you…" Her hands went to his
shoulders. Her eyes burned with a desire she had not been able to
quench, not with all her loves. Throughout the ship's journey he had
managed to evade her, but there was no evading her now. "What nice
shoulders you have, my signore."

*I am losing my adherence to the Way… I can no longer call myself
Wayfarer.*

~

In their lovemaking the torch-illumined lotus flowers on the
wall seemed to sway and dance; the paintings of bronzed Khazidees
took a new life, watching with two-dimensional eyes. It was rapture; it
was delight. But he had forsaken the Way, and he would never regain
it. He had become a creature of the inferior Material World; he had
become the man he once had been, before the years-long opium
dream.

~

Sometime around dusk, their passions spent, they dressed
themselves in preparation for the grand reception.

"We must look presentable for the Imperial Palace!" Astarthe
insisted. "But you, my sweet Signor Lover, must wear your silk robes.
With just Adamantion—excuse me, Anakh—my consort must add
something to our entry. You must be just as exotic to them as I."

Grudgingly, weighed down with guilt, Theon—not Wayfarer—yanked on his silk robes and grabbed his walking stick. But the clothes of the Wayfarer now only served as deceit; he was no more a part of the Way, now, than Astarthe or these Imperials. He had strayed from the sacred path, become a creature of the Material World.

CHAPTER ELEVEN:
A NIGHT TO REMEMBER

Emperor Secondo Janus the God

In the Blue Chamber of the Imperial Palace, the cooks had set out roast quail, platters of stuffed dormice and bowls of pickled eggs; bread and dipping sauces; and jars of wine, all to please the harlot queen of Haroon. She thought them impervious to her scheming; she thought the Imperial government remained blissfully unaware of her son, the Adamantus who posed a serious threat to Secondo. Already he had convened with the Imperial Councilors whom he trusted; he had determined that—by the time the harlot queen left—there would be no threat to his rule remaining.

In the corner he caught sight of Maximian, stewing about the incident with Lemuel the advisor. It had seemed to Secondo a matter of little concern; the augurs were permanently blinded, but thousands of augurs of equal skill roamed the Empire, ready to take their place. Besides, if he prosecuted Lemuel, he would arouse the ire of two of his most distinguished guests—the northman king, Bretonnius, and his beautiful wife Lanabelle.

Crystal cup filled to the brim with wine, he dallied and waited for the southron queen to arrive. Never before had the northman king and the queen of the exotic south met, as far as anyone knew, and it promised to be a spectacle of drama better than any Eloesian play.

At last the first sign of her arrived: her Anakhil warriors. He wondered how on earth a culture could produce something so bizarre: their heads, bald except for a black topknot; their bare copper chests covered with ceremonial golden chains; and swords of bronze that had been outdated a thousand years ago, wielded with undue pride. Of course, Janus reflected, the entire position of Anakhil was purely ceremonial, like the queenship itself. Even a ceremonial queenship lent itself to ambition; therefore, the Empire made it certain she never kept any standing forces.

At last the queen arrived, and Janus managed not to gasp. He had imagined someone much older, but this woman—the one who had written such articulate and intelligent letters—looked barely a middle teen.

"Your Undying Glory." The queen fell to her knees. "May the gods always shine upon you, and bless the nation whom you rule."

Janus smiled slightly. Behind her came the man she called her consort—a southron, he thought at first, but on closer inspection his features were larger, lighter, olive. An Eloesian, most certainly. The queen had never named him, only called him her "consort."

"My signora. A pleasure." Janus bowed only slightly. He went cold when the source of all his troubles arrived—a boy of no more than six or seven—with a reddish tint to his skin, but undeniably Adamantine features on his little, innocent-looking face. To be rid of him was work for the Black Serpents—an order of assassins long-extinguished—but thinking about it, he knew there were many in the Imperial Palace callous enough to put an end to him.

Those strings were yet to be pulled, though; but he promised himself by the time he received his victor's crown in the Arena at the end of the week, he'd put this little problem far behind him.

The heavy musk of Bretonnius' scented oils overwhelmed him, heralding his coming. "Ah, my seigneur." Even now, he struggled to speak the Imperial tongue properly. "Shall you introduce me to this petite beauty?"

"This is Astarthe, the queen of Haroon, in all her glory," Janus said. "She is a most welcome addition to our Empire." Janus was a wonderful liar. "She was recently restored to her place of rule…"

At last Astarthe rose from her groveling stance. "The Empire did me much kindness to restore the Red Throne. But I will have you know, mine is the oldest bloodline in all the world. The first Anakh and Astarthe ruled in the time before the Cataclysm. Our line is pure to the last generation, to me."

"Ah, Astarthe, I think you are boring Signor Bretonnius."

"No, she is not, not at all," Bretonnius went on. "I think the lovely lass is quite charming. It is good for a ruler to have a pure bloodline, and the more ancient the better. By those measurements you shine like a star, my petite seigneura."

Astarthe smiled like an innocent girl, showing none of the scheming Janus knew lurked beneath. "I thank you, signore. What is your name?"

"King Gylles vis Bretagne… or Bretonnius, as these Imperials are fond of saying."

"Well, King Gylles vis Bretagne, I am certain the Empire means no ill toward you by it."

The man she had hooked in her arm seemed uncomfortable, stiff as a board.

"Besides, the name 'Astarthe' is beyond the pronunciation of many…"

Janus could not help but scowl at the queen. The child, the one she privately called Adamantion, walked up to his mother and latched to her leg. His eyes held all the innocent naiveté of youth, but nonetheless he was a problem, a thorn that had to be plucked.

"Mother, mother," the little boy said. "I want to go home."

"Ah, sweet little Anakh. You think you want to, but it's best if you stay here."

How wrong you are.

"Else, you will grow bored without your mother. So act like the king you are, little Anakh, and put on a brave face." Astarthe laughed—infectiously, Janus noted with distaste as Bretonnius joined her. "The little ones never know how to act in public, do they? All they think of are lemon-candies and pretend-play with their friends."

"No, they do not."

Janus turned to look at Bretonnius. The man's dark eyes were fixed on his wife Lanabelle, chatting with the wife of a councilor.

"I would not know," Bretonnius went on, glumly.

In the chance meetings when Janus and Lanabelle were alone,

she had confided in him; she was not the first wife King Bretonnius had. His first wife, Melysse, had failed to conceive, and they thought her barren. The High Priestess of their land, she said, did not grant divorces lightly, not even when the good of the nation is at stake. Soon after the High Priestess denied the divorce, Melysse had fallen from the highest tower of the king's castle to her death; everyone claimed it was an accident. Now Lanabelle—still barren—feared she too would fall victim to a supposed accident, all because the king's life-fire would not quicken. She had wept into Janus' arms, fearing at all times that her husband would find her there, taking comfort in the arms of his rival.

"In time," the southron witch countered his self-pity, "I'm sure there will be many Gylles vi' Bretagnes walking around the halls of your castle."

"Someday, I am certain," Bretonnius answered. "Someday." His eyes had not yet strayed from his wife.

A man cruel enough to kill his wife would most certainly do so again.

From one conversation to another, Janus made his presence known across the room. But though the grand chamber was filled with interesting people from throughout the known world, the only one he truly cared for here was Lanabelle. The woman's pain had only increased his desire for her. Janus, a widower, had never felt such warm companionship than when she wept on his shoulder. The seed of desire had been planted, and it grew every day until now it had become nigh obsession.

At last, crystal cup of wine in hand, Janus found his way to Lanabelle. The northern queen drew back an inch, then glanced furtively at Bretonnius.

"Hello, my petite," Janus said. The northerners had such strange turns of phrase, but they had grown on him.

"Hello, my signor." She tried her best to speak without a northern accent, but traces remained. "Your cuisine is most interesting… this room is charming, in its own way."

The Blue Chamber was square, several hundred feet in area, with dark blue walls and divans, sky-blue pillows and a chandelier of blue-tinted glass.

"In its own way, you say," Janus went on. "That does not sound like love."

"The color is beautiful enough. But in the Royal Castle of Zarubain, we have the Hall of Mirrors, and the Crystal Fountain, and—"

"Stay with me, Lanabelle. Stay with me in Imperial City."

"Stop." She backed away sharply, a recoil. "Don't speak to me like that, seigneur." Under stress her speech reverted to its thick northern accent. "I love my dear husband the king. He is everything to me."

"Until he kills you," Janus snapped. "Just like he killed Melysse—"

"Stop! Keep your wicked tongue quiet. I won't ever tell anything to you again, seigneur."

"Don't do that to me."

But Lanabelle turned and left, managing to keep herself together.

Wounded, Janus walked away, fighting unmanly tears of his own. All the women of the Empire would die to have him; yet the only one he wanted spurned his love.

Soon after, slaves brought out food: great silver platters weighed-down with stuffed quail or even exotic delicacies like ostrich egg and crocodile. The more Janus tried to meet again with Lanabelle, the faster she ran away. Love is madness, Janus thought, but nonetheless it had taken him over, and if Lanabelle left it would take much counsel and perhaps a bit of prayer to forget her. But so too did he realize the only thing would make him happy was her: running his hands through her locks of golden hair, and making her his wife, the first lady of the Empire.

Eventually he gave up, settling into mere observation. Though all of Imperial or southron blood failed to interest him, taking a far second to Lanabelle, he watched the reception go on nonetheless. The Queen of Haroon, her "adorable" son, and her bizarre Anakhil—the ones for whom, in theory, the reception had been thrown—seemed the focus of most everyone's attention. Even the northman king Bretonnius seemed enamored with the spoiled southron brat, and she by all accounts thrived in the flood of the attention. The snake would win their hearts before they betrayed them; but Janus would not give her the chance.

His heart could scarcely bear all the disappointments and failed plans this evening. He walked out into the Sky Porch, into the cold darkness of the summer night.

~

The lights of Imperial City stretched out before him.

Imperial City never sleeps—that is what visitors often said. And it was true; in the dark hours, the brothels did a roaring trade, and many taverns stayed open until all hours of the night. But the streets of Imperial City held infinite dangers at night, dangers that most wise people avoided.

"*Janus.*"

The word, spoken from familiar lips, filled Janus with an emotional liquor stronger than any drink. He turned to regard fair Lanabelle, and nearly gasped. The goal of all his pursuits, the one who had rebuffed his advances, had come for him in the dark of night, and that could only mean one thing.

"I am sorry, my *seigneur*. I am so afraid of him. He is a man of great rage. He terrifies me, *seigneur*."

"I won't let him hurt you, my sweetling. I will not let him touch a hair on your head."

"Being with you takes away all my fear… takes away all my terror."

"Stay with me."

"I cannot."

Janus walked over to her; she did not resist as he wrapped his hands around her chest, planted a kiss on her lips.

"No," she said through tears. "If he finds me…"

"If he finds you I will kill him."

When Janus kissed her again she returned it; his tongue went into her mouth, and hers into his. Her tears continued; tears of relief, tears of love.

"Come with me, to my bedchamber."

"No… no, my *seigneur*…"

"Come with me."

Her resistance was halfhearted as he led her through the outer door.

CHAPTER TWELVE:
THE BATTLE OF THE AGES

Raulus No-Name

He had made a sacrifice with the most expensive goat he could find, before the Altar of Imperium. He had prayed earnestly for the Spirit of Empire to forgive him, and he was certain he could complete the deed. But that did not keep his legs from shaking as he waited from inside the grilled gate of the Arena floor, waiting to complete the very death that Secondo Janus had orchestrated for himself.

The emperor, he had heard, was dressed in the armor, thin-visored helmet, and heavy spiked mace of the Myrmidon; unwieldy without skill—skill that Secondo Janus, despite his Knightly background, did not have—while Raulus wore nearly nothing, clad in the net and trident of the Thartan, the sandals of a commoner, and no clothing or armor. Raulus had heard the women of the Empire most liked him when he fought in the Thartan style—a pride-making thing perhaps, but his domina Leto did not let him meet any of his female admirers because she wanted him all to herself.

Trumpets blared throughout the Arena. The crowd gave a low cheer, marking their excitement. A white-bearded priest came galloping out, carrying the flag of Lorenus the sea-god, white and marked with a dark green trident. From the other gate came the priestess of Leto's and—by extension—Raulus' patron, Seladora the Mother of Nymphs; a woman with long, dark-blonde hair on a white mare, and a flag painted with Seladora's starry crown.

"Thus begins the Game of the Ages!" the Maestro of Ceremonies shouted as he rode across the brown Arena floor. "The emperor himself, His Undying Glory Secondo Janus, fights the no-name Raulus, in a death duel!"

At the news there were a few shocked, irate gasps; a few cheers, and overall a dreadful pall. When he had heard the emperor was fighting in the Arena like a common brawler, his reaction had been much the same.

The gates opened, and Raulus sprinted out. From the gate opposite, the emperor—dressed as the Myrmidon—took his heavy lumbering steps across the dry blood-browned earth.

"Emperor! Emperor!" a small group in the crowd began to cheer, and soon it had become deafening, the vast majority of the some eighty-thousand spectators. "Emperor! Emperor! Emperor!"

The knowledge of whom they favored somehow disheartened him. Still, he was determined to fight him, for Leto. *No, I do not care so much for her,* he thought. *I am doing this for myself... no, for Imperium.*

The emperor continued his slow, iron-shod gait across the blood-caked Arena floor. Raulus No-Name thought of his unfortunate life, abandoned as an infant by a mother who did not care for him. He thought of the woman who had taken him in, trained him from the day he was able to walk to become a gladiator, did her best to feign love. He owed this to himself. He was not responsible for the emperor's mistakes. He would not feel guilty for slaying the emperor; he had chosen to die.

"Emperor! Emperor!"

He sprinted to the heavy-armored Myrmidon, his enemy and not his lord. The Myrmidon raised his spiked mace and grasped the handle tight in iron-lined gloves. He tossed the net at him, but the Myrmidon sidestepped with ineffable grace; the net caught around his left arm and shoulder, and he shook it off.

Raulus suddenly felt cold. He leapt forward and stabbed with his trident; the Myrmidon batted it away hard, and the ring of steel rose above the rising cheers of the crowd. He struck again and the Myrmidon batted again with equal force, nearly knocking the entire trident out of his hand.

Not in a hundred years did he expect this battle to be hard-won; the Myrmidon fought with skill he had not expected, skill he had seen in trained, well-conditioned gladiators. The emperor had been practicing, it seemed, for a long while, and he was a risk-taker not merely a fool. Raulus dove as the Myrmidon struck again, laying hold of the dropped net and then rolling away to his feet.

The weakness of the Myrmidon is his near-blindness, Raulus reminded himself. He sprinted around him, circling like a wolf, and the Myrmidon followed him with his thin visor, going too slow. He tossed the net again, but again he sidestepped and shook it off.

In the midst of his shaking, Raulus darted for him, thrusting his trident at the thick plates of armor. The spiked iron mace bludgeoned him in the back, knocking his breath and slicking him with sudden blood.

"*Emperor! Emperor!*" the bloodthirsty cheers of the crowd rose higher than ever.

Stunned, Raulus grabbed the net again. He could scarcely think; the debilitating pain of broken bones robbed all conscious thought from him. He forced himself through the sharp anguish and again threw the net; at last it caught over him wholly, immobilizing him for at least a few seconds.

Tears of pain welling in his eyes, he ran in and thrust so hard with his trident that the blow toppled the Myrmidon emperor. The cheers of the crowd faded, turned to stunned silence or cries of horror. Caught in a net, the Myrmidon emperor lay like a trapped animal, easy prey for the hunter's knife.

The shocked panic of the crowd, the uncanny silence of the Arena, all the disapproval of the world did not stop Raulus from landing the death-blow. In the end the thing that made him stand there, trident at the ready, was himself. The silence of the Arena was a gift from Imperium the Spirit of Empire. He spoke at a shout: "Men and women of the Empire, the greatest nation in the world, I am the most ill-fortuned of men! My mother and father left me as an unwanted babe. My domina Leto trained me through my earliest years, even when I could scarcely stand it. But the worst thing that has happened to me is this! I will not kill the ruler of our nation, and I will not leave the Arena! To all gods but especially to Imperium, whose Hand I spare, may my blood be a pleasing sacrifice unto your divine glory!"

Into his chest he hammered the three sharp prongs of the trident, and felt the lifeblood trickle from the wounds. He had lived a most ill-fortuned and dreary life; but he had died as a servant of the gods and of Empire, respecting the Hand of Imperium and never failing to honor and revere the greatest nation in Varda.

CHAPTER THIRTEEN:
FAILED PLANS

Emperor Secondo Janus the God

Secondo watched in horror and disgust from the darkness of the Arena cells. His plan to gain respect had backfired, and in the most horrid way possible. The impostor, the well-trained gladiator whom he had dressed in the gear of a Myrmidon, had fallen to the nets of Raulus No-Name. And then, the impostor Secondo had lay there like a lamb for a slaughter, while Raulus committed an honorable suicide for the sake of Empire. The people would never consider him on the level of the Adamanti; now they would remember him as the poor, groveling gladiator on the floor of the Arena, spared by the mercy of a much better man. He had hoped to impress his lady Lanabelle, but she—now, against his wishes, leaving the following morning—would remember him as a poor groveling failure writhing on the Arena floor. And if he told her the truth she would call him a deceiver, a conniver, the lowest of all the low.

It could be worse. He could have killed 'me,' *and then the citizens would know I had lied.* For that Imperium had shown him great grace; he could continue on, even if his honor would never be the same.

He thought of Astarthe. The southron queen made no show of leaving, which would provide ample time to cull the little Adamantus. She had grown popular and well-beloved in the court, but Janus—though humiliated—promised to himself that he would succeed on that end, at the minimum, even if all his plans thus far had come to ruin.

~

His night's rest was badly-needed, but the specter of his failures hung over him like a cloud. He dreamed of his brother Primo, destined to inherit the family vineyard on the west coast of Anthania; his summons to war and his death at the sword of the southrons. He dreamed of his brother Tertio, born paralyzed and helpless. He dreamed of his cold distant father who had despised Secondo from the day of his birth, a hatred that had fostered a near-insane desire to prove himself at all costs… a desire that had served him well, that made him take risks and eventually achieve the Empire's highest office. He dreamed of his first wife Bellana, whom he'd known since boyhood, whom he had worshiped like a goddess; and then he realized he had never loved even Bellana like he loved Lanabelle.

~

The northmen were leaving. In the White Chamber, Lanabelle's eyes had welled with tears. Only Secondo Janus knew what—and whom—she cried for. Her husband's dark eyes were ever-hard with suspicion.

"Emperor Janus… your nation has been… *interesting*."

"Interesting, you say," Secondo Janus says. "Well, my good signore, it has been an adventure, hearing your strange accent and your odd beliefs about the world."

"Indeed," the northman king intoned. The giant steel-armored knights behind him were the only thing holding Janus back from sticking a dagger in his heart. The tone in the room had grown hostile, palpably heavy.

I cannot leave Lanabelle. "Your presence has been most welcome, and your wife is delightful."

The northman king's lips twitched at the mention of her. "I am glad, *seigneur*. She is not used to the presence of common *villeins*, but I am certain she found it a change of pace."

"Common, you say. I would hope you are not referring to me."

"I came with gifts. I came to establish a friendship with you, *seigneur*, beyond the mere exchange of traded goods by our lowborn merchants. Do not let my beliefs ruin the friendship of our nations."

"The beliefs. So you *do* believe I am common."

"The lowborns choose the members of your ruling body, the council; the council must approve the enthronement of the sovereign. Not even the elven nations practice such barbarism, *seigneur.* It is no wonder—"

"No wonder that we are strong and wealthy, have the best military and most prosperous citizenry in the world, yes."

"Goodbye, my *seigneur.* I enjoyed our friendship, and your mummer's play of yesterday."

One of Bretonnius' knights chuckled. They left for the wide-open double doors.

The comment about the Arena flushed Janus hot with shame, and then with anger. Before they had made it out of his sight, Janus shouted the thing he had not yet dared to say: "I made love to your wife, Signor Bretonnius. I suppose despite my mummer's play and 'common blood,' only I am man enough for her. Tell me, signore, does that bother you?"

Bretonnius froze in place, then whipped around in a snarl. He drew his greatsword; Maximian and the Imperial Guard came running in from behind. "You lie. My lady Lanabelle is of Mierese blood, among the oldest bloodlines in Zarubain. She would never let you touch her, you lowborn mockery of a king."

"There is one thing you gave her, Bretonnius, which she alone likes—I have never seen such fine silkwork before I laid eyes on those flame-red undergarments."

Bretonnius' eyes bulged. "Is this true?" His irate gaze turned to his wife. "Is this true?"

Lanabelle shrieked.

"Ah, Lanabelle, you mother of whores. The High Priestess will certainly allow a divorce now. Then I shall shave that lovely gold hair and have you executed before all the country *villeins...*"

Lanabelle ran. Bretonnius charged after her but Maximian and the guards formed a wall of shields. Bretonnius broke his charge an inch before the swords would have stricken him dead. Lanabelle took shelter behind the Imperial Guard; Janus laid his hand around her shoulder and she did not resist.

Bretonnius—red-faced and quite obviously barely holding himself together—flashed even redder at the sight of Janus with his wife. "This means war, common scum. The north and the south will never be at peace, until I have Lanabelle vis Bretagne in my captivity."

"I think you mean Lanabelle Janus, my dear signore. I agree with you. We are at war. Be glad the Imperials are men of honor, and I do not kill you right here."

"No man of honor would steal another man's wife." Bretonnius took a deep breath. "It will greatly please me to see the war won; to see all the holdings of the Empire placed under the authority of the Zarube Crown."

"Fharas, once the largest empire in the world, tried to do the same. But we humiliated them; now, though they fight, they are like spoiled children, demanding to have their possessions back. They wage war but they have not broken past our defenses in decades. I would be very afraid, Signor Bretonnius, to challenge the greatest nation in the world."

"Afraid, you say. Afraid?" Bretonnius laughed unconvincingly. "I would never fear a nation of lowborns, led by a lowborn king. Lanabelle vis Bretagne, I demand you come with me and pay your penalty as befits your honor. As a woman of high birth, the headsman's axe is the price you will pay."

"Lanabelle vis Bretagne will go with you," she answered, and Janus gasped at the thought. "But Lanabelle Janus will not return to Zarubain with the ex-husband whom she fears."

Janus smiled.

Bretonnius' red face paled. "You have wounded me, Lanabelle. But this I promise you: you have written your epitaph."

"Get out of here, Bretonnius, before my honor fails me," Janus intoned.

Bretonnius stalked off.

The double doors of the White Chamber slammed shut, and the War of the North began.

CHAPTER FOURTEEN:
MIDNIGHT VISITOR

Astarthe, Queen of Haroon

The Prior Night

In bed, Astarthe shut her eyes thinking of the night at the reception days ago—by all accounts, a grand success—and the people she had met. The northman king most of all had piqued her interest; never before had a Queen of Haroon met with the sovereign beyond the Wall, at least from what she knew. And now, this night before she departed the following morning, she lay in the arms of her consort Theon Arkadios. All was right with the world—all, except the debacle at the Arena. She had hoped the emperor would have gotten what was due; a man of his station who competed in the Arena like common street-rabble deserved what came to him, nothing less, and her son— the last remaining Adamantus—would have had a serious chance of taking the throne. But there was a thing more important than ruling the whole of the Empire: life—and life, in Haroon, she had to the full.

She drifted asleep in the flickering light of the lanterns, lost in an elysian dream.

~

She startled awake. The lanterns burned low. Her heart pounded, and she sensed her son's fear. In an instant, she bolted out of bed and downstairs.

The door to the House of Lenora was ajar; a man had run out. She did something only done as a last resort. She called up the magic Wellspring, and assailed the man's mind with the power of the gleaming. She ordered him to stay put, immobile, and sprinted into her son's room.

In the fading glow of the candles, the shifting form of a snake, slithering toward her son and almost to him, sent her mad with panic.

"Anakhil! Anakhil!" she screamed.

One came in, heaving his bronze sword. The snake rose up, turned its wicked black eyes toward them, and flicked its forked tongue.

A poisonous snake, she realized. A poisonous snake they could only import from Khazidea, the redtongue viper.

At once the Anakhil charged it; he heaved back his bronze sword, and he and the snake struck at the same time. The bronze blade clove through the snake's scales, decapitating it, and it lay dead, in two pieces.

Relief washed through her, loosening stone-hard muscles and causing her—for just a few moments—to catch her breath and inhale. Adamantion at once began to cry; he got up and ran, and Astarthe scooped him in her arms.

"Take him, Anakhil," she said, "give him whatever he wants. I have something yet to do."

~

The assassin, remaining still as stone, stunned by the power of the gleaming, stood a few yards outside in the street.

"Come with me," she intoned.

The assassin, her pawn, followed her into Adamantion's room.

She slammed the door.

"Kneel."

Her thrall did as she asked. She wanted so badly to order the Anakhil to decapitate him, but that would do no good.

"What is your name?" she asked. "Answer."

"Lycano No-Name."

"Who sent you?"

"A man in a dark hood."

"Who?"

"A man in a dark hood, who did not give his name. He said he would offer me one-hundred gold libra to kill the boy-child of Astarthe and Claudian Adamantus. He gave me the key to the House of Lenora."

At his feet, she noticed, lay a large wooden box—it front-latch opened—where he had doubtlessly kept the redtongue viper.

By his words she knew for certain the Imperial government— or certain nefarious elements within it—wanted to take her son's life. But for the grave error of some, she would never blame or hate the Empire, which had fathered her son. "The House of Lenora will be your prison, dear Lycano No-Name, until you remember everything. The ones who sent you think I will be afraid, that I will leave Imperial City in terror. The Queen of Haroon fears nothing; they will learn as much. I will stay here until I see justice done, with only one change… my dear Adamantion will never leave my sight."

She kicked Lycano No-Name to the floor.

CHAPTER FIFTEEN:
SVARTHAL

Caro, Legionary

"In the beginning, there was only Fire," Septimo read the glyphs which glowed blue as soon as the century entered. "From Fire the world was made; to Fire it will return." He turned, the dim light reflecting off his white hooded medic's robe. "The writing of the Svarthal is ingeniously inscribed. Everything they make is ingenious—wonderful, or terrible. We should beware in this ruin, centurion, for traps and other things."

"Very well," the centurion answered. "I shall beware of 'fire dwarves' and 'efreeti,' and gremlins and sand ghúls, signore."

Septimo's face hardened with disappointment. "*I* shall be careful, in any case."

Beyond the stone entry-hall they followed corridors of low, perfectly-flat stone. The walls and the ceiling, also, had no bumps or blemishes. Caro had heard rumors of the dwarves—especially norgs, the so-called 'dwarves of the forest' that lived in Kalamar—but he had never seen their handiwork, nor thought he'd ever see it.

The corridor led out into a vast chamber ten times larger than the entry hall. All around it lay treasure—urns of gold inset with sparkling white diamonds, silver necklaces studded with forest-green emeralds, statues of gold with flame-red rubies for eyes—worth more than even the padisha emperor was likely to have.

The century rushed in—all except Caro, that is, his friend Halfblood, and Septimo the medic-priest of Sollust—and at once great blue glyphs alighted on the far wall.

"Here lies all the wealth of Arden Stonebones," Septimo read, "greatest of the Svarthal Clanlords, greatest ally of Thu'un Master of the Efreeti, greatest of all mortals."

Below the writing, many yards distant, was a stone sarcophagus, slightly shorter but much wider than those used for humankind.

"A curse upon those who connive to steal the treasure I worked all my life to create: a curse of fire, a curse of pain, a curse of tortured death."

The legionaries were filling their pockets with the gold treasure, stuffing every loose fold of clothing with valuables. At the same time the whole room seemed to brighten; the gold and silver seemed to radiate its own light. Then it all began to unravel: a burning pink sore the size of a silver denar burst into existence above a soldier's brow; he screeched in pain.

On the centurion's cheek a bright-pink sore burst into existence, flaring to bright red and growing in size; he shrieked in pain, like a civilian unused to war, and dropped the diamond brooch he held. All throughout the treasure chamber, similar sores burst onto the legionaries' faces: first one, then two, then three.

Only morbid fascination held Caro in place—Septimo, perhaps a desire to help and an equal desire to flee, and Halfblood who knew?

The treasure increased in brightness, shedding light like the sun, and the screams of the soldiers built to a pinnacle; their very skin seemed to burn, and by now all had dropped whatever bits of treasure they held.

The lid to the sarcophagus flew across the room like a pebble. A man stood up—at times a dry crumbling skeleton and at times a short, wide man of earthy-brown skin and a bright-orange beard, always carrying a crescent-moon axe of shining metal.

The screams of pain at last wrenched Caro's feet from their moorings; he bolted back the way he had entered, knowing that he had to go back to the Empire, to face whatever justice his nation designed for him. In the Southern World, there was only death.

CHAPTER SIXTEEN: THE HAMMER OF GOD

Julian Ultor, Malleus

The Path of Tidus, in the south of the Empire, teemed with inns, shops, and taverns wherever a city sprawl failed to dominate it. Here, in the north, in the shadow of mighty trees, it had taken on a wholly different aspect. All around him the leaves had begun to change color—some had only a few brown or yellow leaves, while others had turned completely gold—and the temperature, though humid, had begun to drop. Inns could still be found about every mile, and more than a few merchant-caravans passed either way. But in the shadow of the giant maples and oaks, the predominating sense was emptiness.

The vile magic weaver—Lemuel, people called him—had in his best estimation already bypassed the Gate of Tidus. Julian would bring the item he stole back from the north, but he would also bring back the man's head, cracked with the mighty hammer of god. Wizards and their servant soldiers he did not fear; with the Just God behind him, all the forces of magic would fail to achieve their target, and all the devices of evil men He would turn back on them. Julian, warrior of god, would crush Lemuel's skull; this had become his sole calling, and all he thought about.

Late in the day, the Wall—a massive work of stone that stretched thirty feet in height—rose above all in its wake. The Gate of Tidus lay open, as it did in times of peace, but as always a legion stood watch. A group of a dozen men blocked Julian's path.

"What is your name, where do you come from, and where are you going?" one legionary said as if reading from a script.

"Julian Ultor, Malleus, is my name. I come from Sanctum, from the Magisterium. I am going to kill Lemuel the wizard, who stole a treasure from our empire."

The legionary's lips perked into a smile. "The wizard slipped past us, Signor Malleus. He vanished and reappeared. He is a mighty man."

"The Hammer of God crushes mighty men."

"You are a paladin, Julian Ultor, young and strong—the youngest that I've ever seen, perhaps—but I would suggest you change course. The legions will take care of him. You will not succeed, Signor Malleus."

"When people tell me I cannot succeed, it only makes me more determined to do so," Julian said, and felt his mood and expression darken. "The Hammer of God crushes the mighty as ants. The Hammer of God fells nations in a single swing. Do not presume to tell me what the Hammer of God can and cannot do, legionary."

"Your courage is impressive," the legionary said, "and I would be a fool to deny you. I am not your enemy signore; I wish with all my being that you succeed, that you prove me wrong. Go, Signor Malleus, and kill Lemuel. May Imperium and all the gods guide your hammer home."

Riding north, Julian Ultor Malleus left without a word.

WINTER 1100

Matteo Alleus, son of Primo

The centennial celebration began with fireworks over the harbor. A recent invention of the Alchemist Collegium, spurred by discoveries along the Silk Route, made the New Year's celebration of 1100 something to remember.

The citizens of Imperial City gathered around, bundled tight in woolen cloaks as a misty rain drifted down.

Matteo Alleus, a young man of nineteen, stood among them, wondering whether the Empire would ever have another centennial celebration again. He had a feeling—a feeling which he had no explanation for, which he had no reason for—that the Empire, and perhaps the world they knew, would not survive another hundred years, perhaps not even another fifty.

Still, the fireworks sizzling in brilliant reds and golds over the dark winter sky did much to ease Alleus' worry. The glass of New Year's sweetwine filled his mouth with flavor. His father Primo had cordoned himself off in their upper-story apartment, working himself to sickness on a history book that probably no one else would read.

"We welcome the year 1100!" a priest of Imperium shouted above the noise of the crowd and the sparkling fireworks. "May the Empire stand supreme for another thousand years!"

Gongs resounded over the harbor, and the winds picked up, spraying Alleus with cold rain. Up on a high stage, a troupe of musicians Alleus recognized—two Eloesians on lutes, an Imperial on drums, and an unmistakable ratling on voice—began a patriotic ballad, "The Unconquered Son," regaling the god Claudio's conquest of Khazidea.

Alleus remembered it was a hundred years ago when that story first took shape. Now, the god Claudio's body lay in its appointed place. "To dust, we all return," he breathed. But he was cremated, stored in a limestone urn in the Temple of Imperium.

Fireworks crackled against the dark cloudy sky, in greens and yellows, in blues and glittering reds. Fire fell like rain.

The Eloesians strummed their lutes. The Imperial pounded out a fast beat. The ratling began his song. *"The unconquered son / the unconquered son / Claudio-Valens the unconquered one…"*

A brilliant blue burst of fire lit up the night. Some in the crowd gasped at the bright display.

"The unconquered empire now rules the sea / It shall never be conquered / It shall reign supreme."

Red fire rained down, sparkling like glitter. He imagined fire consuming the Empire's countryside. He imagined the unconquered empire falling before legions of southrons, or overrun by the encroaching northmen. He prayed to Imperium, and to all the gods, and to Claudio-Valens Adamantus that he was wrong.

~

BEYOND THE CONFINES OF IMPERIAL CITY, WHILE THE REVELERS GUZZLED THEIR NEW YEAR'S SWEETWINE, THE WHEELS OF WAR HAD ALREADY BEGUN TO TURN.

—Primo Alleus, national historian, writer of the Imperial Chronicles

CHAPTER SEVENTEEN:
THE ARCANE EYE

Maximian, Marshal Guard

After the embarrassment in the Arena, many in the palace had come to loathe Secondo Janus—all except his new wife, the empress Lanabelle Janus. Her presence, too, had become an object of hatred to many in the Imperial court, a problem emblematic of all Janus' flaws. The newly dubbed War in the North had begun, all because of Janus' weakness for the northman king's wife.

"How many lives will we lose," one Imperial councilor had told Maximian in confidence, "because of Janus' infidelities? When has a war begun under such pretext?"

But nonetheless, reports had reached him of an army massing in the plain north of the Wall. The northman king, the reports said, had built trebuchets and catapults, siege engines and machinations to break through the Wall. The towns on the northwest coast of Gad reported sights of sailing-ships, the Zarube Navy mobilizing.

Secondo Janus had gotten them into this, but he displayed no regret or shame. Few dared speak against him openly—he, being the Hand of Imperium—but in the shadows and dark corners of the Imperial Palace people began to talk.

And Astarthe—the Queen of Haroon—announced she would stay in Imperial City for the next week or longer. Despite the looming war, Astarthe's prolonged visit was the only thing that seemed to unnerve Secondo Janus. His ire seemed selective. Maximian had heard little glimmers of why she had come: she confided in certain members of the Imperial court that an assassination had been attempted on her "precious little son," which only emboldened her. Maximian admired her courage, but that same courage would prove her undoing if she wasn't careful. And he wondered why Janus had focused his attention on the little boy—he had begun to suspect, judging by the lush golden color of his skin, and his aquiline nose, that there was more to his lineage than commonly thought.

But here Maximian stood, in the White Chamber, an ant compared to the immense White Throne. Throughout the course of the emperor's tempestuous love-affair, it seemed that Lanabelle had a mixture of emotions—guilt being first among them, followed by relief from her former husband's dominating grasp; and also genuine, nigh-obsessive love.

Even now the shapely woman with her golden hair fixed in a long braid, sat in her new husband's lap with her hand around his shoulder as he himself sat on the White Throne.

Maximian pondered what the priesthood of Amara, the Lady of Love, would say about Lanabelle and Secondo Janus' marriage: if it were wrong, if it—by its nature—offended the gods. But Maximian had heard about Lanabelle's prior situation, the very real threat to her life, and wondered how the gods could possibly disagree.

Through the wide-open grand double-doors a visitor walked in, down the long line of red carpet in the shadow of the White Throne. He had the look of a swift traveler, haggard and weak as if he'd ridden all day and all night to deliver the news. "Your Undying Glory," he breathed, and fell to his knees.

"Speak," Secondo Janus ordered.

"The ships of the northmen demolished our navy off the ocean coast. I have never seen such a firestorm… magic had to be involved."

Secondo Janus' lips pursed into a solemn line.

"They took control of Floridium…"

Maximian went cold. The small city on the north-westernmost edge of the Empire had a small garrison of soldiers and ill-maintained fortifications; he could only imagine the ease with which the northmen conquered it.

"The citizens fought valiantly, but fire, lightning, and ice rained from the sky like a judgment of the gods… some managed to escape. I am sorry I fled; and if you wish to execute me I accept it according to the Will of Imperium."

"No… no, I will not execute you. You have done me a service," Janus muttered. "Tell me all you know, signore."

"The ships came suddenly… great ships with many sails, and on each sail there was an eye… the Arcane Eye, they called it. By the time the tempest was done, everyone who hadn't acted quickly was dead. I have no doubts they looted all of Floridium's treasures."

"In times such as these, we must act wisely," Janus began. "The Arcane Eye is an ancient symbol of omniscience… it is used by the wizards of the north. All the Empire's magic weavers must be summoned to fight them off."

"Never in my life have I seen such a display of power," the messenger continued.

Maximian eyed the cause of all this trouble—the hands of Secondo Janus and Lanabelle interlocked—by which their whole nation might come to ruin.

CHAPTER EIGHTEEN:
A NEST OF VIPERS

Theon Arkadios

He had strayed so far from the Way, he could no longer call himself an adherent. Even owning the set of throwing stars which the sage Choh had given him seemed a sacrilege bordering on blasphemy. *These are the weapons of the wise,* Choh had said, *against which the denizens of the Lesser World cannot fight.* Soon after they had both inhaled deeply of their opium pipes, and lost themselves in the sublime dream.

Now, he woke each morning in the bed of the southron queen, Astarthe. The young woman had no flaws that drew his ire, no cross attitude or bitterness; she was lovely inside and out. But the pleasures of the Lesser World—the one that the unwise could see—only drew him further from the way. Scales had begun forming over his eyes; he had lost contact with everything he had once cherished. The image of the Celestial Emperor's face, unchallenged ruler of the Forgotten Isle, flashed in his mind as he woke that morning intertwined with Astarthe. A fearsome face, a face that struck the commoners and slaves with terror… lips which moved to say dread words: *The world is changing. The order of the universe is unraveling. The threads which hold everything together have spun apart like twine.* Then, in the grand markets of Xia, words from sailors who had come from a far country: the land of the *dai ma* in peril. Fire on the mountains. Doom.

Astarthe startled awake, as if by his thoughts. "Morning breaks over Imperial City," she said. "I would not rather be anywhere else. I think I have found my home, in the capital of the world."

"There are many capitals of the world," Theon answered, thinking of Xia, a city which dwarfed even Imperial City in size—a city which he had begun to remember. A city that encompassed many miles, a city of innumerable and diverse people, straddling the edge of desert and ocean. He had been happy there—happy, yet afraid. *Why was I afraid?* "Imperial City is only one capital."

"Well, Theon, you are wise as always. But Imperial City is the capital of *my* world, and of yours."

"Not of mine," Theon said, thinking simultaneously of the Celestial Emperor's court and his father's sprawling mansion in Thénai. At the thought of his father and his father's false son, gooseflesh spread across his skin. He wondered if they would find him here, in the center of the Empire, in the midst of the Imperial Court.

The southron queen arose from their bed. "A new day dawns, a gift of Atman in highest heaven. My brother was his son."

"You had a brother."

The southron queen's silence was unlike her. Even facing away from Theon, he could sense sadness from her, unspoken regrets and despair. "My brother," she at last breathed. "I wish he was here. He was pledged to be my husband, but he betrayed his mission… the mission given him by the Sun God himself."

Theon skirted out of bed and began to dress himself for the day. "Your brother… you were pledged to marry him?" The concept was impossible to grasp—disgusting, perhaps even immoral, like so many Khazidean customs.

"It was a different time. I am the last Astarthe; he was the last Anakh."

"There is…"

"My child is not truly Anakh, though he will certainly rule on the Red Throne…"

The White, you mean.

"My son's father is none other than Claudian Adamantus. Now I hide his divine lineage, disgrace him with falsehood and deception. I call him Anakh, though—to me—he will always be Adamantion. No one can know… not until the right time. One day, the world will know, and I will shout his true name from the rooftops."

"Be careful," Theon said, though he realized he didn't care much about what happened. He could only think of how he strayed from the right path, the sublime Way. He sensed the sage Choh's disappointment in him even here, many thousands of miles and lifetimes away. When he shut his eyes, he could see the cherry-blossoms of the Forgotten Isle, and smell the sweet odor of the opium pipes. That life was long-gone from him, the true Way. He had woken from the opium dream, and he wished he never had.

"Come with me," Astarthe ordered.

Now dressed in his robe of painted silk, Theon Arkadios reluctantly linked arms with the southron queen, and left the House of Lenora with its Khazidean frescoes as her consort.

Guarded only by the bronze swords of the Anakhil, Astarthe led Theon through various thoroughfares like a docile puppy or an obedient child. He didn't question her—not because he feared her, or respected her authority, but due to his total lack of caring. He had severed himself from the Way, and in the wake of that nothing mattered—all joy was muted, all fear was dulled, and nothing that happened could outdo the tragedy of it.

Citizens gawked all along the way; a few giggled at the Anakhil with the topknots sticking from their otherwise-bald heads. Only long after the procession began did he realize where she was taking them: the limestone Temple of Imperium on the edge of Imperial Square, in the shadow of the palace.

At its fore, two heavy-armored guards blocked entry. Imperial Knights, no doubt, they wore thick suits of chain and—over their armor—surcoats bearing the Imperial war eagle.

"What does the southron queen want with Imperium?" a man shouted from behind—a voice barely distinguished against the shouts of merchants and the roar of the crowd.

Yet Astarthe turned her head and said, "Because I am an Imperial, as you."

Then she proceeded past the Imperial Knights, leading Theon again like a puppy she adored, to whatever end she intended.

In the vastness of the temple chamber, a war eagle statue stretched to the tip of the ceiling and its grandeur—at least forty feet in height—stole Theon's breath, breaking him from his malaise for a moment. Its giant beak was layered with a gold skin which glittered in the light of the torch. Its eyes were chiseled from some sort of blue rock; its feathers and body a limestone white. Seeing this representation of Imperium, Theon thought he understood why the Empire had prevailed against all its enemies; with a god such as this at its side, who could fight against it?

From the shadows of the immense statue, the priest of Imperium emerged. He wore a blue robe and clutched a wooden eagle staff in his hands. "Astarthe, Queen of the South. A pleasure."

"Signor Priest," Astarthe began her speech at once. "Do you believe the blood of the Adamanti is divine?"

Theon knew where this was headed. In truth, he hoped Astarthe received what she was asking for.

CHAPTER NINETEEN:
THERE AND BACK

Julian Ultor, Malleus

Beyond the Wall lay a world empty and bereft of civilization. Rolling hills stretched in every direction save for the Path of Tidus. A dusting of snow lay on the ground, swept about by the wind. Julian, though bundled in winter cloaks, had never before felt this miserable. His entire body shivered as he rode down the path. The folk of the frontier towns hadn't told him the truth; he needed twice as much coverings to survive.

But worse than the cold was the overwhelming sense of vulnerability. He now traveled outside the Empire's jurisdiction, outside the rule of the emperor and the safety of the only nation he'd ever known. A few in the frontier towns had told him bands of barbarians lived here, traveling by horse, not as fearsome as their neighbors to the east but still eager for loot. The rumormongers told him that the barbarians collected the scalps of travelers and used their bones in dark rituals. The longer Julian rode through the blasting wind and biting cold, the further he traveled down the road, the more he began to wonder whether he had made a terrible mistake. But to go back now, after he had sworn to crack the skull of Lemuel and bring back what he had stolen, would be to break his vow: an affront to honor, and an abomination to the Just God.

The wind whipped across the road, scattering powdery snow across the pavestones. Beyond, the road stretched for endless miles.

The sun dipped low in the sky when the bright fires of a roadside camp appeared. Truly they could be bandits, but by now Julian had grown numb and the cold would claim him. There was nothing he feared more, now, than the cold; compared to the ice, snow, and winter's grasp, bandits seemed like child's play.

A half a dozen wagons surrounded two distinct bonfires. At one bonfire nearest the road's edge, tall, heavy-set men with swords clipped to their belts rubbed their hands in the flame's warmth. Caravan guards, he guessed; at the other bonfire, a group of merchants—all male, sporting immaculately-trimmed beards of golden brown or blond, and pale of skin—sat in the company of two females. Julian guessed the females were Imperials, and more specifically Eloesians, judging by their olive skin and large noses. No doubt, slaves, judging by their roughspun, brown woolen clothing. These northern merchants had come with human cargo as well.

One of the guards at the bonfire stood up, and Julian noted what a tall and powerfully-built man he was, with a giant greatsword to match. *"Zor… au ellons du?"*

"Do you speak Imperial?" Julian spoke through chattering teeth.

The guard looked to the other bonfire. A man stood up, dressed in a thick winter cloak of jet-black, lined with sable. "Where are you going?" the man said through a viscous northern accent. "You are aware a war has begun?"

"A war? Why?"

"Your emperor has stolen the good king's wife."

"I—" He didn't know what to say. Certainly, the Magisterium would condemn the arrangement; the Pontifex would condemn Secondo Janus, perhaps even ban him from temples, exclude him from the company of the pious. "Are you certain?"

"Another day's travel, good sir," the merchant went on, "and you will run into the good king's army as it moves south. The king is wroth; if he sees an Imperial soldier such as yourself, he will no doubts make a display of you. Go back, behind your Wall, and you shall be safe for a brief while."

"I… Lemuel…"

A faint surprise overtook the merchant's features. "Why do

you speak the name of the wizard? He is long-gone from your lands. He has already returned to the Tower of Pythor with his cargo… and gone back to the Empire."

"Back to the——? How is that possible?"

The merchant smiled. "A *telemancer* can travel many hundreds of miles in the span of a day, good sir. If you are seeking Lemuel, you should head to the city of Floridium…"

"Floridium?" It all seemed impossible.

"Yes, to Floridium… unless the city is already destroyed."

"Destroyed?"

"The Order of Wizards claims to be neutral." The merchant's smile took on a dark aspect. "But more often than not it is in the pay of the king. I would be very surprised if Floridium is not totally gone by now, burnt to smoldering ruin.

"Truly?"

"I would not trust an enemy's tongue," the merchant went on, "but we are not enemies, Sir Paladin. We merely call different kings our sovereign."

"The emperor is not——" His voice trailed off. It did not matter whether this man believed the emperor was a king. Who sat on the White Throne might not—in theory—be determined by blood; but in truth how many times had the rule of the Empire been transferred from father to son? "Thank you, signore." He realized he believed this merchant after all. He had no doubts Lemuel possessed infernal powers—powers that could transport him across the world to commit his evil deeds. Like all magic weavers he tainted and corrupted all things in his path; like all magic weavers he deserved death, and Julian promised himself he would strike the blow.

He wheeled his horse around, yanking the reins, and galloped south toward Floridium across the snow-blown road, back to the nation he called his home. Memories returned to him of that evil night from his childhood, seared into his mind like a scalding brand. To Julian Ultor, Malleus, there was no difference between Lemuel the wizard and Malleon, the one who had burnt his father to death with purple lightning. There was no difference between Lemuel and Malleon, and all of the Augur Collegium.

The world will never find peace until the rivers run red with the blood of magic weavers.

~

He rode into the deeping night. An icy gale blasted from the west, and his charger nickered at the chill touch. Later, shivering in his bedroll, he saw the eyes of Malleon glinting in the darkness; the spears of lightning reflecting purple in those black orbs of darkness.

The next morning, riding through the quickly melting snow, the image of those black eyes remained, suffusing him with all their dread.

~

The Wall loomed above him; and he was an ant before it. The Gate of Tidus, almost as tall as the wall itself, was firmly shut and doubtlessly reinforced. Countless archers stood watch over the battlements, arrows at the ready. He remembered the Empire was preparing for war. The process of shutting the Gate of Tidus was a strenuous process in itself; the task of opening it was something they would only do for the emperor himself.

Without so much as speaking with the guarding legion, he turned and rode west. They would not open the gate for Julian Ultor, Malleus; they wouldn't open it for a Templar, or for the Pontifex himself. Eventually the wall terminated at the edge of the sea. The western ocean awaited him—the shore that would lead him to Floridium, and his quarry, the wizard Lemuel.

Through the next several days, the weather remained cold but the snow did not return. The grass remained bare to the sun, though it had turned a sickly, wilted brown, and he had no doubts it would not regain its lush green color until winter was over. Occasionally, riding along the wall, soldiers heckled him, or in the distance horns blared— a pleasing sound that was no Imperial trumpet. He didn't know whether the horn belonged to the northmen, or the wild nomads said to wander these rolling hills—the Mekari, whom he heard worshiped Balzor, god of death, and wore the skins of civilized men over their faces.

In the middle of the days' journeying, the snow returned suddenly, whirling about him in a cyclone of arctic chill and stinging powder. The same horn blew, harder than ever; the sound of galloping hooves pounding into dirt echoed all around him. The watchmen on the Wall shouted something. Then, through the veil of swirling snowflakes, a face took shape—a man hugely-built, as the barbarians were said to be, with a thick beard of golden-brown and such intense blue eyes that the normally-reticent Julian Ultor, Malleus, jerked his horse back and shouted, "Stop!"

The man rode on a powerfully-built mare, her mane tied in black braids. The man, already a giant, was over ten feet riding on the horse. On his head he wore the antlers of a stag, and his arms— smeared with blue paint—did not touch the reins. Guiding his steed with only his legs, he clutched a giant crescent-moon blade in his right hand, and a leathered wooden shield in his left. At the sight of Julian, his eyes lost some of their bloodthirsty intensity. Behind him, the figures of a half-dozen other Mekari nomads took shape as the snowfall lightened.

"*You…*" the giant thundered. "*Imp-ral?*"

Julian narrowed his eyes. "Do you mean *Imperial?*"

"Aye. *Imp-ral.*"

"Yes," Julian answered, for lying was the greatest breech of honor, the worst offense to the Just God.

"Come wit' me, *Imp-ral.*"

"No."

"Come wit' me, *Imp-ral.* We not hurt you. We want to be-friends *Imp-ror.*"

"No."

"The Zarubes… kill our children, *Imp-ral.* Common enemy, good friends. Good friends for *Imp-ror.* The Zarubes fight you… common enemy, good friends. The Zarubes, they try to steal our land… we be-friends *Imp-ror.*"

"I am not the emperor," Julian answered, "and I am not your friend."

He galloped off. Minutes after he began his ride, he looked back, and the Mekari nomads were nowhere in sight.

CHAPTER TWENTY:
ENEMY LANDS

Caro, Legionary

Caro would never fully recover from the scene in the Svarthal ruin. The image of his fellow-soldiers scouring the ancient treasure and succumbing to its dark curse was burned forever in his mind. Compared to the bright-red sores and the screams of anguish, Halfblood's murky-boots seemed like child's play. But Septimo, medic and nominal priest of Sollust, made it clear murky-boots was anything but child's play; left untreated, the growth would deepen and increase, and eventually Halfblood would lose use of his legs and feet. The thought of Halfblood, the youngster who could once sprint a mile in armor, unable to walk, seemed ridiculous to Caro at first.

Now, in their travels through the enemy lands, when they paused to rest and Halfblood removed his fresh boots, Septimo's statement seemed quite clearly true. His feet had turned scaly and white, and besides the furious itching, Halfblood often stumbled as they made their ill-prepared and likely ill-fated journey to the Imperial border. For all Septimo's knowledge of herbs and medical treatment, it seemed he knew about as much about navigation as the rest of them. He could tell you all about the Svarthal and the efreeti, and point to all the locations of Fharas on the map, but when it came down to survival and actual navigation, he was an ignoramus like the rest of them.

Wheat fields, now cut, dominated the High Plain of Fharas. Stone fortifications of towns, perched on high hills, overlooked the crops and tiny agrarian communities. Those tiny agrarian communities didn't pay much heed to the passersby, and when Caro, Halfblood, and Septimo—surely looking dirty and unshorn—came within close view of the villagers, they went about their business, paying them no mind. Though, Caro figured, on second thought, the married women of Fharas wore veils, so who knew what they were looking at?

They were three days outside the ruin when a broad dirt road appeared. Septimo whipped around and ordered them to run, but a gnawing hunger had consumed Caro. They had run out of roadbiscuits and dried fruit the night before, and now, he gave a half a thought to begging. Gods knew there were enough people on this road.

"*Caro*," Septimo hissed.

"You! You there!" a voice thundered. A cataphract on the road was staring straight at him. When Caro looked back, Septimo and Halfblood were gone. *I should have known my stomach would be the end of me.*

"Signore," Caro answered as politely as he could.

The cataphract's hard face darkened. "I suspected correctly. A northern barbarian. You have come to spy, or worse."

Most certainly a cataphract, Caro thought. Steel plates of armor and fine mail covered the warhorse he rode. An iron breastplate shielded him from all but the most direct of blows. Caro's mother often said he lacked good sense, but he wasn't inclined to run—it seemed stupid. *That,* he reflected, *is what Septimo and Halfblood are doing.*

When he turned to look again, he caught sight of Septimo and Halfblood running away, a bit to the left of where he looked previously. At least, they were running for a few moments—an arrow stuck Septimo in the back, followed by two buried in Halfblood.

Caro gasped and went cold. He turned to face the road—the cataphract still stood there, towering high on his horse. The arrows had come from elsewhere—a woman, he realized, poised on the road with a curved shortbow. A hooded veil of bright red lace covered her face, but most of her body was bare to the sun: bracelets covered her arms, themselves studded with white diamonds and rainbow opals. Twin anklets, forged of gold and studded with rubies, rested on her bare feet. Short but baggy pants of blue silk fell to her thigh.

"Signora," Caro gasped, not knowing what to say.

"Do not disgrace me with your tongue, barbarian," she said, though she spoke Imperial just the same.

"The Arrows of Issa do not know how to be polite," the cataphract said. "Though, I fear, Lady Mirzana's bow might be a preferable death to the one you receive. Pharzanes the Empire-Hater does not view the Imperial-blooded as human… they are dogs compared to the good men of Fharas. But dogs such as you, he says, should die slowly."

"I did only my duty… to the emperor, to Imperium," Caro said. "Much as you do your duty, and Mirzana does hers."

In a flash an arrow was strung to her bow. She snarled. The merchants passing by had stopped to gawk, reining in their horses. "Do not speak of me," she growled. "My name shall not be spoken by a dog."

"Not 'signora,' and not 'Mirzana,'" Caro muttered. "I don't rightly know what to say." He turned to look back, and at the sight of Septimo and Halfblood in their death-throes, tears welled in his eyes. "My friends…"

"If there is one thing the good men of Fharas hate more than Imperials, then it is cowards. Those who turn their back and run die first."

Caro wiped his eyes with his sleeve, which by now had turned brown and ragged through all the travel. He swore he would not cry or show weakness before these southrons, the people whom everyone back home called barbarians. *Strange, that they call us the same.*

"The walls of Seshán are finished." The cataphract smiled. "The barbarian emperor will never wrest the King of Kings from his throne again."

Caro knew little of history, only that Claudio-Valens Adamantus the Divine had started a war, taken Khazidea, and killed the King of Kings. "Signore," Caro said, and at the word Mirzana hissed and drew back an arrow. *Why doesn't she like that word?* "I have done the duty that my lord, the emperor Janus, wanted. However it ends for me, I will know I have done as he, and the god Imperium, has willed."

The cataphract's dark brown eyes glinted. "A man of honor

among the Imperial ranks—a precious rarity. Come with me… *signore.*"

The Arrow of Issa looked at him and snarled. Eyes filled with scorn, she turned and walked the other way. Leaving the arrow-pinned corpses behind her, she moved south down the road with all the alacrity and grace she'd shown as the Fertile Goddess's favored archer.

Caro turned to the cataphract. He had survived, but that was of little consequence. What awaited him was, no doubt, worse than what befell the quickly-dying Halfblood and Septimo. Still he followed his captor north—north, to where the torturous wrath of Pharzanes awaited him.

~

Two days through the arid plain, besides fields of wheat and desolate, dry barrens. On the way, the cataphract bought bread—not the dry road-biscuits the Empire provided—and provided plentiful fresh water. The cataphract, whose name he soon learned was Fharak, spoke little, but it was readily apparent that Caro's behavior had softened his approach; treating him better, even, than the Imperials treated the Fharese.

But soon Seshán appeared, its new fortifications stretching at least forty feet in the air. The walls' giant slabs of stone were so exactly cut they looked handcrafted by the gods, or by the dread Svarthal. *It is best not to think of the Svarthal.* But the memory would never leave him; and he thought of how he lost everything. He thought of Halfblood, his dearest friend, and his eyes welled with unwanted tears. *A soldier should not cry.* He wiped his eyes again, with the shirtsleeves that had already grown more and more ragged and soiled. The gates of Seshán lay open. Without a word he passed through.

The statues of the padisha emperors throughout history were the only human figures besides Caro and Fharak; and they themselves were the only things moving, save for the crackling flames in ceremonial braziers, no doubt dedicated to the elemental god of fire the Fharese worshiped. In legionary camps, some fellow-soldiers had said the Fharese not only worshiped the god of fire, but they worshiped fire itself.

Through the empty city, which could hold many hundreds of thousands of people but now, only held two, they walked. The giant road that cut through the statues, which could hold hundreds of merchants but only held a pair of travelers, continued until it reached a giant mountain. *No,* Caro realized, *a stepped throne.* It had to be two hundred feet high. And they were not alone—a few guards stood watch, keeping their liege Pharzanes safe—and there was another presence that nearly sent Caro, screaming, away. A man only three-quarters his height, yet twice his width, and a thick beard of bright orange. His pudgy hand gripped an axe of blackish metal; his body was covered in leather armor. *No, it is not a man at all… it is a Svarthal.*

He turned and ran, but the cataphract came thundering behind him. He would have to face the Svarthal—either that or his death, and he was not certain which was worse.

CHAPTER TWENTY-ONE:
INTERROGATION

Theon Arkadios

"Lycano No-Name," Astarthe purred in a dim-lit room in the House of Lenora, to the man she had fastened to the chair. There were no whips or hooks or thumbscrews in sight; Astarthe did not learn things through torture, but through kindness. She had fetched the would-be assassin a helping of crisp Khazidean bread, and a pitcher of barley-beer. "If you tell me who sent you to kill my son, you poor thing, then I will buy you a leg of lamb, or a bunch of grapes, or a bowl of figs—"

"*Figs*," Lycano gasped.

"Figs it is."

"And wine. Sweet northern white wine."

"Very well. A bowl of figs, and a glass of northern white, if you tell me who sent you."

Astarthe had chosen the most secluded room in the House of Lenora, stone-walled with a iron door that led out into the sewer-tunnels—securely fastened, the Imperial officer who gave them the tour had said, but even now, the stench of waste hung thick in the air. The water, amply supplied by aqueducts, washed the fetid matter out into the wide sea, but some smells you could never fully erase. Nonetheless, a handful of Astarthe's servants—Anakhil, all, for she would never subject her handmaids to such bland decor—remained in the doorway, waiting for the unarmed, unclothed assassin to make an incriminating move on the queen they adored.

"Anakhil," Astarthe snapped, and they jerked to attention. "You heard my sweet captive."

The word "sweet" stung him. Only seconds later did Theon realize he had felt jealousy; the Way was gone from him, as far-gone as the lands where he'd been taught it. He glanced at the small-framed, copper-skinned beauty that had won him over, and the thought of her, sharing a bed with this man hurt him like no dagger-blade ever had—as ridiculous as that would be. He knew it would never happen—no one of Astarthe's mettle would fall for the one who meant to kill her son, and yet Theon found himself wanting to pull her away from him, to urge her not to stand so close. He wanted Astarthe... he wanted to keep her as his own.

"Go," Astarthe commanded, the young woman who held grown men at her beck and call like puppets on her fingers. "Bring my sweet captive some figs and wine—"

Theon physically recoiled.

"—and we will see if he will talk."

~

Once the murderous vagrant had his figs and his sweetwine—after the queen of Haroon rewarded him for his evil intent—he at last began to talk. The wine, and the kindness of the queen, opened his mouth like water from a broken dam.

"I was living off the street," Lycano No-Name began. "I could scarcely keep myself alive... I was seven when I killed a human being for the first time, but I was fourteen when I first did it for pay."

"We didn't ask you for your life story," Theon snarled. Astarthe, still standing a bit too close to him for Theon's comfort, looked at him curiously. "Tell us who sent you."

"Do not be so rude, signore," Lycano snapped, and the murderer's gaze hardened. "Else, I will not tell your lovely domina what she wants to know."

"Domina? I am not..." He stopped himself from saying anything more. To answer his rude comment was to marginalize himself, to give this wad of scum what he wanted—attention.

"He thought you were my slave. Funny, that." Theon wondered if Astarthe knew how much she was hurting him. "Who sent you?"

"Well, my signora, I assure you I never had any ill will toward you or your son. All I was really after was the pay… money that could pay for a Getic horse."

"Perhaps we can arrange that."

Theon wanted to strike someone. Either that, or admit she had wounded him.

"My sweet signora…" His hands touched Astarthe's, and she did not resist; Theon felt he would go mad. "The man who hired me to kill Anakh was an Imperial councilor, Vitellian was his name—" Theon had a crazy thought, of Astarthe, the woman he loved, bedding this vagabond, of baring herself to him like she had bared herself to Theon. "—and Vitellian, I know, he was sent by, ah, who was it?—" He wondered what it was about this vagabond that could possibly draw Astarthe in, perhaps some bestial magnetism Theon did not see. Perhaps it had to do with the universal truth, that humans crave whatever is forbidden to them. "—the emperor, Secondo Janus, sent me, by way of Vitellian." Astarthe, still holding his hand, drew nearer to him.

Theon's hand dipped into his bag, and within the lapse of a second, two throwing stars stuck from Lycano's body. One shiv of metal emerged halfway from his throat; the other well-aimed blow had buried the throwing star in Lycano's chest. Blood trickled like water across his bare chest. Lycano tried to speak, but all that came out was a gargling sound. He charged Theon, but he had collapsed into his death-throes before he was halfway across the room.

"Theon Arkadios." Astarthe broke her stunned silence. Her eyes seethed with storm. "Were you truly jealous of him? Who do you think I am, Theon Arkadios, that I would fall in love with the man who tried to kill Adamantion?"

"I was wondering the same."

The anger washed away from her eyes. "Oh, you poor fool. If I had half a mind I would send you away—even send you to Thénai and collect the ransom your father's put on your head."

"A ransom?"

"A ransom. I would keep your emotions in check from hereon, Theon Arkadios. The carelessness with which you take a life worries me. And all because of this ridiculous notion."

"I saw the way you looked at him… the way you touched him."

"Leave me," Astarthe snarled. As he turned and left through the door, she could hear her sniffle—and he wondered if the tears were for a lost life, or a lost love.

Not long after Theon retreated to the uppermost story of the guest house, staring at the scene of Kings Terrace far below, he sensed a presence behind him. He had no idea who it was, until the little boy's voice said, "Theon?"

He turned to regard Adamantion, the source of all the emperor's woes, the child whom he wanted dead by any means. It was Secondo Janus that wanted this prince dead—yet the culprit was perhaps not who Astarthe wanted. Who could punish the emperor? Who would dare to?

"A man melted downstairs."

Theon turned to face the little boy, innocent to the evils of the world. "Melted, you say." The infantile description chilled him. Adamantion's innocent face had two hawkish eyes and an eagle nose— two things Imperium's chosen ones were said to have—set on a canvas of reddish Khazidean skin. The combination of peoples seemed the perfect complement.

"My mother says my true da is her brother."

A well-intentioned lie.

"But she has made me call many people da, and I never knew my real da. But you are my favorite da, Signor Theon."

The words unraveled him. Adamantion ran across the room and Theon scooped him up, slinging him over his shoulder. Adamantion burst into giggling. *If not for Astarthe, I will stay for him.*

The young woman herself appeared through the door, a presence despite her small stature. Her face was no longer twisted in anger. There was something else, now, deep in her eyes. Her eyes had grown moist; they revealed a woman who saw Theon in a new light, as a partner, as a helper, and as a friend. He saw love.

~

That evening, at dusk, Theon took a stroll, shunning the protection of Imperial guard regiment and the useless, attention-drawing Anakhil, he wandered Kings Terrace and left it, finding the concerns and conversations of the wealthy too petty, too familiar, for him to care about. No; he could feel the beams of twilight drawing him outside the gates of Kings Terrace, progressing further and further down the road. As the light to seep from the sky, he found himself in the cesspools of Imperial City, where he wanted to be.

The folk here, who lived in squalor and filth, eyed his silk garments, sizing him up and guessing how much the flower-painted robe from the Far East would gain them in the black markets of Imperial City. But he had the peasant's staff that the rice farmers used for self-defense in the paddies of Cathay, and behind his back the lacquer-filmed saber the warriors of the Forgotten Isle. He did not fear them.

Why am I here?

He walked further into the Suburro.

The graphic pictures above the brothel doors left no doubts as to what they offered—*The Fertile Land,* he saw on a sign, and below the words a picture of the legendary gardens of paradise, filled with Khazidean beauties... Another—*The Silver Candlestick*—where the catamites went and indulged the vice that the desert peoples deplored.

At the thought of the desert peoples, his thoughts turned eastward. He spun around; though winter, the air here felt warm, and the rays of sun glanced over the low rooftops, burning his eyes with their red and gold beams. When he shut his eyes, he lapsed into a twilit dream.

Years ago—or was it decades?—he stood among the squalor of Xia, where spiked iron fences protected the giant mansions of the rich from the mass of poor and starving outside. *And I am poor. I am one of those outside. I am of the House of Arkadios and I am standing here in the midst of all the rabble. How did it come to this?*

~

He had shaved his beard. He had dyed his hair to black all to fit in. He remembered—he had murdered the Celestial Emperor and thrown the Forgotten Isle into peril. How could he forget? He went off into the streets of Xia, penniless yet starving for his next puff of opium. *Why did I leave home?* He had killed the Celestial Emperor by the advice of Choh, the wicked man who could stop the sun in its path and reverse the course of rivers, yet whose greatest power was over the minds of mankind... He had fed him all this nonsense about the Way... And now, what was there to do on this hopeless day? He left west down the street, as the setting sun burned red and gold through the burning smog, in search of more opium, and wondering how in Varda he could come upon some.

~

The realization sucked the wind from his lungs as the sunrays glared in his eyes. Had he truly committed regicide? Had the talk of the Way really been nothing more than Choh's scheming? He had a feeling he was just beginning to wake from the opium dream... that the past would return to him, like little bits of a veil torn away. He had a feeling there was still much to remember, though he did not want to.

But I have a home, now... a home in the Lotus Court with Queen Astarthe and her flower maidens. A home with the queen, and with Adamantion.

The thought of the little boy gave the deepening darkness a more and more haunting aspect. As the shadows lengthened, and the air took on a dry chill, he knew how easily all things in life could be snatched away—how fleeting all precious things were, how vulnerable and quickly stolen. He had not stepped another yard before a voice stopped him: "A nice robe you have. I have never seen the likes of such fine silk-work. Pray tell, where'd you get it?"

Theon turned.

"An Eloesian, I see. Good signore, tell me, where'd you get it?"

In the gloaming light, Theon could make out few distinct features—only that he was dressed in plainclothes, and in his hand a dagger glistened orange. "A wise assassin would come upon a man quickly, put the dagger to his throat before giving him time to react."

"A wise assassin knows his quarry," the man said. "You're the southron witch's consort. You're bedding her, aren't you? And enjoying it, too, I gander."

"I would leave, if I valued my life." The thought of this man going after Adamantion was enough to ready himself for killing. The lives of men had lessened in value to him—a grim token of his past.

"A fine *lupa*..."

At the word, Theon fingered a throwing star.

"A looker, too, but she's a man eater, signore... You must be her hundredth."

Theon nearly lost control at the man's insult. He summoned all the discipline of the Way, and restrained himself from attacking him recklessly in defense of Astarthe, waiting for the opportune time to strike. He used the discipline of the Way, which the past—broken from the opium dream's veil—now proved a sham, a manipulation by the wicked miracle worker Choh. "Who sent you? Was it Secondo Janus? Thank the gods she is not here with me..."

"Secondo Janus? You say the emperor wants to kill your lady wife?" The street folk had gathered around them, poking their faces through alleys and upper-story windows, as if watching a pantomime or an Arena show. "No, signore, I am not looking to kill your lady wife. I am looking for a man who came from far away, who abandoned his family in Thénai and was last seen in Haroon—"

The throwing star left his hand, whistling through the air, but the assassin dodged at just the right time, turning it into a glancing blow that ripped his tunic. He charged.

"Ah, so it is you, Theon Arkadios, you runt."

He came within inches of landing a dagger-blow when Theon whipped the peasant's staff around his head and landed a stunning blow. Theon had become the peasant rice paddy farmer again, his only protection from the Forgotten Isle lords his wooden staff.

By the time the assassin recovered he was headless, his blood dripping from the lacquered blade of Theon's saber. In the blink of an eye he had become the Forgotten Isle warrior-lord; for a follower of the Way was all things at all times.

But I have abandoned the Way, he thought, *and for my own good.*

He ran all the way from the Suburro back to Kings Terrace. By the time he had reached the calm streets, the wealthy folk who lived in worriless luxury had retired indoors—to bed, perhaps, or to a dinner party, or to the things the wealthy did in secret, far from the public's prying eyes.

In the dark of the night he nonetheless felt illumined. Illumined and afraid. The Way was a sham—or was it? He knew for certain he had remembered the past correctly—he had murdered the Celestial Emperor by the advice of Choh. But there was so much more to learn. There was so much more to remember. Little by little, life tore holes in the veil that covered the truth—holes that reflected the raw reality, which the opium dream had barred him from. The opium dream was long gone. Now, there was only truth. There was only truth—and there was Anakh.

He wiped the remaining blood off the Forgotten Isle saber, and then—with immense relief—shrugged the baleful events of the day and headed home.

CHAPTER TWENTY-TWO:
THE VOTE

Emperor Secondo Janus the God

It took a while to learn, but eventually the empress Lanabelle adjusted to her new position. She still spoke the Imperial tongue through the lens of a spitting Zarube accent, but she had strived to learn and perfect it. The palace slave-girls curled and braided her bright gold hair in the latest fashions of the East; her old gowns and skirts from the north, Secondo had his servants sell, and replace with the thin but elegant scarlet dresses of the Empire. Her pallid complexion indicated northern heritage—and the Imperial councilors had no end to their criticisms of Secondo's wedding a barbarian—but Empress Lana, as she was called, had not and would never do anything wrong in Secondo's eyes.

In her land, a man and woman could not divorce without the agreement of their local priestess—to her, the former queen, the High Priestess herself. "The priestesses," she told him, teary-eyed, one night as they reclined on the veranda, "will not grant a divorce without reason. Only if a spouse is unfaithful, or defames the Lady—"

Their goddess Feanara was patron of the fairies, revered by all the knights and high lords.

"—and only then if the Lady herself gives consent."

Lana was his only source of warmth in the chill winter night. Beads of water, vestiges of a recent rain, covered the wooden boards. He went in for a kiss and Lana at first shrugged him off. Still, she fought guilt at what she did.

"Your husband would have killed you," he whispered. "You did nothing wrong by marrying me."

"I—"

"Emperor." A voice he recognized instantly as Augusto Vitellian—his plant on the Imperial Council, who told him all the whispered words of the court, and did whatever Secondo bade—startled him from the pure relaxation of Lana. "A word… in private?"

Lana pulled back from his embrace, stood to her feet.

"Now, Vitellian? Truly?" Secondo stood up himself. "Can't this wait until tomorrow?"

"No; no it cannot, Your Undying Glory."

"I will go…" Before Secondo could respond she had pushed by Vitellian and slinked through the door. "A messenger arrived, Secondo… He came from Floridium."

Secondo bit his lip to stem off his irritation.

"He brought news of total destruction—not a single building remains. The northmen's wizards annihilated it, signore. There were no survivors… and the damage has—according to our best estimates—lost over twelve-thousand libra in revenue. To rebuild, at this point, would be unprofitable…"

"Does it matter to me, Vitellian? Was it worth rousing me over?"

"Oh, it is." The wan moonlight illuminated something Secondo never saw before in Vitellian's eyes. "The navy has left… they may be going south. To Imperial City, perhaps—so in truth it is everyone's concern. But especially yours. The Imperial Council questions your judgment. Tomorrow they are taking a vote of incompetence. You brought us into this war—"

"Impossible!" Secondo hissed, and his blood ran hot. He jerked toward him, wanting to clobber him right there.

Vitellian instinctively jerked away. "Don't blame the messenger, signore. You must act. A bribe, perhaps… but the councilors are angry, Signor Secondo, even irate. They think this entire war could have been avoided, were it not for your poor judgment. Bribes may work in the short term—but most likely will not—yet the court is collectively growing angrier and angrier. As your friend, I suggest you accept the vote of incompetence, and retire to some villa on the sea…"

Secondo Janus could see his father laughing at him. *See? I said you'd never amount to anything. I told you…* "A friend would never suggest that."

"Your wife Lana will not come with you. She will be delivered to Bretonnius."

"An embarrassment not just to me, Signor Vitellian, but also to the Empire. To have the wizards assault a town, level it with fire and destruction, and then, for the Empire—Imperium's chosen nation—to run back to the northern barbarians with its tail behind its legs. Such a wrong should be avenged. Such a wrong…"

"You have heard my advice, Signor Janus. Perhaps with enough convincing, you could convince the council to keep Lana by your side."

Secondo sneered. "You have shown your mettle, 'friend.' Leave me, before you rouse me to violence."

Vitellian turned and disappeared through the door.

CHAPTER TWENTY-THREE:
A PROPOSITION

Maximian, Marshal of the Guard

In the White Chamber, Maximian had almost begun to nod off where he stood when Secondo Janus appeared. The young man's face had a cherry red color Maximian had only seen a few times before—when he was about to kill somebody, usually.

"Maximian," he said, "I have a task for you."

"A task?"

"I will pay you four-hundred libra for it."

Maximian's ears perked up. That much money was more than most were like to see in their lifetime. "And what task is worth so much gold, Your Undying Glory?"

"I want you to kill every last sniveling worm on the Imperial Council." His voice shook with rage. "I want you to cut their throats… I want you to make it painful if you can. I want them all dead before morning."

"Signor Emperor, you must be joking."

"*You* must be joking, to question the Hand of Imperium."

Maximian had never cared much for all that religious superstition. "Signore, if you expect me to kill the Imperial Councilors—elected by the people of the Empire themselves—then surely, *surely…*"

Secondo Janus swept the bluish adamant sword from its sheath, his face now a bright apple red. "*Traitor!*"

Maximian drew his own in kind—not as large or finely worked as the emperor's, but wielded with a better hand.

"*I* am the Empire. *I* am the people. The Imperial Council answers to me, Signor Maximian, and they dare to hold a vote of incompetence…"

"Ah." Maximian had heard whispers of such an action, but

now they were confirmed. "Perhaps they will not have a majority, signore."

"I have known some of the sniveling worms since they assumed office. If you will not do your duty—"

"To protect the emperor against violence…"

"—then I have no choice but to see you dead." He struck, and the two adamant swords kissed, ringing through the White Chamber.

"Calm down!" Maximian snapped.

"No. You… you calm down. Do as you are told… you are my servant, my slave."

"I am your protector."

He struck again, and Maximian moved in to disarm him. The emperor's blade went flying across the room.

"Protector… that is what you say you are… so why… why won't you protect me?" Janus' face turned to white splotches. For the first time Maximian saw tears in his eyes.

"I will protect you, but I won't kill anyone without cause. I will protect your life, to the end of my days."

Janus embraced Maximian, and peering over his shoulder, the face of Augusto Vitellian appeared through the open door. Secondo Janus was by any accounts incompetent, and had dragged the Empire into a conflict neither it nor the Northern World needed—but Secondo was his friend. Vitellian looked away and vanished from his sight. Maximian would protect him, but—as the emperor showed weakness for the first time, sobbing over his shoulder—he knew the Empire would be better off without him, though Maximian was his friend.

CHAPTER TWENTY-FOUR: THE DARKEST NIGHT

Maximian, Marshal of the Guard

The sound of screams jolted Maximian from his sleep. Outside the night sky was pitch-dark. A commotion had engulfed the palace. Breathless and covered in sweat he grabbed his *Imperium's Rebuke* from his nightstand, and—clad in nothing but a loincloth—he rushed out to meet whatever challenge awaited.

The screams came from downstairs, he realized, and as he dashed down the twisting hallways the sound of crackling flame and searing ice resounded through the walls. More tellingly, the air had taken on a familiar chill, a chill Maximian recognized as magic. In its dread embrace he ran, bare-chested and bare-legged, through the halls filled with frantic screams, even as the booming voice below dawned on him with startling recognition—Lemuel, the man who had fled the palace, who had somehow evaded the guards. He told himself it was impossible. He told himself it couldn't happen. Lemuel had gone north—the guards had seen him. So how had he so suddenly reappeared?

On the main floor of the Imperial Palace, where once foreign emissaries had made their first appearance, the fine couches and divans now burned with searing fire, and in the flames the blackened corpses of court-members told of Lemuel's grim handiwork. A soldier was rushing across the room to face Lemuel as Maximian approached, and the wizard himself floated a few feet in the air, dressed in his slate-blue robe with a crystal wand in one hand and a staff in the other.

The soldier had come within a few yards of Lemuel when a green ray burst from the oustretched wand then sheathed him in its light. Within seconds the soldier and all he wore had turned to a fine black powder. That was when Maximian ran at him, aware of the madness of his actions but angry—shaking, blood-burningly angry—

at this wizard who had brought so much misery on the nation.

Lemuel's eyes met his, flashing white-hot with anger or eldritch power. But Maximian's rage seethed within him, boiling his blood, consuming him; he lifted his *Imperium's Rebuke* over his head, screaming. Lemuel fired the green ray but Maximian rolled under it, and the wand lost all its color.

The adamant sword was inches from the wizard's neck when green light burst into dazzling existence, and Lemuel was gone.

~

All available augurs from the collegium arrived shortly afterward—three-dozen men and women with winged caps and staves, not the least of them Silvana, whose long blonde hair and piercing blue eyes momentarily distracted him from his failure—and Maximian joined them as they ran through the corridors of the Imperial Palace.

When has a disaster like this ever befallen the Empire? Maximian wondered. The Imperial people had thought the northmen savages, at best a pale shadow of themselves. How wrong they had been.

Numerous fires had started throughout the Imperial Palace. Some rooms had totally engulfed in flames. But Silvana—her wisps of golden hair sticking out from her leather cap—led the charge, and Maximian, enamored with her as much as ever, followed gladly.

At the topmost level of the palace, after a tiring sprint, Silvana and the augurs stopped their running.

"He is gone," Silvana said. "I wonder what he has taken this time?"

"Silvana." Maximian's words spurred her to turn around. The piercing, regal blue eyes met his. "We need to kill him—"

"Easier said than done… sweetling." A trace of a smile touched her lips.

Maximian smiled in response.

A group of Imperial Guards came barreling down the hall—Quintus, he recognized, and Mateo—their faces ashen. "Marshal!" Quintus shouted. "The bastard has taken the empress…"

Empress Lana. He could only imagine what they would do to her in the north. His heart sank for her—but the Empire could not do anything about it. "Where is Janus?"

Both Quintus and Mateo's face grew grave. "Secondo Janus," Mateo answered, "is dead."

CHAPTER TWENTY-FIVE:
A CHANGE OF HEART

Theon Arkadios

"The emperor is dead, burnt to ash by the northmen," Astarthe had told Theon last night. "I suppose the old fellow cremated him in a way… at least he had that honor. And now we needn't worry about Janus killing sweet Adamantion."

Now Theon accompanied Astarthe and Adamantion to where the funeral had begun—in the severely burnt chamber in the Imperial Palace the northman mage had seared with hellfire—and in sight of the limestone jar which supposedly held Secondo's remains, soon to be stored in the Temple of Imperium.

All thirty Imperial Councilors stood there in the room— mostly old, white-haired men—and the Imperial Guard in their red half-cloaks, as well a hundred other members of the court whose names and positions Theon did not know.

"The will of Emperor Secondo Janus the Divine, chosen Hand of Imperium, sovereign of the Six Nations, lord and god." Crispus Servillius, Speaker of the Council, read the words from a vellum scroll. "I donate all my acquired wealth and personal affects to the Empire itself, to its advancement and good governance. I pardon Bathalomer No-Name, the Market District murderer. I pardon Nicator the assassin. I pardon…"

Theon found himself drifting off, tempted to fall asleep. But he righted himself when his thoughts turned to his father—fierce and angry—and his false son, the one he called Theon.

"I leave the Empire in the care of Maximian, Marshal of the Imperial Guard, and name him emperor."

A man stepped back, dazed—an Imperial Guard in a red half-cloak, dark-featured and muscular—Maximian.

"He is not an August… not even a Knight!" one of the

councilors snapped.

"But," Councilor Servillius muttered absently, "it is the will of Imperium."

"Is it?" Astarthe asked, and from the folds of her robe she drew a slip of paper—written by the priest of Imperium not long ago. "The blood of the Adamanti is gods' blood."

All attention focused on Astarthe, the woman they called the "lecherous southron witch."

"I have with me a child of a living god."

In his mind's eye, Maximian saw dark clouds of purple, and fearsome mountains the color of burnished bronze. He saw pools of bright green acid, haunted by hulking beasts. He saw the ancient land of the *dai ma* which so many feared—the land he saw when he became a sailor, changing his *persona* by virtue of the Way.

"The priest of Imperium," the southron witch went on, "made a sacrifice before the god of the Empire, a goat bled dry then burnt in a fiery brazier..."

In his mind's eye, Maximian remembered poisoning the Celestial Emperor, of changing his *persona* to the wine-tester, even as he dripped nightflower's-milk into his glass. He remembered the furor that overtook the Jade Palace as the Celestial Emperor passed on from the mortal world. He remembered changing his *persona* again, into that of a Forgotten Isle knight, and riding through the cherry-blossom orchards to a seaside town, and taking the first available ship to Xia.

"The blood of the goat pleased the god of the Empire, and here, here I have his will—written in goat's blood—that the White Throne should belong to an Adamantus. I have with me the son of Claudian Adamantus, the living god, and by the will of Imperium it is he who should reign."

A few councilors gasped. A woman shouted, "She is mad!"

But Theon only reflected as more of the opium dream faded, as more of the veil was torn away, baring the secrets of the past. He had gained so much power, by virtue of the Way. He had become nigh invincible; he had outshone the sage Choh in his mastery of the Way.

He had played all the petty empires around the Sea of Stars like a grand game. At last the sage Choh had found him, given him opium until he had lost his mind and forgotten all the secrets of the Way. Forgotten… until now. He flexed his fingertips, and felt them bristle with power.

A furor had taken the Imperial Palace. But it was Maximian—the one who Secondo had proclaimed emperor—that did his best to calm them, to force them to listen to the southron witch and let her have her say.

It didn't matter to Theon, anymore. He called on all the powers of the Way, all the secrets of the wise sages. He changed his *persona*, becoming an Imperial Councilor in the eyes of the foolish and uninitiated. He fled his forced friendship with the Queen of Haroon. She looked back at him, eyes filled with anger yet understanding—understanding, perhaps, of what was going on—then turned to face the furor. Theon the Imperial Councilor departed from the palace, heading toward the center of the city. He would go to Thénai to face his father and the false son, and who knew what awaited him? The Way would guide him, and no ignorant denizen of the Material World would stand a chance.

CHAPTER TWENTY-SIX: THE EMPIRE-HATER

Caro, Legionary

"S-Svarthal," Caro stuttered, convinced he sounded like a lackwit. "S-Svarthal…"

The short, yet strongly-built man with the flame-orange beard only smiled in response. His complexion was dark despite the brightness of his hair, a sooty earthen color nearly as dark as the leather armor he wore. "Svarthal." He spoke Imperial in an accent Caro did not recognize. "the ancient name for an ancient race. Things have changed since the Silver Age, my good man. The Fire Lords are gone, though their worship remains among the magi. The ancient wonders of my ancestors remain—locked in tombs with deadly traps—but you… you, my good man, may call me Arran. I am a mere advisor to Pharzanes the Empire-Hater, the Beloved-of-His-Father, the Good."

Caro still didn't like the idea of speaking to a Svarthal, even if he didn't claim to be one. *Especially if he doesn't claim to be one.*

"Still afraid?" Arran said. Caro eyed the curved black axe in his hand, thin and small yet quite capable of cutting out a man's heart. "Nonetheless, you should be, though not of me. Pharzanes…"

The mountainous throne stole his breath. At the top of the ziggurat was a great stone, carved with the Four-Pointed Star. The brightly-colored figure of Pharzanes was an ant before it, barely distinguishable from the stone edifice, sitting high above them, up the many hundreds of steps.

"At all times, two magi stand guard over him," the cataphract behind Caro said. "The great error of our forefathers was to let him stand unguarded; we never thought there was a man so vile he would venture into Fharas, the ancient and holy kingdom, and steal her ruler from his throne. But Claudio the Destroyer proved himself so vile."

"Claudio-Valens Adamantus, the god… overcame you." The

supposed God Manifest who could strike men dead with a glance, whose gaze could reverse the course of rivers and turn day into night. But before him, the unconquered son, the soon-to-be god of the Empire, the King of Kings was merely a man, a hunted prey, a prize to bring back to Imperium's chosen nation.

When Caro became Caro again, the very air had changed.

Pharzanes, not having dared to breathe for seconds now, began to gasp for air. "Such wonder I have never seen… *Be gone, Claudio! Be gone!*"

Caro—not Claudio—turned and stumbled down the steps. He ran past the Svarthal warrior and the cataphracts, through the main road of Seshán past the towering statues of long-dead King of Kings, and at last into the open plains of Gor Ilán.

The normally dry, dusty land turned wet and earthy as clouds drifted in, heralding their presence with a crack of thunder, and rain began to pour. Caro—*not* Claudio—wondered what in Varda had happened, whether his ominous transformation was a phantom of the past, or a portent of things to come.

He ran north through the building rain, thinking only of home.

CHAPTER TWENTY-SEVEN: WHERE THE WALL MEETS THE SEA

Julian Ultor, Malleus

Julian had ridden for more than a week, and eaten all the salted meat he brought with him, leaving only the dry, tasteless road-bread which he came to hate more and more every day. By the time a pair of low mountains appeared, and the Wall quickly changed directions, going southeast toward the sea, he had only one day's food left. Nature provided plentiful water—snow had layered the rolling plain for the past few days, and it was easily melted.

The legionaries remained a heavy presence on the Wall, but even from such a height and such a distance Julian had no doubts they knew his allegiance—to the Empire and its people—and thus, unmolested, he followed the Wall all the way to the sea. The wall ran along the edge of the western ocean, and Julian knew that should not have surprised him. But nonetheless he rode forth, thinking only of the northman-king's wizard, and by extension the sorcerer who had slain his family.

Above the calm rush of the waves, and the foam steadily washing in along the pebbly beach, the shouts of the soldiers became unmistakable: "Get away, you rascal! You are forbidden here!" But it was only the shout "Stop or I will shoot!" that forced him to pull his reins and stop his gallop.

The Wall was so high their shouts barely rose above the waves.

"I am an Imperial!" Julian shouted. "I am a paladin of Hieronus, a hammer of god! Please, allow me into the Empire!"

"If you intend to return, your point of entry is a mere five-hundred miles east! You only overshot just a bit, signore!"

"I must—" Julian began at a shout.

"None may enter except by the Gate of Tidus!"

Julian sighed. He knew very well these soldiers could help him, but he knew in a way they were enjoying his grief. "I have a task that needs doing! For the sake of the Empire!"

A few of the soldiers, mere ants before the massive stone wall, broke into laughter.

"The magic weaver, Lemuel, I must—" His shout broke off.

"You have overshot again, signore! The wizards of the north passed by our watchtower, mayhap three days ago! Their ships are gone into the north sea!"

The news hit him like water on this cold day, sapping his strength. But if he abandoned his oath, his stated desire—his goal of crushing Lemuel with the hammer of god—then it would be a grave offense to the Just God, a shame upon his name. It would be a disappointment to the Lord of Justice. But more importantly, it would be a disappointment to himself. Not for the first time, and not for the last, he shut his eyes and became Julian Tyrenas, the seven-year-old boy who lost his innocence on a sweltering summer night. The memory spurred him north toward the tree-covered mountains that ran along the coast of the western sea.

A fleet of wizards would spell certain death to a common soldier, but neither fire, lightning, nor storm conjured by magic—nor all the armies of the underworld—could stand against the hammer of god.

He rode off into the twilight, to a place he'd never been nor knew anything about, his only food the command of Hieronus, his only weapon his hammer, his only map the oath he swore to god. He peered out to sea. The ships of the wizards now drove through the waves, unaware of the coming storm: the judgment of Hieronus, the Just God.

CHAPTER TWENTY-EIGHT: THE GOD, CAPTIVE

Emperor Secondo Janus the God

The night had seemed like a bad dream, but light dawned over the Western Sea, and the nightmare had continued. He stood with the wizard Lemuel on the deck of a tall ship, and his dear Lana stood trembling at his side. He did his best to comfort her, but even he had begun to question all the decisions he had made. One thing was certain: he knew Lanabelle did not deserve this. Perhaps he did, but not her.

The tall ships of the wizards, their sails emblazoned with the so-called Arcane Eye, were many miles out to sea. Lemuel had traveled all the distance in the blink of an eye, after leaving a trail of destruction and fire in his wake. Now, it was just Secondo Janus and Lanabelle. Secondo was her only protector, and what a poor protector he would be. The wizards would burn him to dust before he landed the first blow. Little wonder, then, that the wizards did not bother to shackle either him or Lana.

"Lady guard me," she whispered. "Lady protect me from death."

"The High Priestess of the Lady," Lemuel said, his eyes peering intensely into hers, "is most displeased with you and your conduct."

Secondo had never seen such intense eyes, such a terrifying stare, on an old man—actually, on anyone. The wizard was surrounded by lackeys, magic weavers of lesser import, who scrambled to control the sails. Lemuel had discarded his crystal wands or perhaps expended them all, and now only wore his slate-blue robes and clutching a gray birch staff. The thought that this Lemuel wasn't the best of the wizards in the north terrified Secondo—not necessarily for himself, but for the nation he had ruled, the nation he had loved.

"I do not put much stock in priests and priestesses, however,"

Lemuel finished the thought. "The High Priestess may be wroth, Lanabelle, but she would only advocate a dissolution of the marriage, to put you in a convent with some Green Sisters and shut you away for the remainder of your life… but alas, your husband Gylles will want you dead."

Secondo wrapped his hands tighter around her shoulder, but even to himself his comfort seemed false, and an overwhelming sense fell upon him that he was not only responsible for his country's trouble, but also for the distress and danger his new wife had fallen into. It was enough to consider flinging himself overboard and drowning—but then, who would poor Lana have?

"Signor Lemuel, I can offer you money beyond your wildest fantasy. Money enough to purchase a villa, and slaves to fill it…"

Lemuel laughed darkly. "A villa. No, *seigneur.*"

The man's accent angered Secondo.

"I think my manor house on the coast shall suffice. Not to mention my tidy yearly sum from the Wizards Council itself."

Secondo didn't know what to do, what to say, or how he could get himself out of this situation—and more importantly, Lana. But for the first time since Secondo Janus was a boy, when his father made clear his favoritism toward Primo, he was powerless.

"And what will they do with me?" Secondo asked, though in truth he was only concerned for the moment about Lana.

"Ah." Lemuel's voice was like a cold autumn vapor. "You, *seigneur* Secondo. King Bretagne most certainly would like to see you disemboweled, or worked to death in the iron-mines. But if he is not rash, he will see you as you are – a prize to be bargained for, a source of no small wealth."

He couldn't imagine the Imperial Councilors sending any money to pay his ransom, not after they nearly voted him incompetent. He could see his father—still kicking on to life—in his home in Nichaeus… the news reaching him as he drank hard liquor. The words, from his old lips: "I knew Secondo would never amount to anything…

I knew he would wreck our country once put in charge… if only Primo was still alive…" The haunting words coalesced around him. Primo was long-dead—his body slashed wide open, the legate said, by a Fharese scimitar—but his elder brother the well-favored lived on in Secondo's mind, a phantasmal presence which would not leave him until his dying day.

"We in the north," Lemuel began, his deep voice unwelcome, "have been fed tales of the Empire's magnificence. We have been told of its megacities ten times the size of Zarubad… but a nation ruled by the wellborn will easily overcome a nation ruled by serfs. It is the natural order of things."

"If I could," Secondo answered, "I would cut that irksome tongue from your mouth so it would never bother me again. Then I would chop off all the northmen's legs, so that they could never trouble our nation."

"You started this war, fool," Lemuel said, his voice turning caustic in an instant. "We had come to make a diplomatic visit, and you—because of your sexual offenses—"

"You did not come for diplomacy," Secondo answered him. "You came to steal a treasure the Empire had long held. Bretonnius distracted me while you snooped about the palace—my guard, Maximian, saw it all."

"Ah, Maximian—lowly born even by the Empire's standards. I do wonder, *seigneur*, if your people will make him emperor as well, since your nation has a habit of making slaves princes, and princes slaves."

"Oh, to cut off your tongue." A man of such beliefs could not be swayed—not until his nation burned and the Empire had conquered King Bretonnius. But even that seemed a flight of fancy, a phantom no more real than Secondo's long-dead brother. Secondo prayed to heaven that the will of Imperium would prevail, that the Empire would overcome the prideful enemy, that the king and— especially—this magic-weaving blackguard would get what he justly deserved.

But Lemuel was smiling, and Secondo Janus had a feeling the Empire would never give him what he deserved; his powers were too great, his ability so far beyond that of the Imperial augurs and the theurges of Eloesus.

Through the expanse of the sea, a trace of high hills—which these barbarians likely called mountains—emerged, a trace outline against a blue haze. He wondered who lived there, if anyone lived there. He could only imagine what men roamed such rugged terrain.

CHAPTER TWENTY-NINE:
INTO THE WOODS

Julian Ultor, Malleus

The giant forested hills, which the Mekari called mountains, soon swallowed him. The trees had all shed their leaves, forming a mat of gold and gray. A recent rain had washed over the slopes, slicking the hilly path and all but covering the road with mud, leaves, and thistles; but Julian Ultor's path was his heart, and the guiding spirit of Hieronus, Lord of Justice and Just War, and the only motive that spurred him on was the oath he had sworn solemnly to his heavenly liege.

Night, he soon learned, fell early here; and when it fell Julian had never been colder or darker. The wan shadows of the moon and the scattering of the leaves in the wind were his only companions. Then, sometime well after the sun had set, a low horn blew. *The hills are not empty.* Memories returned to him of the horseman that wore antlers on his head, of his loathing for the northmen—and worst, of Julian's refusal of him. Rumors wisped around him like troublesome ghosts—of men in taverns, speaking gleefully of the northern barbarian's practices: removing the scalps from their enemies' heads as trophies, even eating their enemies' flesh.

Suddenly, Julian had never felt so vulnerable or alone. Only the oath he swore before Hieronus kept him here, in this backward hill country; but even then, rest was impossible, and he only slept an hour, at most, before the sun dawned.

His charger nickered nervously as Julian mounted him. He clucked and shoved his heels into the beast's sides, but the canter he began was half-hearted, and soon Julian knew why.

Out of the brownness of the forest, up the hill and down from its summit, emerged the natives.

The men had thick brown beards. Both men and boys wielded crescent axes. A few women had come, too. All wore blue paint over their skin, and few wore more than buckskin leggings or loin-cloths. Julian jolted aright. Drawing a hammer was a tricky business. "Signors… signoras…" Julian's voice betrayed his worry. "I mean you no harm."

One man in particular—larger than the others, wearing antlers, and smeared with red paint rather than blue—fixed his eyes especially hard on Julian. "A southlander, if I have ever seen one." His accent was thick, yet his Imperial grammar was perfect. "I rarely—no, never—see his kind, here. Surely he has a good reason."

"You speak—?"

"Hush," he said, "I once spent two years, living among the southlanders like one of them. Small wonder, signore, that I speak the tongue of my master."

"Master—?"

"Aye. A slave, I was, captured off the coastal islands. Served nine months at a farm outside Floridium. The town's a burnt ruin, now."

"A burnt ruin?"

"Aye. A fool, you are, to go into the mountains by yourself. But you don't have the look of a fool in your eyes." The man's eyes narrowed. "You have come to the lands of the Mekari. Why?"

"Why? I… the wizards." Julian Ultor, Malleus, cursed himself for letting the mere threat of death trip up his tongue.

"The wizards, you say. The men of the Far North are your foe." His eyes grew wild, manic. "Steadily the city-dwellers have gone south into the land of our cousins. I hate them, too. And the wizards say they never favor any nation or tribe… but more than once they have tipped the battle in the Zarube king's favor."

A wind blew, scattering the leaves. The earthy hues of the forest seemed to grow in color, a burnt red like autumn fire.

"I am a wildheart, signore. Do you know what that means?"

Julian shook his head firmly.

"You are going after Lemuel, I have no doubts. I felt his aura as he crossed the sea. He is the northman king's ally for now, signore, but he only serves his own ends. The high lords have called him Lemuel the Meddler. He is always concerned with his enigmatic goals, which none—not even the most cynical high lords—can divine. You are after him, aren't you? Do not lie; a wildheart can see the soul."

"A paladin of Hieronus never lies," Julian snapped. He didn't know why the *wildheart* unnerved him but he did. "I *am* after Lemuel. Lemuel the Meddler, you call him. I call him a demon that must be destroyed."

"No, you are seeking something far greater than Lemuel… you are seeking something far more deep-seated."

"A paladin of Hieronus never lies." Julian growled the words this time.

"I never said you were lying. Nonetheless, signore… you will not succeed in your goal as you are. You need some help, and some advice."

Thankfully, Julian's building anger kept his lips shut tight.

"Lemuel is ready for an assassination at any time… and the second he suspects anything, he will vanish and reappear a hundred miles away, with his captives in tow."

"Captives?"

The wildheart's red-painted face lit up with delight. "Ah, you do not know… how strange that a 'barbarian' will tell you the news. Lemuel the Meddler has your emperor and his wife with them… and King Gylles vis Bretagne will no doubts have both their heads."

Julian drew in a cold, shocked gasp. For a moment he couldn't think, let alone speak. But soon, beyond his stunned reaction, the seeds of anger bloomed into hatred. "I… I will crush him."

"You will not," the wildheart said, and Julian nearly throttled him. "Not without my aid. But with my aid, *signore*, you may just achieve your goals."

Julian's eyes narrowed. He knew this wildheart may well be a magic weaver himself and deserve death, but neither could he spare the opportunity for vengeance. *The audacity, of kidnapping the emperor and his wife.*

"The wildheart is the agent of change," the man continued. "The wildheart is a weaver of wills, a shaper of fortune. He is blessed by Harron the Green Man…"

"Help is what I want. Not riddles."

"Then you must come with me, to the Sacred Well."

~

A cluster of tents surrounded a natural well. Stones lined the edges. Though nowhere near a river, its waters shifted and bubbled with no apparent cause.

The wildheart entered a tent and emerged with a leathern watercask in hand. "Only a man such as you, not touched by the gods with the Hand of Magic, can rightfully accomplish this task. Only you…"

"Quiet!" Julian snapped, having at last lost his patience. "Do what you will, and do it quickly."

From beyond the tents and the brush beyond, great hulking warriors stirred, but these barbarians Julian did not fear in the slightest. They were wild men, nomads, with none of the weaponry and armor that Imperials possessed. *I am surprised they even have iron weapons,* Julian thought. Yet his true weapon was the unseen Hammer of God, which imbued all of his strikes with divine power, and guided all his actions toward the supremacy of Hieronus.

The wildheart scooped some of the glistening, swirling water into the leathern pouch. He breathed into it, and the air around Julian wavered and chilled. The chill he recognized—the side-effect of magic which he had learned to detest—and it brought him back to his seventh year of life, when the frenzied wizard had ruined him, had stolen the life he'd known and loved, and robbed him of his innocence.

Julian felt himself grasp the handle to his warhammer, preparing to crack the skull of this wildheart, this devil. But in the end he stayed his hand, and felt it go back to where it needed to be—his side.

The water, scooped into the leathern pouch, smoked and took on a pale crystal glow.

"Go," the wildheart said. "I cannot spirit you away to where Lemuel sails. But this gift will make your impossible goals possible. Whoever drinks it will become invisible in the eyes of all around him. Not even Lemuel will be able to see."

Julian walked up to the wildheart, snatched the draught with perhaps too much bitterness—bitterness at having to rely on a demon-friend magic weaver—and turned to mount his horse.

"Be careful, *signore*. Not all tribes of us Mekari are so friendly. And as you have heard—the rumors are partially true—some wildhearts *do* feast on the flesh of men."

Julian sneered and took off down the lonely path through the woods on his charger, kicking mud behind him. The path went on many days, he'd guess, perhaps weeks. But worse than the long journey was the fact he would use the aid of a magic weaver—all of whom deserved to die, as he decided long ago.

CHAPTER THIRTY:
A NEW RULER

Maximian

Though the winter night was dark and rainy, lanterns washed the White Chamber with light. Rain pattered against the high arched ceilings. Maximian stood, still in the red halfcloak of the Imperial Guard and bearing *Imperium's Rebuke*. The boy-child—once called Anakh, whom his mother now called Adamantion—remained alive, though many Imperial Councilors spoke of assassinating him. In the end, it was Maximian who did all he could to keep him alive. The boy was innocent—but he was also an asset.

As Servillius, Speaker of the Council, laid the glittering silver Imperial Circlet on the boy's newly-combed hair, he spoke in a voice that resounded across the chamber: "I name the little boy Adamantion emperor, in accordance with the divine will of Imperium, and because of his youth I appoint Maximian as regent."

Maximian had no illusions that Adamantion's mother Astarthe—the southron witch, as the men and women of the court liked to call her—wanted the regency. But she kept her calm, unwilling to show even a hint of that desire. Instead, luscious brown eyes beaming, she said, "Congratulations, Maximian. It could not happen to a more deserving *signore*."

Maximian smiled and bobbed his head. All around him, the Imperial Councilors' eyes hardened with suspicion. None of them liked the idea of a southron-blooded emperor—an Eloesian, perhaps, or even a wild Getan, but their minds were filled with stories of widespread brother-sister marriages, and a nation that in its darkest periods of crisis sacrificed children to their gods. But Maximian had been to Khazidea before—few married their siblings outside the monarchy, and even that custom had been put to an end with the death of the queen's brother; and the sacrifice of children, he'd heard, was a relic of a past so far-distant it was ancient history when the Fharese first seized their land.

"I will do my best to protect my liege, the true sovereign chosen by Imperium," Maximian said. The little boy was a handsome thing—it seemed Khazidean and Imperial blood mixed to a pleasing whole—but his innocence would not save him against the scheming of the Imperial Court. "If anyone tries to harm a hair on his head, I will slay him without a second's thought."

A few Imperial Councilors squirmed uncomfortably. Astarthe laid a hand on her son's shoulder, and her beaming smile grew almost sunlike in its radiance.

Overall, though, the set-up couldn't be any more perfect—Maximian was in control of the Empire, and he had in his care a boy he could shape into a strong man, a man worthy of the name Adamantus, who would finish what Claudio-Valens began: the conquest of the waking world.

~

Three weeks passed, and a sense of tension permeated both the Imperial court and the Empire itself. Word came back from the frontier that the northmen, with all their soldiers, knights, and siege weaponry, had not shown their faces at the Wall as had been expected. Yet Maximian, regent, cautioned himself never to relax, never to ignore the great threat that remained.

~

The rain had cleared and the air had warmed when Diego—the new Marshal of the Guard—approached the White Throne in his red halfcloak.

"Regent," Diego said, and fell to his knees.

"You are my friend, Diego, not my servant."

Even dear friends think ascension to the White Throne transforms you into a god.

Diego righted himself, standing up, but couldn't bring himself to smile. "Signore… a messenger from the northmen has come."

Maximian nodded.

Diego turned in a twirl of red cloth.

Moments later, the messenger revealed himself, walking in with the same strident bravado that so epitomized the barbarians. He wore an oiled woolen cloak, dyed scarlet and lined with sable, and beneath it a fustian blue tunic. A beard, considered unstylish in the Empire, marked him for what he was.

"*Seigneur emperor,*" he began in that spitting accent Maximian had grown to detest. "Word from His Royal Highness, King Gylles of the line Vis Bretagne… his treacherous wife Lanabelle has been returned to meet her former husband's justice. Your king, the one you call Secondo Janus, is also in His Royal Highness's care."

"Secondo Janus is dead…"

"No, *seigneur.* He is kept under arrest in Zarubad, as he well deserves."

Maximian snapped to his feet.

"I am Methusiel, an emissary sent from his Most Royal Highness. I have come to discuss the terms of our new peace."

"Peace?" Everyone had said Janus was dead… but Lemuel had spirited him away along with Empress Lana.

"No doubts you have heard of the vast destruction wrought upon the town of Floridium. No doubts you understand the might of Zarubain and the vast strength of the Most High King. Our knights and our allies among the wizards have defeated you again and again, and I have no doubts you wish to end this war and put the matter aside."

"I think you are mistaken, Methusiel," Maximian said.

"For a sum of ten thousand marks, paid over a period of seven years, we will return your emperor Secondo Janus, and make a solemn oath before the Lady that we will not harass you or make war upon you. When you agree, signore, then we will consider this matter put to rest. The Most High King, Gylles Vis Bretagne, bears no especial enmity toward you, any more than he bears enmity toward his subjects."

"Subjects," Maximian sneered. The word tasted like gravel in his mouth. "In the Empire there are no subjects. There are citizens. We are anything but your king's subjects."

An arrogant, derisive smile fell over Methusiel's face, a smile that said, *"Oh, you poor, foolish serf."*

"Diego!" Maximian snapped.

And the Marshal of the Guard came running in.

"Hold this slithering worm and make sure he doesn't leave. I will call the Imperial Council for a meeting."

~

When Maximian shouted the words he'd been told, barely able to rein in his anger, the faces of the Imperial Council remained somber, reserved, unmoved. "He dares come here, demand peace, after all the destruction he's wrought… He dares—"

"Peace," Servillius, Speaker of the Council, began. "Is that not what we want?"

A few of the councilors muttered assent.

Maximian remembered the hatred that Claudio-Valens of old bore toward the doddering Imperial Council, and now he couldn't help but feel a small portion of that. The councilors wanted peace at the expense of honor. They would rather see their country humiliated, rather than purchase a victory in blood. "Men of the Council, I demand you reconsider." But all he could see were thirty faces, solely concerned with their summer vacations in Paradise Gardens, unwilling to consider the honor of the nation.

"Signor Regent," Servillius said, "I understand how you feel.

Yet you are young, not even thirty.”

“My age doesn’t matter,” Maximian said.

“I suggest you reconsider your position,” Servillius said. “Know, Maximian, that as ruler it is most important to overcome passion and the inclinations of the heart, and to use your mind in a calm detached manner. What would we gain, signore, by having more of our countrymen’s blood spilled, and more needless deaths?”

“‘The moment a nation stops its fighting, the moment it quits waging war, its days are from then on numbered.’ So said Claudio-Valens Adamantus, a warrior and a god, but also a student of the past.”

Servillius’ expression turned bitter. “The Empire has all it needs. The citizens are content, our granaries are overflowing, and all our labor is amply supplied on the backs of our slaves. Why should we spill the blood of young men in their prime of life, for no real purpose?”

“‘All things of worth are purchased in blood.’ So said King Anthans.” He could quote ancient rulers all day, if need be.

Servillius’ expression turned bitterer. “Oh, to be a young fool again. There is no pretext for war… I do not know how you could justify it. Enshrined in our laws is ‘no war without cause.’ If we pay reparations to the northman king and recall Secondo Janus, there truly is no pretext for war. Not even King Anthans invaded the mainland without cause. Through all our wars—even the ceding of Khazidea—there has been cause.”

“I have ample cause for you,” Maximian growled. “The cause is the theft by the northmen of the All-Seeing Orb, which we took from the Theomancer years ago.”

“By our laws, a theft is proper cause,” added Vitellian. “If not, the abduction of the emperor will suffice.”

Vitellian, Secondo Janus’ pawn, might just have his use. “I bring to you a proposition,” Maximian growled. “I demand that you continue this war—else, I will continue it regardless, and when the north burns and its cities lie in ruin, and all the wealth of the barbarians flows into Imperial City like a river of gold… then, I will make sure the citizens know you did everything to stop it, that you tried as hard as you could to tarnish the glory of the Empire."

Servillius bristled at the words.

"Now, the custom would be to ask for a vote," Maximian growled, his glare hardening as he examined Servillius' face, as he saw in the Council what Claudio-Valens Adamantus the God had seen long ago. "But I will not ask for the consent of thirty doddering, senile fools."

The insult tasted harsh in his lips, but he did not go back to apologize.

Instead, he summoned the citizens to Imperial Square, and prepared to declare his intentions, to continue the War in the North.

CHAPTER THIRTY-ONE:
A THOUSAND FACES

Umar the Pious, follower of Mazda

Against his brothers' best counsel he had come to the Land of the Enemy, where every unclean practice was displayed as a badge of pride, where the people brazenly ate the flesh of swine in the daylight, and drank wine—the devil's water—with no sense of shame. Against the orders of his brother the Theomancer he had come this far, to the filthy land of abominations, where the common folk were free to do as they wished—to err grievously against Mazda, and escape the punishment of fire that was due.

Trumpets blared and the common merchants in the square turned their heads. The unclean emperor would make a speech. The men who dealt in swine flesh and devil's water had turned their heads, distracted, and Umar wondered if he should act now and upturn their stalls, these wicked fools who disputed the true god's Holy Law.

Umar's black-gloved hand gripped his scourge; its nine tails, ending in flesh-rending spikes, had not drunk the blood of the unclean in some weeks. He had no doubts Mazda wanted to see these unrepentant, unclean abominations stripped of their flesh; but Umar was not the prophet Mahul, who feared nothing and had no qualms flying into blood-hungry rages against impossible odds. Umar kept his actions in check, remaining silent and inconspicuous, his face obscured by a hood and an iron mask.

Soon the unclean emperor had taken his stand on the podium, behind the High Lectern. "The northern king has sent a messenger, demanding we call off the war and pay an indemnity to the king!" the shout issued from his unclean lips, lips that no doubt drank devil's water and consumed swine flesh against Mazda's Holy Law. "I have responded to them with true words—that the Empire values glory over peace; that the northern king will not receive a single aes from the

Imperial Treasury; and that we will not stop fighting them until they grant an unconditional surrender."

Umar slipped through an alleyway, cursing the arrogant emperor, praying to Mazda that his Law would prevail, and that the destruction of these unclean folk would come soon, that all its cities would burn from fire in the sky.

Megarion, Merchant

Megarion, richest man in all of Ten Cities, who bought a mansion on the sea with the moneys he earned from silk, stepped out of the alleyway and onto a great thoroughfare. The streets of Imperial City swarmed with people, as he should have expected, but there were folk here he didn't want to see—men of Gad with their bright blond hair and blue eyes, their giant physique and their glazed, stupid looks. Though they wore Imperial finery, they couldn't hide their barbarous origins. Megarion, a man of Ten Cities to his innermost sinew, had dealt with the barbarian thugs as little as possible, though they were fond of spices and Korthian wine. They were outsiders of the Empire, and though Megarion's vile mother had run off with one, even married him, Megarion would never view them as anything more than what they were—something less than human, something that deserved to be taxed onerously or better yet, sold collectively into slavery—along with all those who betrayed their family and married a barbarous thug.

"Signore! Signore!" a voice called out. Megarion half-turned his head—a man across the street was shouting, apparently desperate for his attention. An Imperial citizen, obviously, not too pallid, wearing common yet not-too-common clothes and wearing a wide-brimmed felt hat to avoid the sun's glare. Worth talking to. "A man of Ten Cities, I see. I can tell by the splendid silk-work. Say, are you heading there?"

"I am heading to Thénai," Megarion answered. "I have… unfinished business there."

"Do you have a carriage? I can offer you two *libra* for the journey."

"Very well."

When the man removed his hat, he revealed a head of bright golden hair.

"Actually, no," Megarion hissed. "I do not pay barbarians."

And he hurried on down the road, ignoring the barbarian's shouted curses.

The path wound about but eventually the great piercing avenue that led directly into the outskirts of the city overtook the confused network of roads like a beam of light in shadow. The afternoon was growing late, and a swarm of people had overtaken the road. Megarion himself could not quite remember just how he had gotten here. He had a way of getting to Thénai, surely. He had his own carriage, as every serious Ten Cities merchant did.

Kelsus the Mage

Kelsus emerged from the swarming crowd like a god born from the primordial dragon's womb. He forced his way ahead, using his black staff like a cattle prod. His dark robes and darker staff made the common folk think he was some sort of magic weaver—a truthful statement of course—and the garb would make his colleagues in the Theurge Collegium suspicious. Not suspicious enough to question him about the truth—that he was what they called a black theurge, a trafficker in dark powers, an evoker of fell creatures, and a devoted servant of the "demon" prince Barguril'a. Cleon, Maestro of the Theurge Collegium, likely wouldn't care. These days, few theurges— magic weavers who communed with otherworldly powers—only dealt with the Heavens, and those who did were mocked as pious do-gooders.

Within the hour, Kelsus the Mage had found his way on a carriage for the long journey to Thénai, using money he didn't know he had, heading to where he had unfinished business—unfinished business, which, on second thought, he couldn't recall.

Theon Arkadios

Theon was splashing his face with water in his cramped quarters on the carriage. The insides of the carriage car were luxurious enough—an ample bed, a bottle of wine, and a nice basket of bread—but a shaking had consumed him. His thoughts swelled with terror at what he had become. And what had he become? A thousand people, a thousand faces, each more terrible than the last. And he had done it all unwillingly. He didn't want to return to Thénai. He had forsaken the Way, and he wanted to remain with Astarthe as long as possible, not face the very thing he dreaded the most—Father.

"What have I become?" Theon wheezed. He grabbed a mirror, provided by the coach-driver, and stuck his tongue out. He was Theon, now, fully Theon. But how long before he became someone else? How long before he changed into someone more fearsome than Kelsus the Mage, more terrible than Umar the Pious, more greedy than Megarion the merchant?

He grabbed the bread and devoured it. He drank in the water, which he spat out instantly—dirty and sickening. *This is for washing,* he realized as he laid eyes on a bottle of Korthian wine, nestled in the bread basket.

The car lurched as the carriage hit a bump in the road. He grabbed the wine and popped off the cork. *I am riding to my death,* he thought, *but at least I am riding in luxury.*

But luxury was against all the best principles of the Way. Luxury was the enemy of the Way's asceticism—the Way's transformation of the material world. He recalled the words of the sage Choh: *"You have come so far, my dear student, but now we must make a midnight journey… we must leave the Forgotten Isle, and there you will become one with the*

Way. You will learn the highest wisdom of the Way. You will become a man of a thousand faces, and with this power you will fell the mightiest of kings... even the Celestial Emperor, if it were possible."

The words, recalled as more of the opium dream peeled back like a veil, sickened him, and he vomited in the midst of the carriage-car.

What is happening to me? He knew beyond all doubt he was heading to his end, yet he didn't know exactly what the sage Choh had done to him. He didn't know what Choh had planted within him. A thousand faces granted Theon—and Choh—infinite power, and he pitied his father for what was to come.

CHAPTER THIRTY-TWO: THE FINAL STRAW

Astarthe, Empress Mother, Queen of Haroon

A calculating woman, a supremely wise and supremely wicked empress mother, would try to assert herself even now, find a way to eliminate the regent from the picture. Astarthe didn't know how she could or if she should. Now, though Adamantion sat proudly on the White Throne, it was not he or Astarthe that ruled the Empire in the regent's stead, but the thirty Imperial Councilors, elderly and prone to arguing, taking three hours to make a decision that Astarthe could have made in a second's thought.

She held her son's hand, squeezed it as he sat, an ant before the colossal throne, and recalled the blessing of the priest. In secret he said—following the sacrifice of a ewe lamb—that the Spirit of Empire would bless her son with the White Throne, that one day he would rule in earnest. And another thing he said, which she didn't like and would never say before her beloved son—that it was not Claudio-Valens' Adamantine blood that made him great, but instead Claudio's divine favor and his great merit. *And the passing of the Imperial throne by adoption is what made our Empire great while southron monarchies have fallen… a kingdom is only as good as its king.* But Astarthe knew the priest of Imperium was a fool, that when her son Adamantion ruled in earnest, it would not be some northern notion of mettle or courage, but instead his Adamantine blood—the blood of the living god—that ensured he would rule well. The favor of Heaven was upon him, as it was with his father Claudian Adamantus, and his long-dead granddad Claudio-Valens.

When she closed her eyes she thought of Theon. She would return to the Fertile Land without a consort without him—or so it would seem—and the common farm-folk would view it as inauspicious, and expect the River Khazan to flood disastrously. *But I will not return any time soon, if I have anything to do with it.* And besides, the fear and unease of her subjects was a small price to pay in the wake of what she saw in Theon's eyes. At the thought she shuddered. She could use her power of *gleaming* to shape a person's emotions—even, in times of extreme duress, to overpower a person's spiritual defenses and assume control of his body—but after honing it throughout her childhood, she could sense things about people: deep, unbidden secrets, little glimmers of who they were beneath the mask. The moment before Theon left, she saw something she had never encountered before—something deeply dark inside of him that she never would have imagined. Theon was rash, perhaps even hot-tempered, but there was something else inside him—another person, another entity besides himself, clawing its way out. Something far beyond her ability to cure.

On the White Throne her son was muttering to himself, playing with toy soldiers. She wanted to stay his hands. *I need to protect him.* She needed to face the fact that she feared for his life, that some in the Imperial court would do anything to have Anakh removed from the line of succession, and wouldn't think twice of killing them both. *The Anakhil are no comfort, either—they only serve as a running joke to the Imperial Council.*

Footsteps echoed through the White Chamber. Someone appeared at the door. Astarthe gasped and drew back—an ill-advised show of weakness. She gathered herself. "Greetings," she said to the messenger, but he did not so much as turn his head to look at her.

The Imperial Council is running the Empire, and we are less than a puppet—observers, powerless as shadows, and hated as much as a foreign enemy. It was far less than what he wanted for her son—far less than what she thought he deserved. *A son of the living god, with Adamantine blood in his veins. Yet they only look upon him as the child of a 'southron witch.'* They would learn to respect them in time.

That night, when she retired to her bedchambers, she locked the door and made sure that Adamantion was locked tight in her arms. She drew the covers up. She knew Adamantion hated being smothered, but it was all for his protection. The palace was a nest of vipers.

That night her dreams were dark and haunting. She remembered her youth, so long ago now—it seemed—with her brother, the last true-blooded King Anakh, and their caretaker Issachar—the priest of Atman who would seem so very bizarre in the Empire… a eunuch who dressed in the garb of a woman as his god demanded, but a member of an order so inextricably linked to the flooding and fertility of the Khazan. She dreamed of the year she spent in Qarn-El, and the hot, nigh unbearable summer when the sun baked the forest, and the wild folk of that village feared that the woods would catch on fire. *A stray spark of the campfire, and our town will be up in flames—* so had said Rasheed, an elderly man she had taken to. Yet the worst thing that happened to her in Qarn-El wasn't the heat or the threat of fire, nor even the oppressive laws she had to follow, but one night when she awoke with a snake wrapped around her body, dark green with a bright red stripe, and clearly venomous, and the hushed whispers of the village folk saying, "She must be a murderess or an adulteress—for Justice has not allowed her to live." Paralyzed she had sat there, not daring to move yet desperate to get away. The snake wrapped tighter and tighter—its yellow eyes so cold, so murderous, so ready at any moment to snap at her and dig its white poisonous fangs into her neck.

She awoke covered in sweat, and found herself living the childhood nightmare. A black snake had coiled around her legs and chest, and its head was moving toward her neck. Its forked tongue flapped at her. She wanted to scream but instead she lay still. *I am going to die.* She could not control the mind of a snake like she could control the mind of a man or woman; she was a lamb for the slaughter, waiting for the wicked creature to snap at her, puncture her throat with its poison fangs.

The damned Councilors will do anything to see me dead. At least the snake will not kill Adamantion. Her blessed child slept soundly just inches away. She watched, mortified, as the snake's head grew closer and closer. She knew she should do something but she didn't know what. If she made a single move the snake would surely snap at her. Instead she lay still, not daring to move, lying perfectly immobile and praying silently to the Twin Gods—to Issa the Fertile, Lady of the Moon, and to Atman the Progenitor, Lord of the Sun, sister brother, man and wife. She asked that if she died by the venom of the snake, that she would spare her son's life, that she would keep him alive if not her. *Let my death be a pleasing sacrifice to you, Mother Issa, and in exchange let my son live on to an old and happy age like his father.*

The snake wound tight around her, so tight she could scarcely breathe. Every muscle of hers was stiff as a board; she dare not breathe lest she provoke the serpent.

Then, the worst sound she could possibly here: "Mama!"

Adamantion rose out of bed, eyes panic-stricken. The snake hissed, then struck, laying its fangs into his innocent neck. Astarthe screamed and yanked the wicked creature's head from her precious son's skin, the son she loved more than herself, the son she adored more than anyone in Heaven or on earth. With its head in her left hand she crushed its neck, and the doors to her bedchamber in the House of Lenora burst open to reveal the Anakhil. A dozen strong bodies entered, but they were too late.

"A second attempt… a second attempt at my son's life… and now, I think they have succeeded." She fell into weeping, clutching him tight, but one of the Anakhil came rushing in from outside with a thin cord; quickly he cinched it around Adamantion's skinny arm until he screamed in pain.

Then he met her eyes with his own. "My queen," he said in Khazidean, cinching it tighter and tighter. "This is a yellowback viper. Very poisonous, not native here."

She cried out again. She wept at the thought of her son being harmed. She wept at the thought of living without him.

"It is not incurable if we act fast… we must get him water."

"Water?" Astarthe shouted. Instead she clutched him tighter and began to weep.

"Melkhor!" the Anakhil shouted. "Go get some powdered dragon-lily from the apothecary."

Adamantion twitched and fell limp.

~

Throughout the remainder of the night and the fullness of the day, Astarthe remained with Adamantion. He had gone unconscious, having broken out in a cold sweat. Yet his little heart continued to beat; his breathing, though short and raspy, kept on unabated. Many times she broke out in weeping as the Anakhil fed him the water, mixed with all manner of cures.

Yet in the twilit hours of the following day, Adamantion sat up from the bed and drew in a breath.

"We have overcome the poison, my queen," the Anakhil said.

"And yet," Astarthe began, "I have realized something… something I wish I was wrong about. I cannot lose my sweet son; I value him more than my own life."

~

The next morning, Astarthe led Adamantion into the midst of the Council House. The thirty men, all old with cold, uncaring eyes, stared at her dully. She wondered which of them had ordered the assassination, or if they all had, collectively.

"Councilors," Astarthe snapped. "As I'm sure you know, a

snake was let into my bedchamber to kill both me and my beloved son. I know you will never answer for your crimes; it isn't in your nature."

"A harsh accusation to level, Your Grace," one of the councilors snapped.

She grabbed the Imperial Circlet from her son's sweet head. "I am certain his father—now deified—is glaring upon you now. I don't know why having him as an emperor fills you with such loathing. Do you hate the Khazidees, with a hatred that overcomes his Adamantine blood?"

"The Empire has been ruled by barbarians before," a different councilor sneered. "The emperor Amaraeus, the emperor Carnassus, the emperor Jordanus…"

"Why is my son an object of hatred to you… such hatred that you would kill him?"

"Careful with your accusations, southron witch," the councilor from before sneered.

At his words she felt herself grow rigid. A calm coolness overtook her. "That is what I am to you. Very well. Ah, councilors, know I still love the Empire… though I detest you, I love the Empire, and the son it bore me, the Adamantine god. I am leaving Imperial City. The sea still swells with storms, but I can catch a ship from elsewhere. I will be long-gone by the time the night falls. If you ever regain your senses, councilors, and want Adamantion, son of the living god, to rule your Empire, you know where I will be… in the City of Issa."

How I miss the Red City. The safe comfort of the palace awaited her. She would leave the viper's nest of Imperial City, go, perhaps, to the city of Bregantium or somewhere nearer; then, when the winter storms calmed, she would sail.

CHAPTER THIRTY-THREE: THROUGH THE MOUNTAINS

Julian Ultor, Malleus

The journey through the hills, in the midst of the giant trees, was lonely, and Julian Ultor, Malleus, would have been terrified if he had not conquered fear long ago. The mountain folk were legendary for their terrible customs, which Julian could neither confirm nor deny—that they collected the heads of their enemies for some spiritual purpose, even that they ate the flesh of men.

In all he had been riding for two weeks. He had nearly grown a full beard; he hadn't bathed since the journey began, and he relied on the kindness of these tribal folk to eat. Thus far they hadn't offered him any strange meat, only scarcely-cooked deer and boiled vegetables. When the road drew near the sea, they'd offer him cooked mussel or crab legs, or fish stew.

But the further north he grew, the more he heard from the tribal folk that the northmen—the ones with whom the Empire had gone to war—had embarked on a mission not only to conquer the wild men's land, but to sell them all into slavery. *Slavery,* he had heard a wildheart say, *is worse than death.*

When snow fell it rarely stayed; the forces of winter were held back somehow by the sea, and even now in the dead of winter rain and ice were by far more common than blizzards.

But at last, at dusk, at the apex of one of the low mountain peaks, he caught sight of what he was looking for along: below, the rush of a swiftly flowing river echoed through his ears—one too vast to cross by swimming. Beyond lay farmers' fields—green rows of beans, and in the distance, likely cities of the north.

He recalled what a wildheart had told him many days ago. As they sat around the campfire, he told of how he'd been captured by the northmen after a battle and taken to their capital to face trial. He had escaped by magic—a detail Julian didn't want to consider—but he had said the capital lay along the sea, where a river bled into the ocean. *Yet is that where Lemuel is?* How on earth would he know?

At last, the folly of what he had done came crashing down on him. He didn't know how to find him. *But I will find him,* he promised himself. *I will find him.*

And he rode toward the river to where his goal—the goal he had sworn in a solemn oath before his god—awaited him. He would find Lemuel and bring him to justice. He had sworn before the Just God himself.

All the warnings and fearful exclamations of the wild-men vanished from his ears, replaced with a determined focus, to crack the skull of Lemuel with the hammer of god. He rode toward the river as it rushed across the countryside, without a hint of fear.

CHAPTER THIRTY-FOUR: SURPRISE ATTACK

The winter faded across the Empire. In the capital, the rain and moisture gave way to dry desert heat. In the fertile land of Khazidea, the air grew hotter. And in the north, where Maximian waited with his troops, the snows of winter melted away, baring the ground for the five legions that waited at the still-shut Gate of Tidus.

Maximian, Regent

As the Gate of Tidus rolled open, Maximian rode at the vanguard with the Tenth Anthanian Legion following right behind. With each legion, ten scorpions, two ballistae and a catapult had been generously furnished. To truly conquer the north, they would need the best weapons to break down their city walls. And in truth no one had as good siege works as the Empire, formulated by the wisdom of the Eloesian academes and the Imperial engineers. The only true advantage they would have against the full unbridled might of the Empire was their wizards—and by his side, Maximian had an answer for them. Silvana the Windborne rode next to him in her leather jerkin and winged augur's cap. He grabbed her hand, perhaps too harshly, and peered into her imperious blue eyes.

The winter they had spent together had not produced what Maximian wanted—Silvana the Windborne was a hard woman to catch within his net. She had spurned all his advances, yet now she didn't resist as his hand held tight to hers. Her superior, the maestro Fausto, had recovered from his blindness, as had the others stricken by Lemuel's wizardry, but Silvana and a large contingent of augurs now walked with him. And Maximian had everything he needed for war—the hand of a beautiful woman in his right, and the hilt of *Imperium's Rebuke* in his left.

Maximian made sure he rode out first, sallying forth on his white charger. He drew *Imperium's Rebuke*, its bluish metal refusing to glint in the bright daylight. In his right hand he waved it before the sun, proclaiming the Empire's strength as he rode down the Path of Tidus at an easy clip. The north would have no idea what was coming to them; they lay in idle peace, thinking the so-called Southern World would stand idly by while its sovereign, the Emperor Janus, lay in a foreign grave, his body not given the proper disposal that the Imperial ruler so well deserved.

The stamping feet of the Tenth Anthanian gave way to the grinding wheels of the scorpions and catapults. Soon all six thousand soldiers had passed by, making way for the Third Harak Legion and its legate Barachus, a dazzling array of southron barbarians and Imperials walking side-by-side in the same military gear, the same scale-mail armor and helmets with red horsehair crests. Then came the two Getan legions—the Second Bregantine with their legate Nestorian and the Twenty-First Bregantine with their greenhorn legate Marcus Junias. The fifth legion, the last of them, the Seventh Sanctonian, began its march through the gate. It had its origins in the province of Paladium, to some a backwater cesspit and to other the center of piety and faith, the origins of the holy warriors of the Magisterium. Yet neither its legate Pilatus, a full-blooded Anthanian with only tenuous connections to his legion's provincial origins, nor any of its legionaries, had any real connections to the Magisterium or its sanctimonious Pontifex.

There was likely no paladin or Magisterial agent in the whole north, Maximian knew. *Likely, there is not a single man of god.* But who was Maximian to talk?

~

The sun rose pale and cold over the low hills of Mekara, yet quickly as a fog grew it warmed. They were three days outside the Gate of Tidus and the Empire itself, and the Path of Tidus had grown rather less cared-for. They had brought much food, but thirty-thousand men were hard to feed, and scouts went out daily, scouring the green hills for farmers to harass or coax into feeding them. Yet the folk who lived here were wild hunters, nomads, men who rode horses and herded wild beasts. They dared not strike the Empire's much more powerful force; yet they did not show their faces… until the third morning.

A giant of a man came riding in on an equally large horse. His bare muscular chest was smeared with blue paint, and on his head he wore a headdress of stag antlers. Behind him, a great host of wild riders looked on at Maximian. Maximian knew he had little to fear from such poorly armed savages, yet something about the man's towering physique and his immense antler headdress unnerved him.

"*Southlander.*" His accent was rolling, thick and syrupy, less harsh than his cousins across the River Gad. "Do you… make… war against the north, the Zarobo?"

"Zarobo." Maximian sounded out the word in attempt to understand it. The northman king, Bretonnius, and his companions had called themselves the Zarubes. The answer to the man's query, of course, was 'yes.' But did he truly want to alert these people and let them know of his plans? Surely not.

"We would like to join you, southlander," the chieftain went on. "I am Getorix, and these are my warriors the Veroni. There are five hundred of us. We know the way to the north, my good southlander king. We know how to surprise them."

Maximian peered deep into the man's hard gray eyes. Silvana's piercing blue eyes then met his. A gust of propitious wind blew around her.

"Your Undying Glory," Silvana said, "I do think this is a risk worthy of taking. He knows the lay of the land."

Silvana the Windborne had wisdom much greater than Maximian, who he was glad to admit had blundered into the position of regent. Maximian met the chieftain Getorix's gray eyes once again. "Very well," he said. "We could always use an auxiliary."

A smile grew on Getorix's face, wide and beaming. "You will

not regret your decision, my lord king."

Not king, Maximian thought of saying but stayed his tongue. *The citizens of the Empire may hate kings, but the barbarians love them.* He should let them think that. "Getorix, stay nearby. You say you know the lay of the land."

"Indeed," Getorix said. "This road will take you to the capital town of the Zarobo, southlander. But I don't think you should go about this route. The merchants are just starting to make their way down the road—the ones that don't fear us at least—and you should go about a better way, to surprise."

"Getorix—I am sorry, but how do I know you aren't leading us in to an ambush?"

Getorix narrowed his eyes. Silvana snapped toward him, her face puckered in a sour grimace. "Do it, Your Undying Glory. The risks are minimal, the rewards great. We should not spurn his help."

"Very well, Getorix," Maximian told him. "Show us the best way into the north, so that we can wreak the most distraction."

"Onward, then, to the Bridge of Arafell. They won't know what is coming." Getorix's insulted expression faded into a bright beaming smile again. "At last, all these years of injustice will be answered."

Maximian started to ask what injustices he meant, but Getorix had already rode forth off-road, and Maximian followed. The stamping feet of the five legions left the safety of the Path of Tidus, leaving it like a path of light into unknowable darkness.

Yet with the presence of Silvana, Maximian felt always enveloped in warmth and light.

A day passed, and Getorix provided all the food they needed from his allies throughout the region. For all the barrenness of the low brown hills, the barbarians seemed quite eager to share their stores of food—dried fruits and berries, salted meats and bread bartered at a high price for coal and tin. Those that provided food unfailingly joined ranks with the legion. By the end of the third day, Maximian's army had swelled from a force of thirty-thousand trained legionaries to a sea of some sixty thousand, the original equaled in number by the late-comers.

Swelled, Maximian thought, *and yet these barbarians likely fight a tenth as well as a true Imperial.* They paid great attention to their weapons—each individual crafted and emblazoned with personal insignias—but their forging from what Maximian saw was cheap; and some fought like nomads that had never strayed from the hill country of Mekara, wielding clubs affixed with stones or rods of bone. Much more disconcerting still were the ones they called "the wildhearts"— men bare-chested and wild, smeared with blood-red or gut-brown paint, whom the Mekari barbarians feared and spoke of their ability to vanish at a moment's notice, and the grand rituals of their private religion, the blood-stained altars of the Wild Lord, prince of entropy.

As the days went by, the air grew warm. The relative chill of the first dissipated, giving way to hotter and hotter days. By the time the fifth day ended in a throe of twilight, the air had grown hot and humid, almost oppressive.

"We draw near the River Zaros," the chieftain Getorix murmured by the fire. "To the Bridge of Arafell… It will be good to see vengeance."

In all this time, I haven't asked at all about why they had come. For politeness' sake he would. "What have the northmen… err, Zarobo… done to you, Signor Getorix?"

"What have they done?" The man's hard eyes softened.

Silvana's blue eyes met Maximian's, and he couldn't tell if she was urging restraint, or merely gazing at him with her normal severe expression.

"Ah, what have they done?" Getorix muttered. "A hundred winters ago, it began. Not long after their war with the Alfar—"

"The Alfar?"

"—the Zarobo got their first taste of slavery. There is no

sweeter labor than unpaid labor, it seems. They thought—if the Alfar, so small and slight—paid dividends in the fields, then surely the Wild Mekari so tall and large and strong would serve the nation even better. But they misjudged us. The heart of the Mekari does not accept slavery; it would rather choose death. And there is something else, too, which the wizards want—beneath our feet, and in the mountains of the west, it is thick with mooncrystal. The land has good bones, my lord king, and the Zarobo will do anything they can to steal it—steal the earth beneath our feet, steal our lives and our labor, steal the souls of our people…"

Maximian had already lost interest. Their plight was grave, indeed, but his duty was first to the Empire—to wreak vengeance upon the treacherous King Bretonnius, to bring the Northern World to its knees, and to repay his friend Secondo's death with total annihilation. "My good Signor Getorix, we will put an end to it, certainly. I am sure, in time, the Council will name you official Friends of the Imperial People." And it was true; the Imperial Council named all manner of people friends, offering protection to those it lacked the motivation to dominate by force. The protection had costs, as everything did—submission to the Empire, influence impossible to be rid of, that perhaps benefited the Friends of the Imperial People in some way but most of all benefited the Empire itself.

"I would be glad to have you as my friend," Getorix answered. "The Mekari have foes everywhere—to the north the Zarobo and the Alfar, and to our east the wild Guthar."

So many names, so many words that he had never heard before. Yet Getorix's naivete was telling; he spoke the word "friend" as if it meant something more than subject. "And we would be glad to have you named 'friends' as well," Maximian answered. Yet as official friends of the Empire, armed and supplied with resources to fight the nation's wars, things would have to change about the wild Mekari. Their strength now seemed only in their mobility, in their ability to run and hide. *And yet, I am fighting a war alongside them.*

As the spring night fell, Maximian once again took in the sight of Silvana's ravishing blue eyes. Not long ago it seemed she had warmed to him; now she had retreated back into her icy shell. He had heard a little of the augurs' beliefs, that love—and related to that, a family—was a severe distraction. Yet Maximian had seen augurs, both male and female, take lovers and even spouses. So why would Silvana the Windborne not warm to him, the regent of the Empire, emperor in all but name? *What,* Maximian thought, *is so wrong with me?* She was a woman of cunning and wisdom, born with a special gift—the power of Wind and Speed—yet by birth Silvana was no August or even Knight. He knew far less than he wanted about Silvana, who on this long and tiresome march had become his supreme goal. He thought she was from the north of Anthania—the crackling-hot Central Valley starved for water, with scarcely enough rainfall for the small bit of wheat they grew. He wanted to know more, about where she came from, about who her parents were and everything about her childhood—but Maximian, regent, Ruler of the Six Nations in all but name, hadn't the courage to ask.

That night, sleeping in the open air, his dreams drifted to Silvana, of she and Maximian in a lover's embrace. In the morning he awoke shaken with the memory, completely unnerved, the sweetness of it turning to poison as he realized it was not real.

Getorix took the lead once more. The sun had not quite reached its apex in the sky when, beyond the greenness of the hills, a great blue river appeared, flowing swiftly westward. Beyond lay farmers' fields—green rows of beans mixed with the black earth, fields of unripe wheat—and right there, a great stone bridge. Yet someone was coming—several, actually, twelve, at the least—and the air seemed to grow colder. Silvana gasped.

Twelve men—all old, wearing beards of gray or white, each falling nearly to their knees—approached them with a stormy gait. Each clutched a staff in his hand, topped with orbs of white crystal. Their gazes were overpoweringly stern. Their robes, falling to their feet and cinched with rope belts of gold or silver, formed a rainbow of color—forest green, blood red, flame orange, and sterling silver.

But one above all—wearing a robe of bright blue, cinched with a white rope belt, and carrying a staff of knobbed white wood—stood out among them. His dark green eyes stood out starkly from his snow-white hair.

"Who are you?" Maximian gasped, failing to mask his wonder.

"Do not presume to speak to me, commoner. You are an enemy of the Zarube nation—but you are, more pitiably for you, an enemy of the Council of the Twelve and its All-Seeing Eye." The old man's expression hardened into a sneer. "I am Odo, archwizard. I know what your designs are—you have declared war, and the cause, you claim, is to retrieve the artifact our agent Lemuel uncovered. To steal the very thing that empowered us, the All-Seeing Eye. I thank the Heavens the orb is outside your common hands, and now people truly practiced in magic may deal with it."

"Do not interfere, Odo," Maximian said, the best thing he could manage. "You may keep your orb… I said that to give a cause for the war, to convince the Imperial Council. Though I do not know how in Varda you knew this…"

"Why, with the very item you proposed to steal." A dark smile fell over Odo's face. "Ah, so sweet, so simple and naïve. The Northern World has an extremely delicate balance of power, my good man, a network of alliances held in check to keep things working properly. If I let you in, my good man, then I would be upsetting this balance."

"It isn't up to you," Maximian growled. He drew his adamant sword.

Yet Odo's dark smile only grew. "I have heard of this metal before. Yet even star steel, forged into the best of swords is useless in the face of magic. Turn back, my good man, or you will quickly come to regret it."

Maximian could feel the chill, far from abating, growing within him—not the chill of growing magic power any more, but the impending sense that his life hung in the balance. For once he wondered if he shouldn't have ridden in the vanguard. "My Signor Odo, I wish you would listen to reason. I gather the Council of the Twelve doesn't act on behest of the northman king… that you are wholly separate political units. Surely we can find a way to help each other. Certainly there is something we can do." He met the gaze of Silvana, and her normally austere gaze was replaced with an unusual nervousness, a dread that he had never seen before, nor wanted to see again.

Yet Odo's smile had widened, growing more exuberant than ever. "You do not listen well, my good man. Believe me, if the northman king had something we wanted, we could quite easily take it. Yet the stability of the Northern World is a precious thing, and we—as a matter of principle—do not wish to upset it. The only way you will escape with your life, my good man, is to call off the invasion. To retreat. The consequences extend far beyond losing your life, which is a small thing in the grander picture. A stifling indemnity, an onerous payment of reparations that will bleed your nation dry and turn you to paupers…"

"Enough, snake."

Odo laughed. Silvana screamed. Overhead, a maelstrom of fire blazed into existence, overtaking the sky and bathing everything in red light. Balls of fire rained down, consuming men left and right, turning them to blackened skeletons, and Odo had become a cackling demon.

But why am I alive? Still stunned, Maximian hadn't realized in his conscious mind that Silvana had drawn up a shield of wind and pushed their horses to faster than a gallop with a powerful gale, and he was riding across the fiery battlefield of blackened bodies and scorched grass, screaming *"Retreat! Retreat! Retreat!"*

Yet the maelstrom of death only worsened. As the fire rained down on them, spears of lightning struck dead those legionaries and centurions that had avoided the flame and unendurable heat. The burning and burnt-up bodies lay like a sea across the now-grassless ground, and all he could see north, west, east, and south, was a hellish landscape of fires and burned-up bodies; far beyond where the wizards' magic weaving had not yet touched them, the horns blew a note of retreat. Not for the first time Maximian thanked the gods that Silvana was with him; without her he surely would have died.

Yet worst of all, as the devilish cackling of Odo faded from his view, was the sight of a pair of antlers, its original headdress burnt to ash, and the thought of the Mekari barbarians—the so-called Friends of the Imperial People—who had lost their lives all thanks to Maximian's folly.

He asked the gods, and most importantly, Imperium, to forgive his misdeeds.

CHAPTER THIRTY-FIVE: HOMEWARD FLIGHT

Caro, Legionary

Down the northward road Caro ran, heedless of anything but escape, of returning to the country he knew, the place he had always called home. The men of Fharas wandered the road, with nary a veiled woman in sight—warriors guarding merchant caravans, clad in loose white shirts and pants, wielding wickedly sharp scimitars; a magus in a white turban and a purple robe, clutching a heavy burden of codices and tomes; a pair of gaunt, pallid men in roughspun wool, perhaps penitents asking the gods' forgiveness. To Caro it would have been so refreshing to see women traveling the road unaccompanied, even in the foreign garb of veils, a sweet reminder of home.

But it was not to be.

The thundering of hooves echoed from behind, a storm of noise. Caro whipped around, drew his standard-issue Imperial sword, and met the sight of a dozen oncoming cataphracts without flinching. Their muscular horses protected with mixed mail and iron plate, and the iron-armored men of steel that rode them, would perhaps unnerve the most hardened of truths, but a film had fallen over Caro's eyes and over all his person; the deaths of all his century, the murder of his two best friends, and the certain threat of execution, had made his own death inevitable. So why would I fear twelve iron giants, riding in to cut me down?

"Sorcerer," one of the cataphracts boomed, as his fellow soldiers circled around him, hemming him in with their spears.

"I am not a sorcerer," Caro answered.

"Ah, but the King of Kings says you are; and thus, you are," the cataphract growled.

"The King of Kings may think that," Caro began, "but that does not mean he is right."

One of the cataphracts cursed him, jabbed a spear closer.

"What happened in the city of Seshán I can't explain. But I know I am not a sorcerer, my good signores. I am as common, as ungifted as they come."

"You are too modest," the cataphract said darkly, so darkly Caro sensed a note of sarcasm in his voice. "His godly majesty, Pharzanes, King of Kings, Ruler of the Nation above all Nations, Champion of the Gods and of Mazda…"

"Champion of the gods, you say," Caro muttered. "I thought he was god himself."

"No," the cataphract sneered. "Your view of history is narrow. Pharzanes does not practice such blasphemy, as your people do…"

Not everyone took the emperor's divinity seriously. Though, among these highly religious southrons, perhaps certain things, certain beliefs, were too charged to be argued, too sensitive and zealously held.

"He is their champion… the champion of the gods, and of Mazda."

Caro had heard the name Mazda before, an already-dim recollection of a recent war—when the emperor Claudian Adamantus and the Fharese padisha joined hands to battle the devotees of Mazda. How quickly, how inexplicably, had things changed? *Ah, yes.* Memories of their hatred of certain meats, the loathing they had for wine and beer and music, everything that brought mankind joy. "So he has forgotten what went on before… he wants me back to face the crime of intruding on his territory—"

"Quiet," the cataphract snapped, and Caro obeyed. "The padisha emperor cares little for you, a minor soldier in a grand war. We are sent by another. All of us are obeyers of the law."

"That is good," Caro said. "It is wise to obey the government's laws…"

"Quiet," the cataphract snarled again. "Not the law of the padisha emperor, but the True Law, handed down by the destroyer of the unclean himself, Mazda."

"Mazda?" A curious lump grew in Caro's throat. He knew nothing of Mazda, only vague passing words spoken by his fellow-soldiers. He didn't know why the name unsettled him.

"You must come with us, lawbreaker. You stink of wine and beer and every unclean thing."

Lawbreaker. But the only crime it seemed Caro had committed was intrusion, and he knew these supposed law-abiders had an entirely different idea in mind.

~

On the next road the cataphracts led him on a sharp rightward turn. The few fields of wheat around him were green and unripe, and beyond, along the brownish hills were sheep pastures ringed with stones. In all, few people lived in this area, and soon, as the day waned, the region grew even sparser—a scorched, dry land strewn with pebbles—and by the time night fell the only habitation in sight was a wooden watchtower burnt to a black shell by Imperial torches.

The heat of the day dissipated quickly, giving way to a chill. Caro shivered but the cataphracts did not give him anything to warm himself; an unclean lawbreaker, they said, had no value in their eyes, and did not deserve the common courtesies of even a pagan Fharese that honored Mazda's law.

Though stiff and sore from the night's cold, the cataphracts pressed him harder than before the next day. The land remained desolate, but by the time the sun fell once again, they turned down a road in sight of a great brick fortress.

Down many winding corridors they took him in the dim light

of torches. But then, in the great room, sitting on a stone chair, was what could only be their end target, the lawgiver official himself.

"Soldier," the black-turbaned man said, and his wily-looking eyes narrowed. His gray beard was long and greasy. Beside him were two Imperials: a man with short-cut hair and a clean-shaven face, and a gray-haired woman carrying a book. Both wore woolen clothes embroidered with the Eloesian laurel-wreath.

Caro wondered why in Varda they were here.

"Soldier!" the lawgiver chief snapped. "You will look at me when I am addressing you."

Even if the cataphracts hadn't stolen his sword, he'd have little chance against these odds. Reluctantly he peered into the lawgiver's crafty eyes. "What is it?"

"Many thousands of your legion were killed when they tried to destroy Seshán. But many survived. Those that have, I and my fellow lawgivers give the chance to swear a pact to Mazda, to make war against the Empire they once served. And many thousands have."

The familiar cold lump grew in Caro's throat.

"These two fellow-citizens from your empire have come all this way to speak with me, to negotiate and see if our... *interests*... align. The Fharese are just as pagan and abominable as you Imperials are; the padisha emperor is a mere puppet in the High Theomancer's hand... He listens so trustingly to the archmagus Sidathra, who himself has sworn allegiance to Mazda unbeknownst to the pagans." A broad smile grew over the lawgiver's wizened face. "Know you are not special, my good legionary, but only one of many thousands who are offered the chance to redeem themselves, to spurn their many gods and turn instead to Mazda, and wreak destruction on the unclean Empire."

"You wish me to betray the gods?" He imagined the Mother, Amara, in heaven, ruling the heart of man in her infinite love. He imagined Imperium, the War Eagle, the Spirit of Empire whose image flew on every flag. Caro fixed his eyes on the two Imperials in the room, who had no reason to be here in the heart of the southlands, in the company of this zealous lawgiver.

At his gaze, they seemed to draw back, growing perhaps uncomfortable.

"Betray the false gods," the lawgiver said in a patronizing tone, like Caro was a child unable to grasp simple concepts. "You may swear an oath to Mazda, and gain your life, or you may spurn your chance and lose it."

"Mazda is no friend of mine," Caro said. "I have honored the gods thirty-three years and they have never done me wrong. May they damn me if I deny them now."

"Fool!" the gray-haired woman snapped.

The sight of a fellow Imperial so close to this lawgiver nearly undid him. *What has become of our country? What has become of our people?* What more mournful end could the Empire, and Varda itself have, than if the lawgivers ascended and gained sway? What more terrible end, without wine and feasting and song? What worse life than one shackled under Mazda and his infernal law, which destroyed the joys of life and replaced it with an eternal mournful sky?

"Fool?" Caro said. "Shame on you. Gods damn you, woman."

"Only a fool would willingly die for something," the man added. "For he could be wrong."

"A fool I am, then," Caro said. "A fool, I have become."

~

When the lawgivers flailed him outside the brick fortress with a scourge, bloodying his naked back yet supremely certain of their own piety, the worst thing was not the salty tears stinging his fresh wounds, nor the shudders of pain that tore at intervals through his body. The worst thing was not the sight of the executioner coming, a giant scimitar in his black-gloved hands. No, the worst thing was the thought of his nation, the Empire, dissolving, unable to adhere, having lost the ability to make war, unwilling to see the enemy as what it was. He died imagining the lawgivers' final victory, of the Theomancer riding amidst the flames of Imperial City, of the world destroyed under the wages of Mazda, burning, and forevermore under a gray and mournful sky.

CHAPTER THIRTY-SIX:
THE GLORY OF THE NORTH

Julian Ultor, Malleus

Julian had foresworn his beloved charger, his steel plated armor, and his helmet. He had even left behind his gilded warhammer in the brush near the Bridge of Arafell. He had entered the north in plainclothes, never forgetting the charge that had brought him here—to slay Lemuel—and only had a knife to protect himself, and the elixir that the wildheart had brewed for him to aid his quest.

Beyond the Bridge of Arafell, Julian entered a realm more green and well-watered than any he had ever seen. Even now, at the cusp of summer, the grass was verdant and rolling, and the ash trees and the pines dripped with water. Though all roads save the Path of Tidus were dirt, the thatch-roofed cottages of the peasants and the roadside inns made Julian feel he was at home, though he was not home. The grand castles in the distance, the wells and innumerable streams, the orchards and farmland that seemed never starved of water, gave Julian the impression of a land of plenty, a land though separated by a great distance, more kin to the Empire than he expected, more warming and welcoming to his soul than he'd guess the Far South would be.

In all, it was a wonder the regent Maximian had continued the war; but by all accounts the war raged on, as furious as it was ill advised. For now, though, Julian made his way across this region called the Western Heartlands, so close to the sea Julian could smell the saltwater breeze. Inn by inn he learned the simplest of words—"Hello!" "How are you?" and "Good!" as the Path of Tidus—which the northerners called the King's Highway—and in all the folk of the north, especially the peasants, were remarkably polite.

Yet even amid the greenery, the endless water and the abundant food, a shadow hung over Julian, the memory of why he had come. As the King's Highway drew inexorably near the capital, he began to ask questions of the common innkeepers, mentioning the name Lemuel, which was invariably met with a snarl.

"Lemuel the Meddler!" one innkeeper said in Zarube. "I wish he would stay out of the country's affairs! He is always in the presence of the king, concocting wars, yet the king is blind to it!"

The next innkeeper down the road, a day from the capital, offered slightly more help. "Ah, my good man, it is anyone's guess where Lemuel is, for he vanishes and reappears a thousand miles away in the blink of an eye, damned wizards! But I think he may be in the king's company even now...."

That evening an army marched by: at the front a group of a hundred knights in full-plated armor, with great feathered plumes billowing from their helmets and heavy lances in their hand; and behind a column of archers and foot soldiers so long it did not end while Julian was still awake.

"The southlanders have declared war," the innkeeper said. "Who knows how it will end? Such warlike folk, those southlanders... though you would know, wouldn't you?"

Is it so obvious? Julian tried to smile, but failed. Even in plainclothes, his accent would mark him as an outsider. When he reached the capital, he would need to keep quiet as much as possible, to blend in, perhaps even drink the wildheart's draught as soon as he arrived.

He relaxed with a glass of wine in his hand; he fell asleep in one of the inn's spacious chambers; and by the time the morning sun arose, the seemingly endless column of footsoldiers had vanished into the cool morning gloom.

Julian continued down the Path of Tidus as it wound steadily northwestward. Villages sprouted up every half-mile; the gentle rush of rivers and the babbling streams drew ever closer to the path. Castles loomed high above the already-immense firs and pines. Then, the cobblestone Path of Tidus arched into a great stone bridge. Under it flowed what the locals called the River Zaros; and Julian Ultor, Malleus, knew he had at last reached Zarubad.

Hugging the edge of the River Zaros, to the left and right of him, was the city sprawl: the grand thatch-roofed houses and shops of the merchants, mixed with the shanty shacks and tents of the urban poor. The stench of habitation overwhelmed him; far greater than Imperial City—Julian wondered if they had a proper sewer system here. Yet the quaint northern beauty was undeniable, especially beyond the bridge. The true city was built among a dozen or more bridges that spanned small islands in a river. The islands themselves had all been fortified with stone walls, and an especially large one boasted what could only be the king's residence: a towering castle with numerous turrets and towers, each bearing the blue-gold lion banner of the north. It was, in fact, so tall, Julian had no doubts the common urban poor always lived in its shadow.

Not far from it, and nearly as tall, was a grand cathedral, its pink and green stained glass windows portraying the nymphs and sprites of the fairy faith. Julian had heard of these buildings, constructed to bring the worshipers closer to the Otherworld, but he also had no doubts the common folk were never allowed to enter.

And that included him. A group of armed men stood watch over the bridge, two dozen of them in heavy plate armor. Two, clearly knights, were mounted on horses and wielding giant lances.

Regardless of it all Julian approached them, hoping that his biases were wrong, that these aloof noblemen allowed commoners into the city proper. He walked in, toward the wall of armed men.

"Stop!" a knight snapped in his spitting Zarube accent. "It is not a high holy day. Do not take a step closer, lowborn scum."

Julian's love for the north evaporated quickly then, and he yearned to be home, to a land where all citizens were equal under the law, where power and wealth was not inherited but earned and deserved. He bit back a retort, and vanished into the alley, the realm of the supposed lowborn scum.

He did not know how long the draught would last, or if Lemuel were here; but he would have to trust himself to fate and try his best. From the reports Lemuel was here, yet the wizard could be half a world away in the blink of an eye.

The potion tasted foul and dirty, but the magic inside sizzled his tongue like lightning. A cold chill, a deep well of power, sprang from within him in an instant—a sensation he had never felt before—and when he walked out into the street, the soldiers standing guard at the bridge showed no sign of seeing him.

He walked past them, invisible to their ignorant eyes. For the first time, perhaps in history, a common *villein* had entered the royal city of Zarubain unasked-for.

Through the city of the nobles Julian walked, invisible, hearing traces of their conversation. Amid the married noblewomen in their wimples, shopping for spices in the open air, the conversation was heavy with talk of war and of tumult in the royal court.

"Ah, poor Lanabelle," one said. "A woman of such good breeding, locked up like a common criminal."

"A woman of good breeding who betrayed herself to that southlander," the other answered.

"Why not execute the southlander already, and have her committed to a nunnery?"

"Ah, my good Tanda, the king does not forgive so easily as you…"

At the words, spoken within one of the walled islets, Julian felt his blood blaze through him hotter than ever. Emperor Secondo Janus was still alive; it was his duty to free him, then, as an Imperial citizen. *But I am a citizen of heaven, a willing slave to Hieronus.* Hard though it was, he knew his oath to Hieronus outweighed his duty to the Empire.

Soon it became clear that the royal castle was accessible only by a boat—no bridge went there or beyond—and Julian without a second's thought leapt into the current, splashing off the bridge. Passersby looked aghast at the strange sight—an invisible object hitting the water, but Julian ignored the ruckus he had caused and found his way to the castle. A guard stood watch at the boat landing, but paid no heed to the invisible Julian, and he slipped in.

The royal castle smelled of cooking meat and spices. The guards in the basement failed to notice the invisible Julian. It crossed his mind, then, that he was in a place no one in this backward land would ever see; a place where the king ruled and starved his subjects of resources, living in luxury yet unwilling to grant them any of it.

But Julian was hardly impressed with this dingy underground area. He followed the passageways, past—to his surprise—rows of iron-grilled prisoner's cells, until he reached the upward leading stairs, terminating—to his anguish—in a giant locked door. He cursed under his breath, wondering how he was going to find keys, when a voice called out, "Ah, you faithless southlander! You would bed my wife but I knew you would just as soon betray her if I gave you your freedom!"

Like a hound catching on to a scent, Julian turned and followed the noise, knowing he had few other options. He turned down the corridors, following the angry words through the dim gray passageways, and at last found an open cell door.

In the midst of the small room, the sovereign of the Empire lay miserable in chains, all of his youthful charm gone. His ribs protruded from his chest; scars ran the length of his body, and fresh cuts lined his shoulders and arms. His face was pale and gaunt; his eyes had lost their life, their purpose. A few of his teeth had been knocked out, and the shackles that bound him were rusty.

The person standing before him wore a black cloak, stylish even in its simplicity and lined with sable. A great jeweled golden crown lay on his black hair. Julian prayed to Hieronus for self-control, that he wouldn't stab the northman king right here and compromise the mission.

"You are trapped, my *seigneur*," Bretonnius went on. "And if you escape my friends in the Wizards Council will find you, snatch you up again. Did you think, *seigneur*, when you stole my wife you would escape punishment from the King of Zarubain, the gods' divinely appointed hand on earth?"

Poor Secondo Janus merely groaned; if he had any response to the foul king's words, it was all lost in his supreme misery. Quietly, wordlessly, Julian entered his daily commune with the Just God, asking for guidance.

A command appeared in his mind, that he should, in fact, assault the northman king.

He grabbed his dagger, then had second thoughts about the blade. Instead he rushed forth to the northman king, and kicked him in the back with all possible strength.

King Bretonnius staggered forward and gasped for air like a dying fish, so totally unused to true battle. He fell hard onto his back, and grasped an amulet that hung around his neck. "Ah! An assassin!" he cried. "Invisible."

A flash of green light burst across the room, blinding Julian for a bare second. When it faded a tall figure stood there in a flannel robe dyed slate blue. In his hand, he gripped a tall staff of dark birch. His white beard was so long it grazed the floor. He seemed twenty feet tall in Julian's mind, yet his head did not even graze the ceiling.

"Ah, King Gylles vis Bretagne," the wizard said. "You have summoned me many miles at great expense to my power. How will we possibly win a war if you plea for help willy-nilly?"

Bretonnius staggered to his feet, still gasping for air. "An invisible assassin," he managed to say through all his wheezing. "Please, Lemuel."

"An invisible assassin." The wizard's voice dripped with derision. "You have grown very inventive, my good king. Perhaps, I should not have given you the amulet. If there were an invisible assassin, my good king, I would sense his magical aura. There is no magic weaver here, you poor man. I have a war to win. Ask for my help so wantonly and I will take that device from you once and for all."

"No," Bretonnius breathed. "No…" He was clutching his heart, the pathetic fool.

"Goodbye, Gylles." A trace of green light appeared—the beginnings of a spell—and Julian, Ultor Malleus, struck with his blade. The knife shredded through his robe, biting deep into his flesh and immediately drawing blood. The wizard Lemuel shrieked like a banshee and the magic exploded all around them, totally uncontrolled, an arcane storm.

~

Wherever Julian, King Bretonnius, Secondo Janus, and a huge piece of the wall appeared, it was clearly not where Lemuel intended to go. They were in the midst of a forest with pine trees as large as towers, veiled in a misty rain. Lemuel, however, was still screaming, breaking the normally tranquil scene, and blood drenched his slate-blue robe. The green light burst forth again, and Julian stuck him in the chest once more, harder than ever. The scream became shriller, more desperate, but still the magic consumed them, and they vanished together.

~

They appeared in a realm of high winds and biting, deathly cold temperatures, and thin, unbreathable air. At the top of a mountain, Julian realized. The wind was shrill, but Lemuel's panicked screams were shriller. Bretonnius remained in shock, and the green light appeared again. The green light burst more uncontrolled than ever, a giant vortex of light that consumed them. Julian stuck him with the knife again and Lemuel's screamed reached its fever pitch; the light exploded, consuming them all again.

~

When they reached their destination this time, in the midst of golden sundried grass, Lemuel at last collapsed bleeding. His slate blue robe was drenched in blood. Abovehead, the skies were clear and blue. Neither Bretonnius nor the stones that had once composed the prison cell remained with them, and who knew where either of them were.

Secondo Janus gasped for air; his rusty chains still clung to his hands. "We are in the Central Valley," he said. "We are in the Empire. Thank the gods for you."

"I only did my duty to Hieronus. My oath is fulfilled, Your Undying Glory."

"You are a priest," Secondo panted.

"A paladin."

"You will be the Pontifex soon, if I have anything to do with it."

Julian felt himself smile, something he thought he had never done before. "Ah, my good Secondo Janus. Let's get you back to Imperial City at once."

"And we will bring Lemuel with us, too. I can think of no better trophy... vengeance is served, my friend. And the wicked Bretonnius is dying somewhere, at the top of a mountain peak. Yet the war... the war may not, at the end of it all, be won."

"The war," Julian said, "is the least of our concerns right now. I must bring you back to the Imperial Palace at once."

"Thank you, friend," Emperor Secondo Janus said. "You will be the Pontifex, if it is the last thing I do."

Julian had an inclination to argue with him, to say that the emperor should not force his will upon the White Synod, but the poor man had been through too much, suffered too greatly to correct him. "Thank you, signore," Julian said instead. "You are too kind."

Soon they found the Path of Tidus, a paved and well maintained roadway that led southward toward Imperial City, southward toward home.

CHAPTER THIRTY-SEVEN: OLD FRIEND

Astarthe, Queen of Haroon

The ship docked in the harbor of her home. Astarthe had never before been so glad to see the red sandstone buildings of Haroon, the City of Issa. She would never return to Imperial City; of that, she was certain. She, Adamantion, her handmaids and her Anakhil had all boarded the first ship after the winter storms quieted, and now... now, she felt safe in the realm of the Moon Goddess her mother. She strode out of the harbor with her normal pomp, and the trumpets blared, announcing the return of the queen. The people's faces were somber: a disappointing harvest, it would seem. There was little doubt as to the cause: Astarthe had no consort with her, preventing the fertility of the land. She gave one last passing thought to Theon Arkadios, the man she had lost to dark powers, and shuddered.

CHAPTER THIRTY-EIGHT:
TO THÉNAI

Theon Arkadios

The carriage ride was bumpy, the trip was expensive, the personal library mediocre and the lighting dim, but Theon forced himself through it, nursing a bottle of cheap wine and feeling himself drawn inexorably by the hands of fate to his father's dwelling, and his father's false son.

"I must be avenged!" The memory of the sage Choh, in his pointed silken cap, hissing at him with a contorted angry expression on his face, was clear as dawn in Theon's mind, as more and more of the opium dream parted like a veil. The sage Choh had been so good to him up to now, so supremely wise, so eager to impart eternal truths. But now he had come up with a mad mission, insisting that Theon the Wayfarer kill the Celestial Emperor himself, all as repayment for snubbing Choh.

"No!" Theon had shouted, and drew the lacquered blade of the Forgotten Isle warriors. And for once they had fought, master versus student, in the midst of cherry blossom fields. Yet Choh, with only a peasant's staff, overcame him; he had shoved a gauze over Theon's mouth and nose pungent with some foul liquid. Almost instantly Theon had fallen asleep; and when he woke, he was in the hull of an oceangoing ship.

From then on, the vision was blank. Theon gulped down the remainder of the wine in the privacy of the carriage car. He opened the windows and let the morning light flood in. The warm spring air meant the threat of winter storms was gone, but they had already crossed into Eloesus, so there was little point in hiring a ship now. He eyed the four books in the personal library, which he had read twice each: "The Unconquered Son, Being a Biography of Claudio-Valens Adamantus" by Marco Tullius—fabricated and thoroughly biased; "On

Agriculture" by Lucius Geta—astoundingly tedious and dull; "Love Poems to Claudia" by Leppo—sentimental garbage; and "The Demon Cult in Ancient Paladium" by an anonymous author—the only one he found remotely interesting and realistic. On the many days he'd spent crossing Paladium he would often imagine demon shrines peeking through the weeds of the salt marsh, or mad orgiastic worshipers looking to sacrifice innocents. It provided a bit of sweet relief for him throughout the day, which were punctuated by sudden transformations into other personalities, other selves, both good and evil, which he wanted no part in.

At the thought he felt one coming on, like a birthing pain. He shut the windows and welcomed the total privacy, allowing the dark transformation to take part. How long, he wondered, before he would at last reach the House of Arkadios where his father stood so haughtily, eager to meet him? And which part of him, which self, would greet the man who eschewed familial bonds and targeted his own son in a personal blood hunt?

CHAPTER THIRTY-NINE: IMPERIAL CITY

Days Later…

Secondo Janus

Secondo Janus basked in the familiar sights and smells of Imperial City. He had spent what seemed like years in the dingy Zarube prison, but this kindly Julian Ultor, Malleus all but nursed him back to health, bringing him all the food and wine he could possibly want, and now, he had returned to the city he loved. *I have proven those who doubted me wrong.* He could see his father now, grimacing at the success of his son, seeing that it was not Primo his favorite that had succeeded, but his second born that had been named emperor, been captured, and against all odds returned triumphant.

The walls of the grant apartment blocks were painted in the bright lurid colors that he remembered: "Demetrio's Elixirs," one said, and portrayed many bubbling potions and drinks that sent Secondo's already parched tongue to near madness; "The Baths of Faustus," read another, portrayed with images of towel-clad men and women in the steaming heat; and "Lady Leto's House of Pleasure," with graphic paintings Secondo fixed his eyes to, and remembered Lanabelle, the woman he had lost.

Yet despite all their efforts, in the midst of the thick swarm of people, Secondo Janus and Julian were drawing far more attention than he wanted. Julian Ultor, Malleus, was heaving a cart behind him like an ox, and on the cart was the ripe and rotting body of Lemuel, his maggot-covered corpse still clad in the slate blue robe he wore in life. The stench, too, was unbearable for anyone besides Secondo or Julian, but after many days of walking near it he had grown accustomed to the awful stench. For the people of Imperial City, however, it proved far too much, and soon the guards came running.

"What are you doing with that corpse, you idiots? No burial within the city perimeter!" The guard's tone indicated clearly who he thought Secondo Janus was—unworthy street trash.

"You do realize you are talking to your emperor, Sovereign of the Six Nations?" Julian boomed from his side.

Yet Secondo had no doubts he looked terrible, with a long-grown beard and a starved, malnourished body, nothing like he did months ago, in his prime. But despite it, a note of uncertainty fell over the guard's face. "The emperor. I expect if I summoned the Imperial Guard, they would recognize you."

"They would," Secondo Janus answered, "and the ripe body you see here is none other than Lemuel the Wizard—quite dead, now. My friend here, Julian, dealt him the death-blow."

Something changed about the guard's demeanor when he laid eyes on the dark birch staff topped with white crystal, and the slate-blue robes the maggot-infested corpse still wore. "Ah, signore. We will see. Follow me."

An Imperial Guard met them at the long walkway that led from Imperial Square to the palace proper. Diego, he recognized, in a red half-cloak and steel breastplate, and by his side a sword.

"This man claims to be Emperor Secondo Janus," the guard said.

"Emperor Secondo Janus is dead," Diego answered him.

"He is not!" Secondo said. "Look at me, Diego."

"Maximian is regent. Secondo Janus is dead."

"Diego! Gods, man, look into my eyes!"

"When Maximian wins the war in the North, the Imperial Council will have no choice but to elect him emperor." Diego's eyes recognized Secondo, but his lips stated deception. "If Maximian loses the war, the Imperial Council will have no choice but to elect someone else, or one of their own. Get rid of this impostor, guard, and do not trouble me again."

"He lies!" Julian hissed. "Diego, were you there when this wizard stole a treasure from the Imperial Palace? The wizard Lemuel that lies before you now, covered in maggots?"

"Get rid of them, my good signore," Diego answered, and turned, leaving for the walk.

The guard threw him into Imperial Square and Julian caught his arm to steady him. Secondo Janus' eyes welled with tears. All this for naught. He wondered if he would rather die in the north, if that would be better than disgrace. He could see his father now, saying, "I was right… Primo Janus was better than his brother."

Only Julian's words stopped him from suicidal frenzy: "We will right this wrong. The Just God hates all liars, and Diego and his friends will be punished. I will do whatever it takes to help you, friend… even if it means going into the north, into the war-zone, and finding Maximian ourselves."

And that, Secondo thought, *is the best option of all of them*. That is what they would do.

CHAPTER FORTY:
UTOPIA

Diego, Marshal of the Guard

"Secondo Janus has returned alive," Diego reported in a dim-lit room of the Imperial Palace.

Crispus Servillius, Speaker of the Council, hissed some indecipherable curse. "He will cause trouble if left alive. Much as Maximian is proud of his position, the two have always been close. If Maximian finds out, he will demand Secondo Janus be reinstated—the very Secondo that got us into this awful war by his foolishness. Curses! A curse on both their heads." Crispus looked down in thought. "Keep this quiet, my good Diego. Do not tell Vitellian, or anyone. We must deal with this quietly."

Servillius had his own ideas on how the Empire should be run. In truth, he liked Maximian as little as Secondo Janus. Maximian was as much a traditionalist as Secondo, and Servillius had grand ideas on how to reform the government. All his time spent in the academies of Eloesus had filled his mind with grand notions, but Diego didn't much care one way or the other about that. Servillius had promised him a country estate and wealth untold if he agreed to help him. Silver and gold, Diego knew, is all that matters in life.

"If we go to the city's underbelly, I am sure we can procure some help. Perhaps you would know…"

"Why? Because I grew up in the Suburro?"

Servillius smiled faintly. "Yes."

"I will see what I can do." But as soon as he left the squalor of the Suburro for the wealth of the Imperial Court, he had become anathema to people there.

Servillius' eyes filled with a fire Diego had not seen before. "With our traditions gone, with the myths that make up our identity banished, the people of the Empire will have no choice but to change our society from the ground up."

Diego had heard Servillius' grand utopian goals before, his ideas of perfect harmony, but he had never seen such hatred in his eyes, nor in anyone's. It was almost enough to make Diego reconsider.

Almost.

SUMMER 1100

Primo Alleus, National Historian, Writer of the Imperial Chronicles

Primo Alleus basked in the new warmth of summer, but not all was fully well. The easy passage of roads and the newly comfortable climes paved the way for messengers: messengers who spoke of the Empire finally finding its match, of a disaster in the hill country north of the Wall and a scattered army. Worst of all, here in his small rural cottage on the edge of the western sea, dissent and disillusion had begun to seep in among his countrymen. Some questioned whether the Empire had the strength to fight its enemies.

He had worked furiously throughout the years, but especially this winter. He felt like he was on the edge of a breakthrough. Pen in hand, he began to narrate the events of one of the most minor struggles of the Empire—the Kheroan Rebellion, or, as the more cynical philosophers and historians called it, the Seánine War.

"Magon, Great King of Kheroe, found himself in the midst of a great rebellion. Worst of all, the southron padisha emperor aided the rebels, providing them with arms and all manner of support. On the cusp of certain destruction, Magon begged the Empire to intervene. Yet the Imperial Council was hostile and opposed to them, not wishing to meddle in an affair they said 'has nothing to do with them.' The Emperor Julio Seánus convinced them over a matter of weeks for limited intervention... yet when His Undying Glory at last turned the tide of the rebellion, the Imperial Council made clear their wishes to interfere no further."

When did it all change, Primo Alleus wondered. How, in the span of a few decades, did the Empire suddenly alter its course, seize Khazidea from the southron empire? Clearly it had the means to; clearly such an action was possible from the very beginning. But the Imperial Council had shackled and reined in the Empire's power at every turn.

It was the elite, the blueblooded aristocrats, the supposed intellectuals and philosophers that stood in the Empire's way. What had changed? What had broken the Empire from their restraining hand, from their desperate desire to maintain the status quo?

In a flood it came to him. Primo Alleus shut his eyes, and saw in his mind's eye the emperor Claudio-Valens Adamantus, the so-called living god, who—after his sudden rise by the wings of fortune—forced every sitting member of the Imperial Council to resign, then executed them. The change began with Claudio-Valens, Primo realized, and to truly understand the story of the Empire's latter years he would have to begin with him.

An eagle flew across the yellow grass. *It is the elite, the blueblooded noblemen, the philosophers and academes, that cause all the country's ills*, he realized. The academies of Eloesus would surely disbar him from all hopes of teaching, he knew. But the truth needed to be told. It needed to be told, to reinvigorate the sons of Empire once again, to reach a new height of glory and win the War in the North.

After a brief break, Primo Alleus once again set to writing.

CHAPTER FORTY-ONE:
FATIGUE

Maximian

It was neither cold nor snowing, neither cloudy nor gray; the sky was blue, the air warm yet not hot, but already the travails of the march and the struggle of battle weighed heavy on Maximian as he pondered how he could possibly win this war. The encounter with the wizards, for all the mass death—four-thousand lives cut short in the span of an hour—was the least of his concerns. Silvana the Windborne, foremost of his augurs, had brought news that the king of Zarubain had mobilized his troops, mustered a grand army and now marched to where Maximian had camped.

A great general would know what to do, but Maximian was not a great general. In such times, he needed to take a risk. And as the Zarube army, according to reports, steadily approached them, Maximian needed to decide on an action. The propitious winds of Silvana did not ease his soul as he stood there; the woman had grown colder, more distant to him, more and more unwilling to return his affections.

"Maximian." Her angelic voice resounded through the wind.

"No more bad news," Maximian said under his breath. "I can't handle it."

"You must handle more than bad news if you wish to win this war."

"I fear, Silvana," he began, and pivoted to face the blonde, blue-eyed augur, "that this war cannot be won with what we have."

"The Empire's first defeat in waking memory," Silvana began. "A pity."

The words wrenched Maximian's gut. The Empire would get its first taste of failure in many years—and all thanks to Maximian, the foolish Marshal of the Guard who thought he could rule the Empire.

"No," he growled through gritted teeth. "I will not let my country fail."

Silvana pursed her lips. "We've heard word from an informant. King Bretonnius has vanished, along with Secondo Janus and the wizard Lemuel."

"Secondo is dead…" Maximian breathed.

"That is what we thought," Silvana said, "but it is a lie. The court is in a frenzy. They think the Wizards Council is conspiring against them, it appears. The king has no son… the throne would go to Queen Lanabelle in any other circumstance, but not in such disgrace."

"And the army…"

"The army is less than a day away. We must prepare to fight, or we must flee."

"Flee," Maximian scoffed. "An Imperial does not flee…" The words he spoke softly, weakly.

"Perhaps," Silvana breathed, "we *should*. Perhaps the sun is setting on the Empire, and we are only hastening its demise."

Maximian growled some curse at her. "Leave me, traitor." He would fight like a patriot, even to the bloody end. He prayed to Imperium, the Spirit of Empire, for guidance. Yet he received nothing the following night as the soldiers continued building fortifications, doing their absolute best to stave off what Maximian knew was all-but-certain defeat.

In the cold dawn the army appeared—a line of a few hundred knights riding behind an endless mass of archers and peasant soldiers. They stopped their march a dozen yards from where the legionaries had dug the trenches and laid caltrops. Eventually, a man appeared in a tunic of black wool and a feathered black cap.

The northman general is a coward, Maximian thought. *He won't even meet me himself.*

But the emissary made his way into the Imperial ranks, and Maximian ordered his soldiers not to harass him.

"My good *seigneur* emperor," he said in Imperial, in that phlegmy northman accent of the Zarubes. "I come to you on behalf of Ramir, Duke of Lessant, chief commander of this army. He does not wish for this coming maelstrom of death any more than you do. He wishes for diplomacy most of all, that we can both leave without a single life lost."

Maximian said nothing.

"If you, my good *seigneur* emperor, wish to end this useless war altogether, you have my liege Ramir's full blessing as well as His Majesty King Gylles vis Bretagne. For reparations of seven thousand marks paid in gold and silver, over a period of ten years, we will agree to quit this war and leave your nation in peace."

"That agreement is remarkably one-sided," Maximian said.

"There is only one side, my good *seigneur*, that has a strong chance of winning this war. A wise man would accept Ramir's offer. No blood shall be spilled, and the price is most fair."

"I would give you one more option, my signore, which I hope you will heed." The words were slow to come from his lips; even they seemed like defeat. For the sake of his troops and of his country's honor, he spoke them assertively. "We call off this war altogether, resume trade, and put the matter behind us."

A dark grin crept over the emissary's features. "The duchy of Lessant was once small and insignificant, a petty thing in the scope of the Western Heartlands. Yet Ramir's forefathers expanded the territory—oftentimes against the king's will—and it became the greatest in the region."

"I don't need to know your history."

"Ah, but you do, my good *seigneur*. What I am trying to say is that the Duke of Lessant does not give up, especially against such good odds. My lord Ramir has offered you a deal far better than you deserve. You have been given the choice—to pay reparations of seven thousand marks."

"Then," Maximian said darkly, "I will meet you on a field of war.”

Soon the sky was darkened with arrows as the two sides exchanged volleys. The battle was a maelstrom of death, as predicted, and lasted far into the depths of the night. The dry grass was soon wet with blood.

CHAPTER FORTY-TWO:
ARRIVAL

Choh, Sage

Choh rubbed his hands together and delighted at the seed he had planted in this foolish foreigner, at the designs that had benefited him so greatly and yet cast Theon the idiot into ill fortune. In the end the Celestial Emperor did not suspect him and he had escaped with his life; it mattered little what happened to his pawn.

Theon

Theon gasped, waking from the unwished-for transformation, and grabbed the bottle of wine to find it empty. The air inside the carriage car had grown unbearably hot, and Theon recognized the smells of an Eloesian summer. He peeked outside the window and saw the low mountains that stood guard over the Vale of Isteros. Thénai lay a matter of days away, and for all the power Theon possessed the thought of his father had slowly but surely begun to undo him.

His disciplinarian, authoritarian nature was a major part of what had driven him away from home along the Silk Route. Tharon Arkadios' rages were something to behold, sending even brave men into terror. At the thought Theon shuddered.

Atalantë, Knight of Telantis

Atalantë had no knowledge of where he was—no idea why he stood here in these cramped, uncivilized quarters with these strangely-shaped scrolls—but he could not help but feel a familiar cold dread. When the cataclysm erupted and drowned the vast central plain in water, breaking the power of the Telantine King, he had managed to survive the year-long rain of fire. Atalantë, the last of the true

Telantines, had fought the encroaching forces of shadow until a wraith reached its ghostly hand into his heart, and froze his living soul.

But here he was, alive again, his Telantine blade studded with priceless gems in his hand, his fine starmetal breastplate protecting him. The air bore a scent he would never forget, a scent not physical but spiritual, that the end was coming like the end had come all those millennia ago… *The second End,* a priest had once told Atalantë, *will be final.*

Theon Arkadios

Covered in cold sweat, Theon gasped for air. The transformations Choh had wrought inside him had all felt horrific to him, yet the noble persona of Atalantë was something else altogether. For once Theon Arkadios could sense what Atalantë had in the air— the sense he, and Varda itself, were approaching the end. Worst of all, the image of the sage Choh, cackling at the evil he had wrought in him, Theon did not understand—for he still did not know exactly what he had done to him, and what evil he had planted inside him. Too much of his past, still, was hidden by the veil of the opium dream. Too many dark things still hid within the folds of his mind—things he did not want to, but *had* to remember.

CHAPTER FORTY-THREE:
LAST HOPE

Julian Ultor, Malleus

At the edge of Anthania, two weeks after they had departed Imperial City, Julian questioned his actions for the first time. They had gone beyond the waterless desolation of the Central Valley and its intolerable heat, and now made their way toward the stickier summers of Gad. Julian had made this journey before, and only the fell trickery of Lemuel had brought both he and Secondo Janus so quickly back home.

He was helping Secondo Janus, the rightful emperor, by leading him to his friend. Yet Julian Ultor, Malleus, had sworn no oath nor promised Hieronus the Just God he would accomplish this task. He had completed his mission by slaying Lemuel, as he had sworn. Now, he wondered if—in the hidden depths of his mind—he was doing this for a selfish purpose, for the promise Secondo had made, to install Julian as the Pontifex. He would be the youngest Pontifex in history.

At dusk, they stopped and pitched a tent by the side of the road. Julian's money had nearly run out, and staying in the comfort of an inn would spell immediate financial ruin. As the crickets chirped, he shut his eyes, and entered his daily commune.

The Just God did not disapprove of his actions. Yet his demands were quite clear… that Julian would not look past the Imperial Court's denial of Secondo Janus. Something very dark and very troubling was at work in the upper echelon of the Empire, something that threatened the very foundations of what the nation stood for. And in the Just God's eyes, this War in the North was a useless endeavor in the wake of growing trouble at home. There were traitors in the ranks of the elite, and the Just God's heart burned against them. The elite, far-removed from the people, are a constant source of trouble. *They idle in luxury, pondering grand ideas to shape and reshape the nation yet inevitably worsening everything for the common people.* And the Thenoan Philosophers, some of whom served in the Imperial Council, claimed to believe in no greater power, yet in their actions they would bring about the designs of the enemy.

And the enemy is at hand. The Dark One is again at work; the Devil is reborn, awakened on the Red Mountain. And the worst is yet to come. Images flashed in Julian's mind, of trouble never before seen, of famine and war and tumult, of evil taking physical form, of a shadow falling over all… cities burning, people starving, the Empire faltering and then collapsing in the wake of growing shadow.

And a people from the Southern World, brought at the behest of the elite to serve their own ends, to reshape the nation according to their philosophical designs. *Oh,* the Just God shouted, *how their plans will backfire!*

And Julian Ultor, Malleus, sat up suddenly, gasping for breath like a fish out of water, his entire body dripping with ice-cold sweat. He had a thought of rushing back south to fight the Imperial Council, but he knew he couldn't do anything about it as he was.

No, he thought as he drew in deep breaths and tried to calm his raging heart, *I will continue with my plans.* Julian Ultor, Malleus, could not rein in the Imperial Council, but Secondo Janus—the man who slept near him in such a peaceful angelic sleep—could. With an army, a numerous host, things could be set right for a time. And force of arms was the only way Janus could secure the Empire, to take it by the reins and guide it in the proper direction.

Julian eyed the former emperor, dressed like a poor slave or a prisoner of war in tattered woolen clothing, and realized he could accomplish nothing without Secondo Janus, the true heir to the throne.

The War in the North is useless—the assertion of the Just God sent him into a frenzy, a near panic, as he thought of the urgency of the task at hand. He would need to go north as quickly as he possibly could, and tell Maximian, the regent, to abandon all his hopes of wreaking vengeance on the north.

~

The trees grew larger; the small conifers and oaks of the Anthanian peninsula gave way to the grand maples and towering elms of the north—though now, Julian noted, they were not naked and barren like they had been when he first passed through. They were as he remembered in his childhood: leaves full and green, air warm and thick with humidity. All around the Path of Tidus, towns and villages sprouted up, but Julian and Secondo Janus never stayed in any of the warm inns, electing to camp by the road and eat like paupers.

The experience, Julian could tell, was weighing on his friend Secondo. Secondo, from the wealthy Janus family, was no doubts used to rich dinners and a life of easy comforts—though Julian did his best to keep his spirits high, he knew the former emperor longed for the good life of the courts.

Day by day, week by week, the towns and villages began to fade away into a rustic countryside, overrun by thorns and snares and a land of wet marshes. Soon even the greenery began to fade, the trees lose their number and give way to a grand plain; and then, on the horizon, the Wall appeared.

At the sight Secondo groaned. "I cannot believe," he began, "we have come all this way."

"And yet we have. Be proud of yourself, signore." It was the best Julian could offer, but Secondo only groaned again in response.

The Gate of Tidus lay open, but the crowd of soldiers guarding it didn't seem very welcoming. They greeted the two haggard travelers with stern gazes.

"Signors," one snapped. "What business do you have in the north? A war is raging, you know."

"We know," Julian said, and determined that he would speak honestly. "We seek the regent himself, Maximian. We have an important message to relay."

"The regent Maximian," the same soldier sneered, "is engaged in a war with the northmen. He would have little time for the likes of you."

"For the likes of your emperor?" Secondo said with a strength Julian hadn't heard for weeks. "I am Secondo Janus, rightful emperor, Maximian's close friend. Let us by, my signore."

The soldier's eyes hardened further. "The emperor, dressed in tattered wool like a slave? The emperor who is dead?"

"The northmen lied," Secondo growled back with twice the soldier's anger. "Let us by, signore, or when I again achieve the throne, I'll have your head."

"We are letting most anyone by," the soldier said, "anyone foolish enough to venture beyond. Do not think I believe your story for a second, signore." He beat the butt of his spear into the ground and the soldiers parted.

Julian entered the north for the second time.

~

The plain of Mekara lay barren as ever, a land of browning grass-covered hills under a clear sky. The only difference was the heat.

"And where will we find Maximian?" Secondo said. "How will we know where he is? How will we eat in this country?"

"How will we eat," Julian breathed. "Wander long enough, and you will see." Julian led him off the road, into the wild grassy hills."

They spent the night hungry in the tent, far beyond the road. Secondo Janus was thin and wan, looking weaker than he ever had. Worst of all, a cloud of despair had fallen over him, draining all his hope, all his joy, all his will. But in the nightly commune, covered in his scant blankets, Hieronus agreed with his course of action.

And in the morning, as he expected, they were there.

A dozen barbarians on horses stood there, each wielding a long spear. One, clad in bulky leathers, wore the antler headdress of a chieftain. He had a bushy, light brown beard and blue eyes, and his cheeks were covered in blue war-paint.

"Do you speak?" the barbarian chieftain asked in the Mekari tongue.

And in the Mekari tongue, Julian answered. "I do."

"What are you doing in the land of Mekara, southlander, in the realm of the Tenebri?"

"You are foes with the *Zarobo*, no doubt. As am I. There is an army of southlanders somewhere near…"

"An army." An odd grin fell over the barbarian chieftain's face. "Two armies. I could show you, but you have no horse."

Julian's heart sank at the words.

"I can take you two-a-saddle, good man, but you would have to leave your tent behind."

Julian gulped. It was a risk, but once he reached the Imperial army neither he nor Secondo would have any need of their makeshift tent. He nodded. "Yes, chieftain. I accept."

~

They rode through the remainder of the day at a quick pace, until night fell over the Mekari hills. In the evening the barbarians offered them dried berries and smoked meats, better fare than Julian and Secondo had eaten in a long while.

And in the morning they continued their ride, at a faster breakneck pace than ever. The wind whipped at Julian's face, and though the barbarians had fed them the best food they had, and given them ample spring water, Secondo Janus—in the few scant looks Julian spared throughout the day—seemed to be going quickly downhill, losing his strength, even his will to live.

And when, late in the day, they found the sight the barbarian chieftain was talking about, it nearly did in Julian as well.

Before them lay a scene of unspeakable carnage. The air was thick with a miasma of rot and death. Thousands and thousands of bodies lay unburied in the hot sun. Maggots and worms crawled through the bodies of legionaries; a host of crows pecked out soldiers' eyes while others circled above head. Even Julian nearly gagged. He fell off the horse onto the hard ground and retched. He had never seen such carnage.

And the chieftain of the Tenebri was laughing.

In a haze of nausea Julian staggered to his feet. He walked toward the bodies, still in armor, swords and spears and shields lying undisturbed. Behind him, Secondo was wailing.

And yet, as he went further, surveying the mass death in the putrid air, he saw slight vestiges of hope: mixed among the Imperial dead, among the piles of bodies, lay a countless number of fallen Zarubes—peasant-soldiers and peasant-archers mixed among the steel goliaths of Zarube knights. *We do not know the whole story,* Julian thought. But he did know he had to get out of here.

"The battle raged more than a day," the chieftain began. "I watched from the safety of a hill, cheering the southlanders on. The Zarubes fell back and retreated… but I have never seen such a costly victory."

"They are still alive?" Julian breathed.

"Your magic weavers summoned up such strong winds the

peasant-archers could not so much as land a single arrow. And once the duke's knights fell, there was little chance of the peasant-soldiers overcoming the legion. And yet, in all, I do believe three-quarters of your soldiers are dead. It is—as they say—a victory that lost the war. And the king of the *Zarobo* no doubt has many more armies. The cause is lost, and some tribes of my own people have promised friendship with the king of the *Zarobo*."

"Where are they?" Julian asked. "Where are our people?"

"Camped by the River Gad, due east," the chieftain said. "They are lucky their folly won't hurt them, camped so near our cousins the *Guthar*."

The barbarians east of the River Gad, Julian remembered, were far fiercer than these ones in the hill country. Long ago, the Guthar had invaded the Empire, before Claudian Adamantus drove them back way.

Behind him, Secondo had collapsed, weeping. "Will you show us the way?" Julian begged him.

"No," the chieftain answered firmly, then wheeled his horse around and galloped back the way they had come.

Julian, feeling tears of his own form, grabbed Secondo Janus' arm and yanked him to his feet. "Maximian is alive, my emperor, and we will find him."

Julian had to drag him eastwards, away from where the sun had begun to set. That night, it began to rain.

~

By the time they reached the River Gad days later, Secondo Janus had grown ill, and both of them were so hungry a tremor had spread throughout their bodies. The great waters of the River Gad lay before them, and they had no means to fish. Beyond lay a forest where the cruelest and strongest of the northern barbarians lived. *Though not as cruel*, Secondo thought, *as the Mekari chieftain that abandoned us.*

They filled their famished stomachs with water from the River Gad, and lay still for the remainder of the day and night, too weak to travel.

Secondo woke up the next morning violently ill, vomiting the watery contents of his stomach. Weak and shaking, Julian lay idle. Crows circled overhead, perhaps thinking that the two would be their next feast.

And they will. They will…

At twilight winds began to buffet them, perhaps heralding the beginning of a storm. Or so Julian thought, until a group of augurs in their winged leather caps appeared. Yet Julian, so starved for food and so weak, feeling an illness coming on, did not so much as greet them.

"Secondo Janus!" one blonde augur cried in disbelief, while another scooped up Julian in her magic-strengthened hands.

And then, through the deepening summer night, the augurs carried them through the scraggly woods and brush, beyond the ditches and wooden fortifications, and into the camp, into the legate's tent where Maximian stood.

Secondo Janus, rightful emperor, was still ill when Maximian greeted him the following morning, but a light had dawned in his eyes—a light of hope Julian hadn't seen since he rescued him from the dingy Zarube prison.

"I thought you were dead," Maximian cried, and tears welled anew in his eyes. He grabbed his ill friend and wrapped him in an embrace. "I thought you were dead… I thought you were dead… oh, gods in heaven, I thank you."

CHAPTER FORTY-FOUR:
REUNION

Maximian, Regent

When he first laid eyes on his friend Secondo Janus, he did not question *if* he would hand the governance of the nation to his friend, but *when*. "Oh, Secondo, I have so many questions. Like what happened to you, and who is this young man with you?"

He had blondish-brown hair like burnished gold, and though much younger than either of them, had a stern look to his eyes that made him appear far older.

"This man is Julian, a paladin, and he is my savior."

"Hieronus is the savior—" Julian began, but Maximian cut him off.

"A paladin without a hammer. I've never seen such a thing."

"I lost my hammer in the north," the young man replied, and pulled a small shiv from the rope belt. "I am forbidden to shed blood, but I was forced to."

"He killed the wizard Lemuel," Secondo shouted, "and now the Empire can rest peacefully."

"You killed Lemuel!" Maximian exclaimed. Such a task was beyond the strongest of their augurs, beyond the strongest of their soldiers, beyond Maximian himself—even with *Imperium's Rebuke*. "The Empire will be forever in your debt, young man."

"The Empire is in Hieronus' debt, and all the gods."

Quiet, Maximian wanted to say, but he wouldn't. He would not disrespect a national hero. He wondered how a man armed with only a knife could have slain a wizard of such inconceivable power—a wizard who could appear and reappear halfway across the world in the blink of an eye, whose mastery over magic power was far greater than any in the Empire. "Thank you, Julian, for serving Hieronus, and for giving the Empire a gift it cannot possibly repay. And it cannot... there are less than five thousand soldiers remaining, and I wonder how we can possibly win this war."

"We can't," Secondo Janus said flatly. "We can't win the war."

Maximian turned dour. "I have always known you to be brave, fiery, almost to the point of recklessness. What has changed?"

"There is trouble at home," Julian said. "I know you are not a paladin—"

"You do not have the look of one," Maximian interjected.

Julian drew back a bit, as if the words stung him. "There is something dark in the hearts of the Imperial Council. Are you a reader of history, regent?"

"Not terribly much," Maximian thought, and it was true. He was a man of war, a wielder of the sword and not the mind. A poor thing for a general.

"In the days of Claudio-Valens Adamantus the… God…" The last word was slow to come from Julian's lips. "The Imperial Council was a thorn in the Empire's side, a restraining force that withheld its strength. And now, I fear, they are a problem again… worse than ever."

Maximian had a hard time fearing the ominous warnings of priests—their communes could so easily be nothing more than idle fancy and imagination.

Then Secondo Janus spoke. "I think he is right, friend. The Imperial Council denied me… they said they did not recognize me."

He has changed, Maximian thought, noting the gauntness of his friend's face, *but not that much.* "That is strange," he breathed. "But the War in the North—"

"Gods damn the War in the North!" Secondo hissed, red-faced.

Maximian paused. The fury had returned, but not in the way that he wanted. "If I abandon it now, the Zarubes would demand crushing reparations… indemnities of seven thousand marks. A good twenty-thousand libra… our national budget would be dashed."

"Friend." Secondo Janus held himself together a bit more this time, growling rather than snapping at him. "The War in the North is pointless. I began this war through my own gods-damned folly. I deserve a beheading for the tumult I've caused, for the lives I lost. And now… now, I demand you end the war I started through my own error, and you won't end it. There is trouble, Maximian, we need to deal with, and the Northern World is made of sterner stuff than either of us thought. We need to abolish it altogether. We could win this war, perhaps, if we put all our resources behind it, summoned all our legions… The rain of death would cost our nation hundreds of thousands of lives. And in the end, it isn't worth it. Not when there are dark forces at work in the Imperial Council."

Behind his friend's anguished eyes, Maximian saw a self-serving motive. Secondo Janus wanted to retain his position as emperor. And yet, even through all that, glimmers of truth hid within his words. The War in the North—if he intended to win—would only end in victory at immense human and financial cost. What were twenty-thousand libra compared to that? The legions he used hadn't been able to overcome Zarubain's borders, to inflict any damage on King Bretonnius. "I would hate to see Bretonnius triumphant."

"Zarubain would be triumphant, perhaps," Secondo said, "but Bretonnius is dead."

Maximian had so much to catch up on. "Ah, my signore, very well. I fear I have no choice. We will go south, and ensure the Imperial Council honors its obligations."

The next day, their march began.

CHAPTER FORTY-FIVE:
APOTHEOSIS

Theon Arkadios

The House of Arkadios sat high on a hill, reminding Theon in an instant of the life he'd left behind. From his birth he'd been doted on, given all the best things: food cooked by a staff of slaves, purple garments beyond the means of most anyone, an indoor bath and pool, and on his fourteenth birthday, his own four-horse chariot lined with gold. Yet his father had been distant, never there; his mother even less so. He only punished, never rewarded. All Theon's associations with him—terror at best, nonexistence at worst—had been negative.

And yet, here I am. He was here to set things right. He was here to show Tharon Arkadios in no uncertain terms who his son was, and where he and his impostor child stood in the grand scheme of things. *The grand scheme of things...*

"Kill yourself, fool!" the sage Choh screamed from within him. "Kill yourself, and be done with it! You are no use to me."

Still little bits of his life in the far east remained lost in the opium fog. Yet the sage Choh held him fast even here. He was no longer Wayfarer; he no longer followed Choh and his vile teachings. He was no longer enlightened. And yet, he was not free.

Something lived inside him, something he didn't want to contemplate. Something he couldn't contemplate. A host of spirits lived within him, changing Theon's self at their whim.

Yet even they seemed taken aback at the sight of the House of Arkadios with its great stone walls, its red-tile roof, its towering spires and its grand windows. It stood, a beacon of wealth and power among the dirty sprawl of Thénai. In a sea of hovels and refuse-stained streets, the great privilege of his birth was clearer than ever to Theon Arkadios. But he wasn't here to return to his childhood, the comfort of a wealthy life. He was not here to live or prosper; he was here to destroy. He had left forlorn and dejected, as Theon the Desperate, seeking something in the far east that would bring lasting joy. He had returned to his father's house as Theon the Destroyer, hoping to unmake the fortunes of the House of Arkadios.

I am here to sow ruin, Theon thought. *As the sage Choh wants me to.* He wondered if he would ever know the nature of the evil Choh planted within him. But even now, as he approached the iron-grilled gates to the mansion, he could feel himself begin to change.

A dusky shadow appeared, then a few more. His father's guards. They wore steel breastplates emblazoned with the laurel-wreath symbol of Eloesus, and on their heads conical helms outfitted with bright red horsehair crests. Wry grins had crept over all their faces. He recognized them all; they had aged.

"Theon Arkadios," one said. "You recognize old Lysander, don't you? Why, I'll never. The brat returns after all these years. Your da has found a new Theon, now."

"So I've heard," Theon muttered. He reached inside the pouch filled with throwing stars, and flexed his grip around the peasant's staff.

"I'd be damned if I would deny the little boy I played ball with… Your da may hate you, but Lysander still doesn't."

Theon tried to smile, but found himself unable.

With a shudder and a creak, the iron-grilled gate snapped open, and Theon began the walk up the stone stair and into the House of Arkadios.

Even in the Red Palace, Theon had not seen such beauty and luxury. Each floor tile had a different image: beautiful, nymphlike women of Gad with long red hair; squids and schools of fish; and many depictions of Tharon Arkadios' favored god, Brecko the Satyr King. Beyond the rich red walls of the corridor, torchlight glistening on a glass chandelier illuminated a fresco of the Themurian wilds, an oft-idealized land in the Eloesian hinterlands, where the satyrs drank and enchanted revelers with their magic pipes. There, in the shadow of a great mountain in view of the pines, snow fell often in wintertime, and idlers there never need fear the hot summers of the lowland coast.

"False son!"

Theon gasped and whipped around, snatching a throwing star fully out of the bag. His father stood there in the corridor, the orange light showing just how poorly he had aged. His once-fresh face was covered with wrinkles, his salt-and-pepper hair had turned to pure gray. At this late hour he was still in his bedclothes. His breath reeked of alcohol.

"I am not the false son," Theon said. "I am your flesh and blood."

Father bared his yellow teeth. "So my stories have worked. Oh, the tales I spun to get you back to me. There is no impostor here, my Theon. No false son except for you." He stiffened. "Things have not gone well since you abandoned me. Your mother has left me… she ran off with a westerner, an ignorant Imperial bastard. And you… you were gone. I have grown to hate you, false son. I dreamed in my loneliest hour of what I would do to you… I devised so many terrible tortures." He drew in a breath. He looked weak. "I sent men to hunt you and bring you back to me. But now, looking at you Theon, I cannot do any of that. Though I hate you, I love you. You are my son… my true son."

Choh's face flashed in his mind, angry, hissing, as Father wrapped Theon in a weak embrace. Choh urged him to kill Father, and Theon fought with all his might, to stop what he knew was the final transformation.

Look at me! Choh hissed. *Look at me!* Look!

~

"Look!" the sage Choh told Theon the Wayfarer as the earth trembled all around him.

They had taken a ship for days and weeks along the coast, going beyond the dry barrens, until they came here—the purple-rocked land of the *dai ma*, where—Choh said—true enlightenment dwelled.

Wayfarer's heart beat rapidly for the first time since he had begun his training all those years ago. The clouds glowed overhead, as if they were on fire, and lightning spears crackled and sizzled on the purple rock ground with alarming frequency. In the evil purple light, the shapes of glowing green pools stood out starkly against the bleak landscape, and Wayfarer and the Sage Choh—though in a land uninhabited for millennia—were not alone.

Creatures wandered the pools, creatures clearly humanoid but clearly nonhuman. Eight feet tall, they had the red scales of lizards, and their long tails ended in stingers that dripped with poison. Their faces were obscured in black armor, but traces of tentacle beards peeked through them.

Wayfarer felt his bladder empty. "Teacher, teacher… I cannot." The warm sticky liquid ran down his loose pants.

"You can," Choh said, and an anger Theon had never seen before blazed in his master's eyes. "And you *will*. Drink from the green well, from the Well of Power. You are my student. You are a disciple of the Way. You must heed my commands. You know I want nothing but the best for you. You know I have your good at heart. Drink, my disciple, at the font of power, at the Stygian Well, and you will have the strength of Abol'on."

"Abol'on," Theon the Wayfarer breathed. The word felt grim. "I… I have never known you to do me harm, Choh. I have never known you to wish ill of me."

A wide grin grew on Choh's face—a grin, Theon the Wayfarer thought as he stooped to drink from the bright green well—he wasn't sure he liked.

~

Aboluhon, Prince of Destruction

The walls of the House of Arkadios rattled with the sound of a piercing howl. From within the demon's body, Theon looked at its great iron claws, its scaly black skin, and the tail that protruded, dripping with poison, from its back.

Theon's father Tharon screamed and fell back, hitting the floor. "Please, please, please…"

But the plaintive cries only fed the hunger of Aboluhon. Desperately Theon fought for control. He screamed and kicked within him, but the body of Aboluhon—the body Theon inhabited—lurched forward, razor-sharp claws reaching outward, ready to slay Tharon Arkadios and everyone who inhabited the mansion, and then destroy Thénai, and then, the world. Theon screamed and tried his best to wrest control.

~

Theon Arkadios

In a flash of light and a burn of demon-fire Theon regained control of his senses. He was back in the forsaken mountains of the *dai ma,* his lips hovering over the bubbling green liquid. In this new reality, he had not yet drunk from it.

"Why did you stop?" the sage Choh hissed. "You are my student. If you care for the Way, you will do what I command."

Theon jerked to his feet and righted himself. Under the fire-red clouds, in sight of the baleful purple mountains and the blazing demon pits, he grabbed his peasant's staff in his left hand, and a throwing star in his right. "I do not care for the Way," he snapped at his former master—the one he recognized, in his newfound wisdom, as a fraud.

His eyes bulged, simmering with infinite wrath. From his back he swept free his steel temple sword. "Your master is Choh," he hissed, baring his rotten stumps of teeth. "You are not your own. I rescued from your slime, foreigner. It is far better than what most men of the Forgotten Isle would do to you. War captives from Xia never leave the Jade City alive…"

"I am going home."

"You are not going anywhere." And Choh was in the air, loose robes fluttering, his temple sword shimmering red in the fiery light.

Theon dove under him, choosing the path of least resistance as he had been taught—as Choh had taught him.

He launched a throwing star underhanded but Choh batted it away. He launched another but Choh dodged easily. He charged with his peasant's staff and blocked Choh's sword blow, then slammed the wood into the sage's skull.

~

Aboluhon, Prince of Destruction

Aboluhon staggered backward, stunned somehow. The human prey bolted off down some hallway and Aboluhon stooped over and coughed up the contents of his stomach—the green acid slime. He did not know what was happening to him.

He dashed after the human as it ran.

~

Theon Arkadios

The demons howled in the midst of the evil night, and fireballs crackled across the sky like shooting stars would in the normal world. And it seemed indeed that Theon had left the real world altogether and entered the domain of hell.

He had never seen Choh so angry as he came flying in, heaving his temple sword back.

Theon dodged away, letting him charge by, as he had been taught—as Choh had taught him. He whipped a throwing star at Choh and missed. He whipped another and it bit Theon's former master in the back, drawing blood and tearing cloth. Choh turned around, hysterical with anger, and charged again, having lost all the serene dignity and forethought he claimed to have in the Way. "What has come over you, Wayfarer?"

"Not Wayfarer," Theon replied with calm, retaining his cool collection even in the heat of battle, as he had been taught—a Choh had taught him. "Theon Arkadios, son of Tharon."

He tripped Choh as he ran by. The temple sword went scattering across the black spongy rock. He leapt and grabbed it by the hilt as Choh tried to stand up; a single blow, a clean cut, and Choh was headless.

Years Later…

His poor father Tharon knelt before him like a serf, cheeks wet with tears. "I sent men to hunt you and bring you back to me. But now, looking at you Theon, I cannot do any of that. Though I hate you, I love you. You are my son… my true son."

"But I am here, now, Father," Theon said. The silk clothing of the Far East was comfortable and splendidly-crafted, but it was not his own.

"I am here now, Father," Theon said, "and I will never leave."

As the opium dream faded from his memory, Theon knew he had finally found his true home—the nation, the Empire, that he loved.

CHAPTER FORTY-SIX:
SOUTHWARD BOUND

Maximian, Marshal of the Guard

The crippling reparations would hamper the Empire's industry and wealth, but it was a small favor to Secondo Janus, his dear friend. Besides, what Secondo and the self-righteous paladin said had a ring of truth when Maximian pondered it in his mind. Why would the Imperial Council deny Secondo Janus, the true sovereign, unless there was some dark machination at work? Over everything Maximian did, an ominous cloud now hovered, a dark and heavy curse. He prayed to Imperium, the Spirit of Empire, that they could withstand whatever came to plague them.

For now, the homeland beckoned.

~

From the hinterlands of Mekara to the Gate of Tidus, a journey of many days passed them by. The innumerable host Maximian brought with him to subdue the north had fallen threadbare, like pigs to the slaughter, and the people of Imperial City hated rulers that came back without the spoils of war, without a victory that proved the Imperial nation reigned supreme.

But I am not ruler anymore. And for once, Maximian was glad. Secondo Janus had earned the throne by virtue of his cunning and ambition; the White Throne was a position Maximian had found himself ill-suited. All the dangers and responsibilities had fled from him, gone to their rightful place—on the shoulders of Emperor Secondo Janus the God.

~

Walking by the emperor's side, they passed through the Gate of Tidus. From here, the great stone-paved path would lead them from the frontier into the heart of Imperial City. It would lead them from the furthermost precinct to the absolute center of the world, the Imperial Palace where no small amount of uncertainty awaited him.

But at least Maximian was back where he belonged—in the nation, the Empire of his birth, as a citizen-soldier standing guard over his friend. He intended never to let Secondo out of his sight, from now until the end; he swore an oath no dagger or secret plot of the Imperial Council would succeed against his dearest friend.

Down the path they marched, the Path of Tidus built in unforgotten times, into the heart of the nation, into the heart of empire.

CHAPTER FORTY-SEVEN:
HOME

Emperor Secondo Janus the God

The deadly heat of the Central Valley, the bright yellow grass and the poor, smoky air were exactly as Secondo Janus remembered. What he did not remember, as the legions marched down the road, was the eerie quiet and the sense that he was walking, along with history, into a gathering storm.

Things did not improve when he reached the outskirts of Imperial City. Even the noise of the crowd seemed subdued. At the doorway of the Imperial Palace, with the strength of a cohort to back him up, he expected the false Marshal of the Guard to deny him again. But the gates opened; and he found himself within the luxurious confines of the Imperial Palace.

~

"I do not feel the same," Secondo muttered, half-thinking that no one would hear him. "I am a changed man… bruised and beaten… defeated."

"The palace is not the same, either, my friend."

Maximian's heavy hand on his shoulder reassured him. His newfound friend Julian Ultor was silent as always. "You are right, Maximian," Secondo said. The members of the court were few; the grand hall was missing many of its luxurious couches, and much of the carpet had been torn out, revealing the blackened wood beneath. "It seems it hasn't recovered, yet, from Lemuel's magic."

"Magic…" Julian's voice startled him. "…is the source of all ills."

"Indeed," Secondo muttered. "And now we must show the Imperial Council the extent of their folly."

The Speaker of the Council, Crispus Servillius, met them at the sky bridge that led to the Council House. He had a small dagger in his hands—no match for the masterfully-crafted adamant sword Maximian had already drawn.

"Answer for yourself, slime," Maximian snapped. "Why did you deny the true emperor?"

Crispus drew back, his old frail frame nearly toppling in the effort. "Ah, my signore, I simply didn't believe it was him. We had already elected a new emperor, as you know—the child, Adamantion."

Secondo had heard of the southron queen's devil-working. A living Adamantus would have spelled the certain end of Secondo's reign, if the common citizens found out about it. Yet Claudian Adamantus was a monk, having forsworn all temptations of the flesh. It might possibly be true, but it was in his best interests to deny it. "I expect an immediate resignation," Secondo growled.

"And you will get it… Your Undying Glory." Crispus' voice sounded almost snickering. "The electorate in the Ricci will be quite easy to bend one way or the other, in accordance with your will."

The walled-in, nearly-quarantined district where the ratlings lived would be quite an impressionable lot, indeed. "You are getting off easy, Signor Crispus," Secondo growled. "If you got what you deserved, you would be hanging from a tree."

"And people rarely get what they deserve, in this cold uncaring world." His voice sounded nearly triumphant. "I will be retiring to Dualmis. I predict a great deal of leisurely reading in my future…"

Secondo glared at the feeble councilor as he stumbled by. "Get out, traitor," he called after him, and pondered who would replace him.

~

The other councilors greeted him warmly, with due respect, but late in the day Vitellian his friend pulled him aside, and in a shadowy abandoned room, laid bare all he knew. "There is a conspiracy brewing," he whispered, "of massive scale… a trouble is coming, like we've never seen before. We must be prepared to abandon Imperial City at a moment's notice."

"I will never abandon Imperial City," Secondo Janus told him. "I will never leave it again."

~

The next day, Secondo ordered a clerk to write an official demand to the Magisterium that Julian at once be raised to the position of Pontifex. "If they reject the serene Emperor Secondo's command, they will face the full wrath of the legion."

Secondo handed Julian the scroll with its official Imperial seal, and embraced the paladin, the friend who'd grown closer to him than a brother. "I will think of you always," he said, and bade him goodbye.

~

Secondo Janus sat once more upon the White Throne, the silver Imperial Circlet once more resting on his head. Maximian stood tall and firm at his side, and at that moment he swore he would never leave the nation—he was a soldier, a son, of Empire.

CHAPTER FORTY-EIGHT:
LOVE AT LAST

Maximian, Marshal of the Guard

All things are right, Maximian thought. *Secondo is restored to the throne, and I am here, as Marshal of the Guard, with my adamant sword.* And yet he did not feel complete.

A burst of propitious wind buffeted him from within his bedchamber. He turned and saw what he expected—the radiant blue eyes of Silvana the Windborne. Without a further word he met her, locked her in a deep kiss. She, after all, was what he wanted all along.

CHAPTER FORTY-NINE:
THE WILL OF IMPERIUM

Julian Ultor, Malleus

The ship had docked in Sanctum's harbor. For once Julian didn't feel at home amid the great temple spires and the ringing bells. Monks in their brown habits and vestals in their white robes wandered the streets of Imperial City, looking somber and holy but never quite exuberant and joyful like the denizens of the outside world.

He wandered the perfectly-clean streets in view of the monasteries, feeling like a total stranger though he'd spent most of his life within the White City. The letter he clutched, bound in an Imperial seal, was likely to get him killed. But wherever Julian walked, Hieronus walked also.

~

At the gate to the Magisterium, two Templars in white surcoats and great steel breastplates stood guard, warhammers in hand.

"Julian!" one said. "Where is your hammer?"

So strange, he thought, *that I don't recognize them.* "I swore an oath to Hieronus—and I lost it. I must see the Pontifex."

"Once a paladin, always a paladin," the other Templar said, and let him by.

~

In the throne room where the Pontifex sat, his gem-encrusted miter glistening in the torchlight, Julian walked forward with his Imperial sealed letter.

"Where is your armor, Julian? Where is your hammer?" The Pontifex didn't sound half so friendly as the Templars did.

"I lost them," Julian Ultor, Malleus, said simply, and did not bother to explain. "I have a letter from the emperor, Secondo Janus the God."

"The *god?*" the Pontifex roared.

"That is his title," Julian said.

The Pontifex sprang to his feet, rushed over and snatched the letter from his hands. He crushed the Imperial seal and unraveled the letter. The further he read, the wider his eyes grew, the redder his face, the more total his anger. "*Blasphemy!*" he at last wailed. "The emperor has no power over the White Synod. Hieronus does not bend to Secondo Janus' commands! I will have you flogged and hanged before the day is through! And to think you are a paladin—that you come in the name of Hieronus."

"Not Hieronus!" Julian's voice echoed through the great room like a thundering storm. The torches blazed a hundred times brighter. "Imperium!"

And the gem-encrusted miter flew off the Pontifex's head; his rich robes split in half down the front; and he himself went flying, skidding to the floor.

~

By the time night fell, Julian was the Pontifex, and the Pontifex was his underling. *Magic is the source of all ills, but Imperium is its cure...*

EPILOGUE: THE COUP

Crispus Servillius, August

Crispus sat in an ill-lit tavern and cackled to himself, pewter goblet of wine in hand. Secondo Janus was so certain of his own triumph, so self-righteous and so deeply unaware. His doom was coming fast—his doom, and the doom of the Empire as they knew it. The common citizenry, so unwilling to change, so unwilling to expand their small and unsophisticated minds, had no way to fight the new order of the world.

Secondo Janus may have bested him for now, but Crispus Servillius, Speaker of the Council, would get the last laugh.

Priscilla Marianus, Provost of the Thenoan Academy

The fleet rounded the Horn of Zoar, where the stone lighthouse towered many hundreds of feet above the sea. The stone edifices and grand cities of the Empire were nothing compared to the grand vision the Academies had drawn up. With the help of the foreigners and the Imperial Council, a grand new experiment would take shape—the Empire would become a utopia, and the Academies would be the architect.

The hundreds of dhows stretched before her like an army of the sea, ridden with a force of a hundred thousand lawgiver warriors and their horses and camels. A small mind would condemn her for her employment of these foreigners, but these "barbarians" had a tradition far richer and far more excellent than the Empire ever had in its too-long existence. The thinkers of the Academies had debated the topic, and in a short time made a unanimous agreement that the lawgivers were, by far, the best way to create the new world.

A loud horn blew, echoing across the sea. Around her on the deck of the dhow, the lawgiver warriors dropped to their knees and threw up their hands. "Praise Mazda!" they shouted.

Praise Mazda, indeed, Priscilla thought, and relished her plans coming, at last, to fruition.

GLOSSARY

CURRENCY

Aes: A copper coin, the cheapest unit of currency. Also called a copper or an "eagle."

Denar: A silver coin, worth twelve aesa. Also called a silver or a "moon."

Liber: A gold coin, worth eighty denara or approximately one-thousand aesa. Also called a gold, a "crown," or a "sovereign."

TERMS

Adamant: A metal of light bluish color. Its existence was known, but it could not be shaped until the eleventh century, when the Alchemist Collegium created a flame hot enough. The process of making adamant weapons is so expensive that hardly any can afford one outside of the upper tier of the military.

Amara: The goddess of motherly love.

Anthans: (1) Another name for Imperial City. (2) Anthans the Great, the last of the Sea Kings and the first emperor (having achieved the title with the ceding of Anthania).

Archmagus: The chief of the magi, a group of magician-priests in Fharas who revere fire.

Arkadios family: An ancient merchant family of Thénai. As Imperial sympathizers, their wealth continued throughout the occupation and conquest of Eloesus.

Augusts: The higher of the two ruling classes (the other being Knights). They are the descendants of the original Peregothian families through the male line, and are the only people allowed to serve within the upper tier of the government.

Barbarians: A general term for non-Imperials, both to the north and to the south.

Desolation, the: An area of intense fighting between Fharas and the Empire on the southern part of Khazidea. The constant burning and leveling of towns has turned this once-fertile region into a desert.

Demons: The enemies of the gods. Their names are often shortened (marked with an apostrophe) to avoid attracting their attention.

Empire, the: A large nation surrounding the Imperial Sea. Their flag is a gold war-eagle on a red field.

Elders, the: According to legend, a race of mystical beings rumored to live "beyond the reach of the north wind."

Eloesus: An ancient land famed for its wealth and rich culture. Since the 500s YE, an Imperial province. Their flag is a laurel-wreath on a green field.

Fharas: An ancient empire centered in the plain of Gor Ilán. Their flag is a golden four-pointed star on a purple field.

Gad: The northernmost and least populous province of the Empire, known for its light-featured inhabitants.

Haroon Spice: An intoxicant, currently banned in the Empire, which causes hallucinations and feelings of euphoria but—over the long term—afflicting the consumer with severe weight loss and, oftentimes, dementia. Crimson eyes are the telltale sign of long-term addicts.

Hieronus: The god of justice and just war.

Imperial City: Also called Anthans. The de facto capital of the Empire, and the largest city in the known world.

Imperial Council: A body of thirty Augusts (see above), given certain governmental powers, including the ability to remove the emperor. They are elected by the people of Imperial City across its thirty districts.

Imperial Cult: A group devoted to the worship of the emperors, especially the Adamanti, located in Imperiopoli.

Imperiopoli: A large city of Eloesus.

Imperium: The god of the Imperial state, represented as an eagle. His cult was founded in the 400s YE. The theologians of the Magisterium consider him a human invention.

Issa: Goddess of fertility. Worshiped mostly in Khazidea and the southlands, she nevertheless has a large temple in Imperiopoli.

Janus family: A distinguished family raised to the knightly class during the recent Fharese war.

Kernunnos: The wild god of forests, wildernesses, and changing seasons.

Korthos: An Eloesian metropolis.

Khazidea: A southern land along the Khazan River, surrounded by desert.

Knight: (1) A mounted warrior, especially one wearing heavy armor; (2) A member of the lower tier of the Imperial upper class—the other being Augusts—officially tasked with the defense of the Empire. In actuality, not all knights serve actively as soldiers.

Lorenus: The god of the sea, favored by the city of Peregoth.

Magisterium, the: A large religious complex in Sanctum, led by the Pontifex, chief priest of Hieronus.

Malleus: An honorary title given to full-ranked paladins.

Mazda: A god mostly unknown to the Imperials. His worshipers consider him the only good god.

Monk: A member of a religious order. Monks Militant go to war, but are generally forbidden to shed blood; some wield clubs or maces to overcome this barrier, while others are sworn to use their fists. Monks of Peace are often scribes, scholars, theologians or healers.

Paradise Gardens: An elite enclave of the wealthy in the foothills of the Goldenhorn Mountains, a summer retreat popular with the August families of Imperial City.

Path of Tidus: A long paved road running from Imperial City to Zarubad far to the north.

Pharzanes the Empire-Hater: The current padisha King of Kings of Fharas, at one time he fought alongside Claudian Adamantus against the lawgivers. However, thanks to the counsel of his archmagus, Sidathra, he radically changed course and declared war in 1096 Y.E.

Peregoth: The founding city of the Empire, built on an island of the same name.

Thénai: The capital and largest city of Eloesus.

Theomancer: The religious and political leader of all Mazda's worshippers.

Uneasy Peace, the: A period from about 1092 Y.E. to 1096 Y.E. when the Empire and Fharas had declared an alliance. It broke in spring of 1096 Y.E. when Pharzanes unexpectedly declared war and renewed his claim to Khazidea.

Vestal: Generally, the Imperial equivalent of a nun in the north, a female monk.

Wall, the: A large wall separating the Empire from the northern barbarians. Its origins are a mystery.

White Synod, the: A council of seventy priests, with representatives from each branch of the Magisterium, headed by the Pontifex.

IMPERIAL CITY MAP KEY

Suburro: An ancient, poor section of town, flanked by the Equine and Aurean Hills. Though widely known for its poverty and shanty homes, many great Imperials found their origins here.

West Side: Arguably part of the Suburro, a poor section of town predominating much of the western two-thirds of the city. It is filled with parks and spice dens.

a. **Armory District:** Once a center for the production of armaments and siege weaponry, this quiet district northeast of the Suburro is known for its charming shops and sprawling apartments.

b. **Kings Terrace:** An ancient enclave near the center of the city, featuring the mansions and homes of rich councilors and government officials. Most of these mansions cannot be bought and are passed down through families.

c. **Maxima:** Shops and theaters abound in this district, a center for drama and entertainment. Named for the war hero Adriano Maximus.

d. **Villa Regis:** A wealthy section of town, built along the shores of the North River.

e. **Bulus Wharf:** A section of town facing Imperial Harbor, a center of fishmongers and the fish trade.

Celsus Heights: A rich section of town built on a steep promontory. It is named for the infamous shipping magnate Celsus, who — rumor has it — burned down the area to build one of his mansions. Beside the rumor for arson, he was known for his unscrupulous business practices, charging exorbitant rents for those who stayed in his apartments, and was rumored to be a Strig, a kind of undead. Today, the mostly sumptuous apartment buildings overlook Imperial Harbor. Shops and music halls can also be found in abundance.

Harbor District: A sprawling district bordering the Imperial Harbor, featuring docks and warehouses.

Cloaca: The sewer district of Imperial City, flushing effluent into the South River. In ancient days, the first Cloaca broke and gushed forth water into the low-lying fields south of the river, creating the Palladian Swamp. The second Cloaca was built, much larger and stronger, after years of construction.

f. **Market District:** A vast district predominating the center of the city, featuring its eponymous markets as well as slum areas.

g. **Canyon Row:** Shops, apartments, temples and shrines predominate this central section of town. The Walk of Triumph begins here.

h. **Newmarket:** A quiet district of shops and apartments.

i. **Mud Bottom:** A dilapidated, ancient section of town, the most impoverished district.

Avediccus: A section of town facing the Palladian Swamp. Predominated by homes, shops, and small shrines, a concrete stairway into the swamp can be found here.

j. **Meridia:** A section of town bordering the Palladian Swamp and city bounds, featuring apartment blocks, shops and administrative buildings.

k. **Mystia:** A large section of town featuring markets, shops and homes, as well as the garrison for the city watch.

l. **Villa Maris:** A section of town bordering the South River, highly developed, known for its taverns along the river's shore.

Emporia: Markets and shops predominate this central district.

m. **Loud Surf:** A section of town built along cliffs, featuring often more pleasant weather than the city below. Its inhabitants call this section of town the city's most blessed area.

n. **Perrine:** Named after the Emperor Perrius, this section of town has a mixture of wealth and poverty. It is a favored home for members of the military, as it connects to a road to Fort Mettius several miles away.

o. **Gaboline:** Named after the Emperor Gabolus, originally built around a fort then outside of city bounds, this district is known for its quaint stone streets and temples.

p. **West Limes:** A border area facing Wagontown Settlement, it is nonetheless highly developed and features vast theaters and gladiatorial arenas.

q. **East Limes:** A border area featuring many gladiatorial arenas. It abuts a section of cemeteries outside city bounds.

r. **Terrentian:** Named after the legate Terrentius, this section of town is known as a site of public executions. Shops and homes can be found here.

s. **Majorian Markets:** Named for two sprawling indoor market complexes, it is rumored that anything in Varda can be found here on sale.

The Ricci: A walled-off, closed section of town that houses the city's ratling population.

t. **The Strand:** A highly developed area of town known for its lighted roads, specialized taverns and bookshops.

u. **Meletus**: A section of apartments, shops and temples bordering the North River.

v. **Urubus**: A vast section of town below Celsus Heights, relatively impoverished, where the smoke of the city often settles. City administrators consider it a public health nuisance.

About the Author

Cursed at birth with a wild imagination, Andrew Cooper spent his youth dreaming of worlds more exciting than Earth.

He is a graduate of the Odyssey Writing Workshop. His stories have appeared in Morpheus Tales, Fear and Trembling, Residential Aliens and Mindflights, among others.

CONTACT THE AUTHOR

Visit **www.aj-cooper.com** to sign up for the newsletter and stay up-to-date on new releases.

Find him on Facebook at:

www.facebook.com/AJCooperauthor

9 781958 724156